Model Citizen

The Prague Affair

By R. H. Score

eBook ISBN: 979-8-89795-918-1
Paperback ISBN: 979-8-89795-919-8
Hardcover ISBN: 979-8-89795-920-4

Acknowledgments

I want to extend my heartfelt gratitude to everyone who supported me throughout this journey. Whether you listened to my endless ramblings or offered a kind word of encouragement, I truly appreciate it. Your support made all the difference.

A special thank you to Stella Din for her invaluable collaboration in bringing this story to life. To Leah Berg, for providing the images that helped shape my vision of the main character. To my brother Clyde and my sister Donna, whose unwavering encouragement kept me going. To my producing partner, Timothy Bryant, whose excitement is infectious. And to my very best friend in the world, Jen, who stood by me with steadfast support through every step of this crazy adventure—and many more yet to come.

I'd also like to thank Lucas Parez and his exceptional team at Penguin Publishers for their hard work in turning my manuscript into the book you're now holding in your hands. Their dedication and skill have helped to make this a reality.

Thank you, from the bottom of my heart.

R.H. Score

1

As she took one last look in the mirror before preparing to hit the runway at the Metropol to represent Dolce and Gabbana during Milan fashion week, Sloane Harper felt a subtle tension as the tiny hairs on the back of her neck prickled with unease. She couldn't put her finger on it, but she knew something wasn't quite right. It wasn't nerves—she had walked too many runways for that. This was something else.

It started earlier when she was informed that her assistant Marie had been in an automobile accident while on her way to the show. Then she found out that the original gown she was to wear had mysteriously gotten torn, and she now had to wear a replacement that was not to her liking, an ill-fitting substitute that clashed with her usual high standards. Finally, her hair and makeup people were new that morning and were taking forever to get her ready for her first trip down the runway.

Coincidences? Maybe. But in Sloane's world, coincidences rarely existed.

She took a slow, steadying breath, forcing herself to push past the unease. One year ago, things had been simpler and more in control. Cleaner.

Before everything changed.

She had been with Prada at their design headquarters, art center, and idea lab. She had just landed her first Vogue magazine feature photoshoot and was set to go to Bali when the call came. The caller directed her to a bench in the Centro Storico zone, that chic neighborhood known for its parties and other actions. Her bosses looked at her in dismay when she told them she had to go just as they were getting ready to head to Milan Malpensa airport. All Sloane could do was shrug her shoulders and apologize for the inconvenience, to explain that she would see them all in Bali.

She found her car, a used Ferrari 308GTS, but still a classic. She slid in behind the driver's wheel and turned the key. The powerful V8 roared to life, and Sloane gave it a rev. She put the powerful convertible sports car into gear, mashed down on the accelerator, and tore off down the narrow street towards the Centro Storico for her rendezvous. A thrill shot through her—not just from the speed, but from the anticipation of what lay ahead.

Heading down the Via Adalberto Carena at an almost reckless speed, Sloane arrived just outside of the Piazza Delia Scala near the old opera house and parked the Ferrari on a side street. She adjusted her sunglasses before stepping out.

Donning a plain, wide-brimmed sun hat, she set off at a casual pace towards the opera house. The plaza was eerily quiet, the calm before the inevitable arrival of tour buses packed with charters of tourists wanting eagerly to admire the grandeur of the historic site. As she neared the front entrance of the opera house, Sloane spotted a bench tucked near a stand of Italian cypress and walked over to take a seat and wait. She settled in, legs crossed, the picture of effortless sophistication. But beneath the surface, her mind worked like a machine, assessing every movement around her.

Where was the contact? Where was the drop?

Wondering when the instructions from the caller would arrive, she scanned the immediate area with the practiced eye of someone who could never afford to let her guard down. Out of the corner of her eye, she spotted a group of school-aged children playing with a football as they moved toward her position.

Sloane sighed internally, irritation creeping in as she knew this might delay the delivery she was anticipating. But her training as an intelligence operative kicked in, and she smiled at the playful group as they passed in front of her. Even the smallest detail had to be controlled—she couldn't afford to seem out of place. Suddenly, an errant pass from one of the children sent the ball rolling directly to where she sat. A small boy with tousled hair chased after the ball, stopping within arm's reach of where Sloane now sat with the football she had picked up in both hands. The boy stopped in front of her and smiled as she handed him the football.

As the boy turned to catch up with his friends, he turned back again and asked if Sloane knew what time it was. Sloane looked at her designer Rolex, but as she looked up, the boy was gone. In the place where he stood, she spotted a manila envelope on the walkway.

Smooth. Real smooth.

Sloane quickly looked around and reached down to retrieve the envelope. With it in hand, she made her way into the opera house and quickly took a stairway up to the luxury boxes of the balcony, where she would not be bothered.

The boxes were all locked up, of course, but for Sloane, locks were merely suggestions. She took her lock-picking tools from a hidden compartment in her jacket, easily opened the door, and soon had the contents of the envelope before her to read. Quickly scanning the documents, Sloane realized she wasn't going to Bali, but to

Prague. She was being dispatched to infiltrate a secretive and dangerous group of mercenaries intent on disrupting the fragile peace in the region.

Sloane replaced the dossier into the envelope and left the private box, waiting just out of sight for a passing tour group before slipping down the stairs unnoticed. Once outside, she returned to the same bench she had sat on before, removed the dossier, and exposed the paper to sunlight, where a photochemical reaction turned every page to an ebony blackness that rendered it all unreadable.

Sloane stood up and took one last look around before walking casually towards the Ferrari. Passing by a trash receptacle, she nonchalantly dropped the envelope into the opening at the top and continued on to her car.

Arriving at the beautiful classic red convertible, Sloane wondered if she was really ready for what lay ahead. She had been in the game long enough to know that 'ready' was a luxury. Prepared? That was all she could afford. Knowing that she was one of the best operatives in the agency renewed her courage as she turned the ignition key, revved the powerful V8, and headed towards Bergamo airport, where a charter jet awaited to take her to Prague.

2

With an eleven-hour drive in front of her, Sloane has plenty of time to think about what lies ahead and to contemplate how she got to this type of life.

Glamorous runway model during one life with the same look and appeal as her mother, who modeled for the house of Gucci for a dozen years, and a highly skilled intel agent and assassin in another life for a secret offshoot of the Central Intelligence Agency. The very same agency her father worked for as a covert agent —until a contact betrayed him to the KGB. After that, no one knows what happened to him, but Sloane became convinced over the years that the Soviets probably executed him for espionage. In the meantime, her mother had lost herself in the recesses of her own despair, and it was as if Sloane had lost both of her parents to circumstances beyond her control—one to the enemy, the other to grief.

She found herself fighting back the tears as she remembered a happy childhood filled with immense love from both her parents. But there was no time for sentimentality. Pushing the memories aside, Sloane hit the accelerator and pushed the Ferrari to its top speed through the Italian countryside towards the airport she had carefully chosen for its lower profile—discreet, quiet, catering mostly to executives and private charters. The kind of place where anonymity was expected.

As she turned off the main road in her approach to the airport, she bypassed the regular passenger terminal and continued until she spotted the sign directing her to the executive terminal. Turning in, she spotted the covered car park for long-term parking, grabbed a ticket from the dispenser, and found a space for her convertible between a Bugatti Chiron and a Lamborghini Aventador, two hypercars that made her used Ferrari look like a budget ride.

Upon entering the luxurious terminal, she went to the concierge desk, where she checked in for her private charter flight to Prague. Her cover was seamless—just another model jetting off for a high-profile photoshoot. While checking in, Sloane used her regular identification, which went hand in hand with her cover story as that of a model on a shooting assignment for any number of publications.

Because she had pushed the car at such high speeds with only three short fuel stops, she had arrived at Bergamo with a couple of hours to spare. Realizing she hadn't eaten all day, Sloane found the executive lounge where she quickly ate a wonderful crudités plate with a toasted baguette and a glass of Pinot Noir. The food was good, but her mind was elsewhere. As she ate, Sloane started running the various scenarios through her mind based on what her handler had briefed her for. She knew that the agency-supplied jet would hold a more detailed dossier on the mission and on her target, whom she was inevitably ordered to dispatch in any way she saw fit. This, of course, would all depend on how things played out in Prague.

The first thing she had to do was learn all she could about her target and make plans to enter his world with his invitation. Infiltration was a delicate dance of persuasion and deception. She decided this was much like convincing someone to go to hell while enjoying the trip. A dark smirk played on her lips at the thought. Looking at the jeweled Rolex, she saw it was time to board the jet and prepare for the deadly mission at hand.

Sloane soon found herself aboard a beautifully appointed $72-million-dollar Gulfstream G800, which made most of the other private jets look like economy-class "low rent" aircraft.

The jet was soon taxiing towards the private runway and accelerating with its powerful twin turbojet engines. Sloane reached down to a side pocket in the Corinthian leather seat and retrieved the new dossier filled with every detail she would inevitably need to succeed in her mission. She devoured the information before her, flipping through the pages and absorbing every critical piece of intelligence, memorizing faces, names, and routines."

With the jet on the runway and now prepared for take off, the engines roared to life, the sheer force of acceleration pressed her back against the leather seat. The beautiful man-made bird was suddenly airborne and on its way to Prague.

Returning the dossier to the side pocket of her seat, Sloane closed her eyes and pondered what awaited her once on the ground. Soon she was sleeping in a Power Nap with a slight purr like that of a restless tigress emanating from her peaceful looking face.

Sloane awoke to the gentle southern drawl of the pilot announcing the descent into Prague's Vaclav Havel airport. The jet smoothly landed and arrived at another executive terminal where Sloane disembarked from the Gulfstream and headed into anyone's guess.

3

Sloane descended the retractable stairway of the Gulfstream and walked towards the executive terminal. By her walk alone, anyone could tell that her movements were used to drawing attention and holding breaths. Like all the top models in the world, her mere glance was enough to bring a smile to anyone's face, even if they were disgruntled. With an exotic physique and elegance paired with long, dark hair, Sloane's beauty staked its claim in the modeling world like a natural. Soon, she found herself in demand for both runway and photo assignments.

At only 14 years of age, she was signed to the Wilhelmina Models Agency, but by 18, she had rebelled against the structure and its grueling schedule. Freelancing became her saving grace after she left the agency, and four short years later, she was at the top of her game.

But good things rarely ever last.

Just when she had begun to settle into her new life, another tragedy knocked her to the ground. In the blink of an eye, she found herself sitting at rock bottom with her mother as she tried to pry away the empty pill bottle from her rigor-set hands. All she could remember was hearing her own voice desperately calling for her mom while the paramedics tried to console her. The events preceding it went by in a blur. She vaguely recalled hearing terms like "overdose" or "sleeping pills," though, between the funeral procession and her own grief, she couldn't bring herself to spare another thought.

Nothing could help the pain.

Sloane found herself spinning out of control, trying to suppress her anguish. On a path carved by her own darkness, she threw all reason away to live on the edge of decency. A vicious cycle of insomnia mixed with alcohol and pills took her up and down like an out-of-control runaway elevator. It finally came to a head one stormy night in Marseille.

Some fishermen found Sloane unconscious near the docks and rushed her to a hospital. The doctors feverishly revived her a dozen times throughout the night, barely able to keep her from the clutches of death. When Sloane finally came to, she was restrained to a hospital bed with an IV in her arm. She had been comatose for almost two weeks, but upon awakening, she found herself tired, hungry, and absolutely clueless about how she got to this point. It didn't take long for a nursing assistant to walk in and realize Sloane was now awake. Sitting halfway up with barely enough strength, she saw the assistant run from the room. She tried to call after her, but her throat felt parched and sore. It took the nurse only a little while before she returned with the duty nurse and the resident doctors who monitored her regularly.

With a quizzical look on her sunken yet still beautiful face, Sloane listened as the doctor told her about her near-death experience and how she was brought to the hospital. He explained to her that she had seemingly survived by sheer willpower alone to overcome both death at hand and the lethal addiction to whatever she consumed to stay high. Whispering a silent prayer, thanking God for sparing her life, Sloane made a vow in that moment to herself and the universe.

This would be the moment of true change in her life.

4

When Sloane finally signed herself out of the Hospital, it was dusk as the evening began to set. She had no idea what to do or how to start, but was determined to rebuild her life back to what it was and beyond. Luckily, she still had some money left, and her passport was cached in a locker at a local train station. After some shuffling, she even found the key in the insole of the shoes she had been wearing when they found her unconscious on the docks. The only problem was that she had no clue where the locker was or even the train station, for that matter. In fact, she wasn't even sure where she was, and her head began to hurt as she tried to think things through her still somewhat addled mind.

After some hysterical searching, she finally came across a city directory at a nearby local transit stop. She was able to locate the train station, but it was quite a long way ahead. Having no money for transit and fearful of catching a ride with strangers, she had no choice but to set off on foot. She ended up winding through several neighborhoods and districts, still dressed in the grimy street clothes she had been found in. They were the only clothes she had on, and the hospital had returned them when she checked out.

As she made her way along the narrow avenues and empty streets towards the train station, she could feel the eyes watching her. They regarded her with suspicion, like an innkeeper watching a possible thief as they skulked through a shop. She could feel the unease with every streetlamp she passed beneath.

At one point, Sloane was approached by a group of local young men out on the street a short distance away. Given the state she was in, she was convinced they wanted to rob and rape her. The tone of their voices and their way of talking did nothing to calm her nerves. Already feeling on edge, she quickly dashed into an alleyway and crouched behind some trash cans as the group started running in her direction. Covering her mouth with trembling hands, she hid there while the young men stopped and peered intently down the alleyway, listening for any movement or breathing. Hearing none, the group continued on their way while laughing about how "lucky this one had been" to escape their "fun and games."

While sitting awkwardly in the darkened alleyway and trying not to move or make a sound, Sloane felt her hand brush against something hard on the ground. Even though she couldn't see anything, once she felt the object, she recognized it was a handgun and picked it up. Somehow, this singular find gave her a sense of security and comfort she hadn't known for quite some time.

Sloane paused and listened, but she could no longer hear the footfall or the threatening banter from the group of young men. After taking a moment to calm her heartbeat, she climbed out to continue on her way with the newfound courage of the semi-automatic pistol she held in her hand. She wasn't even sure if it was loaded, but it gave her a sense of security anyway. She wasn't afraid of the gun. Her father had taught her when she was about twelve how to fire a weapon with deadly accuracy. She couldn't help but recall how he would take her to an indoor shooting range as he regularly practiced his skills.

As she exited the alleyway and proceeded to continue on her way, somebody suddenly grabbed her from behind and violently threw her against a wall. Sloane fell to the ground as some shadowy figures slowly stalked over her. It was three of the young men she had seen earlier. Apparently, they had doubled back around, knowing that they had missed her the first time in the alleyway. They seemed determined to have their way with this poor, defenseless creature. In all likelihood, they would leave her for dead in the very same alleyway that had once been her refuge.

Picturing the scene in her head, she felt like someone had thrown a bucket of ice-cold water at her.

Suddenly, Sloane came to her full senses. She quickly engaged the semi-auto's slide, pulled the weapon in front of her to a firing position, and squeezed the trigger, not knowing whether a bullet existed or not. It did, hitting her first assailant center mass, causing him to clutch his chest and immediately drop to the ground dead as a stone. The other two attackers shouted, "Get her!" and rushed towards her. But Sloane squeezed the trigger twice more with deadly accuracy, and the other two young men each went down in a heap.

With no time to spare, Sloane picked herself up, wiped down the weapon with the bottom of her dirty and torn shirt, and quickly tossed the gun behind a bush. She ran towards the train station as she heard nearby doors opening and voices clamoring in a semi-panicked state, trying to figure out who had fired shots in the quiet confines of their neighborhood. But for Sloane, it was a turning point as the realization set in that she had just killed someone in both fear and anger.

Little did she know it would not be the last time she pulled the trigger.

5

Sloane suddenly snapped back to the present and hurried away from the Gulfstream. As she entered the well-appointed executive terminal at the Vaclav Havel Airport just outside of Prague, she showed her passport to the smiling immigration officer. He was used to dealing with celebrities, diplomats, and other VIPs who visited Prague for various reasons. People from all over the world came here, from proceedings at the International Court of Justice, where many war criminals were imprisoned, to tours of the prestigious Museum of Decorative Arts, the impressive Saint Vitus Cathedral, or the majestic State Opera House and National Theater.

Once inside the terminal, Sloane spotted a well-dressed young man with a chauffeur's cap and a neatly printed card with her last name on it. When she approached the young man, he immediately straightened up and smiled like all the others. It took him no less than two seconds to recognize her as the passenger he would have to escort to the hotel. Fame came with its own perks. Though it wasn't so much that she was instantly recognized for all her modeling work, it was easy to pick her out with the description of "A tall beauty with dark hair who stands out among everyone else around her." The young man carried a certain warmth about him. While greeting, he noticed that she had no carry-on for him to help with, so he simply escorted her to the car they would be taking to the hotel.

The car was a newer Mercedes; Sloane was too preoccupied to take note of the model. Once inside the luxury sedan, they were soon on their way to the hotel. The lodgings were old, but like all historical structures, they still had the ability to take one's breath away. However, undisclosed to the general public, the hotel and car were owned by the Central Intelligence Agency, or what most people called "The Agency." The young man behind the wheel was an agent himself. He passed Sloane a new dossier of paperwork about her mission details as they wound through the classic architecture of this long-standing European capital. Vigilant as ever, the young man was on a continuous lookout for any suspicious vehicle while driving. When satisfied, he informed her that her agency handler, Edward "Eddie" Stafford, was waiting at the hotel in an adjoining suite to brief her about the remaining details not found in the new pages she was clutching tightly in her hands.

The hotel itself had been acquired by the Office of Special Services or OSS, the forerunner of the CIA, shortly after World War II had ended under a European shell corporation well before the Cold War kicked into high gear. Over the years, it had been used to launch many covert missions throughout the Eastern Block, with the Soviets, East Germans, and other enemies being none the wiser. The century-old town, McGallery, sat in close proximity to the Vitava River, skirting the western edge of this European metropolis that was once home to Wolfgang Amadeus Mozart and several Holy Roman Emperors. During World War two, while occupied by Nazi forces, a small resistance force had staged a partially successful movement to liberate the city. Though it was bombed several times during the war, it was largely spared due to both cultural and strategic considerations.

The Mercedes was soon pulling into the driveway at the front of the hotel. Barely able to keep her eyes open, Sloane saw the waiting staff hurrying to open the passenger door for her. She held on to the dossier more like a stylish notebook than a mission brief as she stepped out of the car and headed up the front steps. A doorman was already waiting for her as he opened the massive entryway and directed her towards a behemoth oak wood desk at reception. It was manned by half a dozen clerks awaiting other guests as they checked in. Sloane immediately bypassed all of the regular check-in windows and approached the VIP concierge, where she was immediately issued a room key. The staff was kind enough to inform her that her luggage had already been delivered to her suite, even though she was familiar with the procedure. After being escorted to a private lift, she made her way to the top floor with the special suites specially reserved for those above the norm to be pampered and treated with a style tantamount to royalty regardless of their actual station in life.

Sloane walked out of the lift and moved to the second room to the left and across the narrow hallway. Upon entering, she discovered a luxurious suite truly meant for those raised with the bread and butter of high society. The spacious living room was decorated in a classic Renaissance style but outfitted with every modern amenity needed to survive in the 21st century. Double doors opened into a high-ceilinged sleeping chamber and sitting room complete with a workstation meant for business. At the far side of the room, another pair of French doors opened up to a balcony with a wonderful view of the old town square. Unfortunately, those doors were sealed for security purposes, as bulletproof glass was installed in the divided light panels gracing the classical doors. Unfazed by all the grandeur, Sloane made a beeline for the wardrobe opening along the wall. She found a large variety of high-end labeled fashion wear already tailored for her beautiful model figure for almost any occasion: from the runway to elegant dining and party wear for club nights. After rummaging through the contents, she pushed down on the armoire floor and released a spring-loaded panel that opened access to a hidden compartment below the main section.

Opening up the panel revealed a medium-sized suitcase. Exactly what she was looking for. She lifted it out from the compartment to the bench at the foot of the bed and set it down to dial in the four numbers she had committed to memory. It was a combination lock for accessing the contents of the suitcase. Once opened, the case yielded all the equipment and apparel necessary for Sloane to carry out her mission. She found two sets of form-fitting all-black jumpsuits made of a special carbon fiber weave for flexibility and protection against everything from knife attacks to small arms fire. Two all-black full-face balaclavas made of the same carbon fiber weave. Two sets of all-black flexible ankle-high boots with special soles for cat-like stealth on any and all surfaces while protecting against slippage, even on ice. Two pairs of perfectly fitting flex gloves of the same material meant for protection and dexterity to the point of picking up something as small as a paperclip. Last but not least, it included smart tips for perfect connectivity to electronics and other smart devices.

Next came the armament with a Sig Sauer 9mm semi-auto handgun with 15 shot capacity. A special ammo vest able to hold an additional eight clips for the Sig if necessary. Three razor-sharp throwing knives. One spring-loaded stiletto knife, meant to be carried in her garter or boot, depending on the situation. A diamond studded piano wire garrote for close-up and personal dispatching of an enemy combatant. It served an added purpose of a diamond saw for cutting through many materials if needed. The remaining items consisted of a custom smartwatch containing a unidirectional, high-frequency pitch generator for disorienting her foes when pointed directly at them and a miniature radio transmitter for close proximity communications. Satisfied after examining all the contents, Sloane immediately reached for the Sig Sauer. She hit a stopwatch function on her smartwatch and then proceeded to completely field strip, reassemble, load, and operate the slide for action in just under 60 seconds. As she adjusted the Sig and feeling of the custom grips in her hand, a coded knock came from the door to the adjoining room. She answered the knock with her own light taps, and after receiving another coded response, she opened the door to Eddie Stafford standing in the doorway with his usual dour expression.

6

“Edward!” Sloane beamed as she greeted Eddie by his proper name with a warm peck on the cheek. This, of course, disarmed him completely and erased the semi-permanent scowl from his face, embedded after years of stress from handling an intelligence network. He gawked for a moment, then replaced his scowl with a big toothy smile. This was one of Sloane's most valuable weapons in her arsenal, as was her charm and sensuality. It had the same effect on almost all men she encountered.

It worked so well that, on multiple occasions, it enabled her to infiltrate international terrorist organizations and tyrannical governments intent on destroying the fabric of American society. These hostile entities were doing their best to see the demise of this government "of the people and for the people." They acted like they could do no wrong while meddling with the affairs of other nation-states following a different political ideology.

On many occasions, Sloane was able to thwart their plans, which posed a real threat to the United States. These threats were relentless, from dirty bombs and terrorist attacks to counterfeit currency schemes meant to take down financial institutions and wreak havoc on the economy to cyber-attacks meant to cripple the transportation systems, infrastructures, and power grids. The list went on. And on each mission, Sloane had successfully disrupted the plans by charming her way into hearts and sometimes bed, when need be, with those in charge of all these schemes.

The disruption came in many forms, such as planting misinformation, which inevitably forced the enemy to self-destruct. It often set back planned operations for years if not ending them completely. She was also an expert at infiltrating enemy cyber-systems remotely or in person by either uploading a virus that fried their systems or downloading plans to forward to superiors for decisive actions But her best skill was getting one-on-one sensitive information from all who fell under her exotic spell only to be executed at the end. Whether by poison made to look like a heart attack or something more intimate like strangulation in a bedroom game with silk stockings or blatantly with a garrote. And if she's in a hurry, a quick stab directly into the heart with her stiletto or a silenced small caliber bullet through the temple, her means were endless.

Since most of the private trysts were kept very hush-hush by the men and sometimes women involved with this part of her life, Sloane could slip away without being noticed. She was good at leaving almost no trace behind, with the exception of a few droplets of blood. But hardly anyone paid attention at first glance, too preoccupied with the "beautiful visitor" as she would breeze through them with the statuesque grace of a runway model.

Now, she sat while Eddie briefed her on more intimate details about the mission she was about to undertake. Her target was the charismatic leader of the mercenary group hellbent on the destruction of this government. He had friendly ties with the US Government because of operations launched from the very hotel where they sat in. These operations hardly ever faced any interference and, in many cases, assistance from intelligence personnel deployed in the Czech Republic since they knew the value of keeping countries like Russia in their place.

His name was Pavel Grovzny, and he was a 34-year-old former officer who led a team of highly trained experts specializing in covert operations. Their services, offered to the highest bidder, included a range of illicit activities, from violence and intimidation to cyber terrorism, kidnapping, extortion, and assassinations. With expertise in sabotage, ambushes, and other forms of clandestine warfare, Grovzny's team was a formidable and feared entity. He was also handsome to a fault, with rugged good looks except for the scar on his right cheek that he mainly kept concealed by a constant two-day shadow of a beard.

To top that all off, he was also a known ladies' man with one or two beautiful ladies constantly hanging off his arm at social events. Hardly anyone realized his position as the leader of a ruthless group of men and women that populated his private army.

As Eddie Stafford related to Sloane, she was to innocently run into Pavel as he attended a high-end fashion show to be staged inside the National Theater. Her job was to charm him into inviting her to a private party at his luxury riverside villa. He was hosting it for many dignitaries and celebrities, both local and international, to kick off a week of festivities for the new Formula One race held at a specially built complex near the old town section of the capital. The appointed track ran past all the cultural icons of splendid architecture specially selected for their incredible appeal to show off this dignified European destination.

There was little doubt that Sloane would accomplish this first task since she and Pavel both exuded charm and sex appeal possessed by only a few others. She could easily play the game of seduction. The next part of her mission would prove to be somewhat more challenging due to Pavel's gregarious nature and the event itself. With hundreds of guests and the chance of privacy somewhere between slim and none, her next step was to assassinate Pavel by any means possible and escape without being detected.

7

Eddie began to fill Sloane in on several standard ops procedures she had heard many times concerning communications or exit strategies in case of failure, however remote. Though she knew these procedures by heart, they always made it a point to remind her of the inevitability that she might very well have to take her own life by biting into an ever-present capsule of cyanide. Fortunately for Sloane, that close of a call never really came to force her hand for this play. Except, maybe once. She was almost caught in action by the East German Stasi while retrieving documents from a highly secured safe that might as well have been a fortified vault. Quick on her toes, she was only able to gain access after peeking at the combination lock of her target through the reflection on the small mirror of her cosmetic compact. It should have been a fond memory, but all of a sudden, her mind was pulled back into the harrowing episodes of her early career as a novice operative.

Feigning a headache, she had asked her amorous target if he would be kind enough to get her a glass of water with some aspirin for her sudden migraine. The man was an overweight senior-level East German bureaucrat, and even a rookie could tell from the way he was pawing at her that he was dying to sleep with her. With nimble fingers, she moved quickly to the safe the moment she was left alone. Spinning the lock to open the safe was child's play. Just as Sloane was retrieving the documents, she froze when she suddenly heard someone clearing his throat. She spun around to find herself face-to-face with the same overweight womanizing pig of a man wearing an angry scowl while pointing a classic World War Two German Luger in her direction. The barrel was barely 18 inches away from her face.

Without wasting a second, Sloane slapped the pistol away from her face and delivered a combination of fast and powerful blows. One to the throat, another to the solar plexus, and a cross-elbow point to the temple left the man stunned, but he still had the gun in his hand. He raised the pistol once again. Sloane immediately grabbed the gun, and a struggle ensued with her enemy to take possession of the weapon. Then, suddenly, the gun went off. Sloane cocked her head up to find the fired shot had made its way through the chin of the man and up into his brain. His death was instant. Unfortunately for Sloane, the gunshot had also caused a deafening bang that would certainly alert security. Sure enough, in the very next moment, two large and grim-looking Stasi agents began pounding on the locked double doors while Sloane scuttled around to figure a way out of the room.

Seeing none, Sloane quickly put the automatic back into the man's hand, placing his finger inside the trigger guard. She then grabbed the stolen papers, folded them, and stuffed them down the rear of her panties. Then, she quickly closed the safe and ran into the bathroom to hide behind the shower curtain and tried to think of an exit strategy. Alarmed by the heavy footfalls approaching the bathroom, Sloane retrieved the cyanide capsule and placed it under her bottom lip, ready to take her own life. She knew more than enough about the Stasi interrogation methods to let herself be hauled away for torture at the hands of their cruelty. They would surely accuse her of espionage and treat her as a spy. As one of the security men entered the bathroom, they found an incoherent and terrified young woman in a bra and panties with tears and mascara streaking her face. The seemingly inconsolable woman was lamenting in a high-pitched wail about her one true love not being able to live without her. She appeared genuinely devasted as she relayed that he killed himself out of uncontrollable grief upon learning that she was leaving him for another, younger man.

Both security agents looked at her with a mix of suspicion and sympathy. The shock and grief consuming Sloane's persona was truly convincing as she sobbed harder when they led her out past the dead body. One of the men even placed a robe around Sloane before pulling out a small radio from his coat pocket. Stealing a quick glance over her shoulder, she saw him call for the house physician to attend to the dead bureaucrat and help this obviously distraught woman calm down so they could get some answers. Forcing a somewhat kind look on his face, one of the agents led her out of the room to sit her down on a small settee just outside the suite door. Thinking she was too upset to be of much concern as she continued to sob and babble incoherently, he left her alone. He was still on the fence as he went back to examine the gruesome scene of an apparent suicide.

With no time to waste, Sloane quickly dried her tears and sprinted toward the stairs. While she quickly descended to the ground floor, she came across a man with a doctor's case in his hand running the other way up. He gave her no more than a perfunctory glance as they passed each other. Once she hit the ground floor, Sloane hurried to the grand entryway and picked up her pace. Rushing through the doorway, she quickly found the Porsche she had been driving earlier. Entering the sporty coupe, she felt beneath the driver-side floor mat for the extra set of keys she kept stashed and nearly exclaimed with relief when she found them. Sloane was soon underway and speeding down the winding drive to the main road leading away from the estate. Only when she was on the highway did she fully settle her nerves and realize that the cyanide capsule was still sitting under her bottom lip, awaiting the lethal bite.

After removing the capsule and placing it in a key tray, Sloane then removed the folded papers she was sitting on. She placed them into the glove box's secret double-door compartment as the car sped down the road. Thinking back to that episode, Sloane realized she had worked hard since then to become more careful about situational awareness when jumping into action. She had also learned to always take out her close-at-hand enemies first before they could do the same for her. Still looking and listening intently, Eddie finished his final instructions for the mission after a full three-hour briefing session and headed back through the door to the adjoining room. Alone once again, Sloane began to ponder and plan her moves for the next day, starting with the fashion show in which she was to be featured.

While preparing a small bag with all her necessary clothing, she also packed weaponry she anticipated she would need for the after-party. She carefully hid it away in an inner pocket of her garment bag, which was usually reserved for fashionable outfits, including several sexy mini-dresses sure to catch Pavel's eye. She paused briefly to stretch her tensed-up muscles by doing some quick yoga exercises. To placate her parched throat, Sloane found and drank a large bottle of Evian mineral water and climbed into the luxurious king-size bed, courtesy of her suite. Donning some satin sleepwear, she set her alarm for 5:00 am and turned off the bedside lamp. She soon fell into a restless sleep. The agitation was familiar; it was the same restless sleep she had always experienced just before starting a mission.

Sloane awoke quickly when her alarm went off. Rolling out of the way-too -comfortable bed, she padded towards the bathroom and turned on the light. After stopping to admire her model's body in a full-size mirror, she removed her sleepwear and entered the shower to get her mission underway. She dried off with a fluffy towel after having a good soak under the warm jet of the shower. Sloane then went to the wardrobe and picked out a smart-looking Givenchy outfit suitable for any number of affairs while admiring the tailored fit as she dressed. She quickly applied a minimal amount of makeup, put on her Manolo Blahnik open-toe heels, and took one last look in the mirror. Finally satisfied with her appearance, she grabbed her fully prepared garment bag and headed down to the lobby cafe for a quick plate of fresh fruit, flaky croissants, and two very strong cups of espresso. After finishing the brief but wonderfully light breakfast, Sloane made her way out front to the limousine. The car was already waiting, and she was soon escorted to the prestigious National Theater for this very first-of-its-kind fashion show staged for an international audience.

On her way, as the limo wound through the quiet streets of the still-sleeping city, Sloane started making plans to get close to Pavel. She needed to capture his complete attention to get the special VIP invite to the biggest party of the year at his riverside villa. The city was also preparing to welcome the world to the festivities leading up to the first-ever CEZ Petroleum / Rolex Grand Prix Formula One race. After all, it would determine the constructors' championship between Red Bull and McLaren. The last race of the season had witnessed a horrific crash and death of one of the world's favorite drivers a mere two weeks earlier. The upcoming race was dedicated to the memory of this champion of champions who could no longer enthrall his fans in the racing world.

As she arrived at the National Theater, Sloane was escorted through the stunning infrastructure, past the massive stage, and into the well-appointed dressing room. This room was specifically closed off for all the top models gracing the runway for the adoration of fashion fans and a massive media presence. The cameras flashed non-stop, bathing all the radiant female and male models. Models walking the grand world stage that afternoon wore the latest in high fashion. All the top designers were sure to give Milan, Paris, and New York fashion weeks a run for their money as it was the most prestigious fashion event of the year.

8

By 1:45 pm, the entire seating area near the runway had already filled up in anticipation of this one-of-a-kind fashion event. Featuring almost every major designer, the theme of the event had a special focus on cutting-edge stylish trends, debuting each designer's one-of-a-kind creations through the convention. This vast array included fashion houses from Italy like Valentino, Versace, Prada, Armani, Dolce Gabbana, Gucci, and Fendi. Not far behind, French Designers Louis Vuitton, Chanel, Hermes, Dior, St Laurent, and Givenchy could all be found in a final frenzy of preparation and last-minute dress fittings. The room was buzzing with excitement as the designers prepared for a grand standoff with the American design houses Calvin Klein, Ralph Lauren, Michael Kors, Tom Ford, Tommy Hilfiger, Donna Karan, and Marc Jacobs, along with the top Czech design brands Laformella, Mira Sabo, Chatty, Nehera, and Jakub Polanka were other formidable fashion giants. Never before had such a powerful continuum of designers been featured at one time on the same stage.

Apart from the design houses here, celebrities from the motion picture and television industries were also invited as guests. In the limelight of the front row were well-known personalities, such as Reese Witherspoon, Nicole Kidman, Sandra Bullock, Jennifer Aniston, Emma Stone, Emily Blunt, Julianne Moore, and Margot Robbie, to name just a few. And then there were the influencers from every corner of the entertainment industry with Christiano Ronaldo and Lionel Messi from the world of international football, Justin Bieber, Taylor Swift, and Ariana Grande from the music business, Kim and Khloe Kardashian and Kylie Jenner from reality TV and a whole slew of other well-known faces from around the globe, alongside local elites like top cabinet ministers and ambassadors plus local socialites.

As a statement against tradition, the models assigned to each designer were picked at random, defying the norm. This included the elite from the modeling world and Sloane, who was thought to be an emerging superstar on both the runway and in magazines. However, new names like Agel Akol, Karolina Spakowski, Lulu Tenney, Dianna Chiu, and Annemarie Aderibigby could also be found in the mix among favorites such as Gigi Hadid, Kendall Jenner, Karli Kloss, Ashley Graham, Linda Evangelista and Naomi Campbell along with other recognizable supermodels from various eras.

At precisely 2:00 pm, the house lights dimmed, and EDM boomed through hidden speakers in the hall, letting all in attendance know that this significant fashion shindig was about to begin. As the host and emcee of the show, none other than Pavel Grovzny himself entered the stage to thunderous applause from the prestigious "who's who" audience that themselves looked like they could be in their own fashion show of celebrity style. Pavel waved and gestured to hype up the crowd before raising a microphone to address everyone in attendance. The crowd quieted down as Pavel began thanking them profusely for their generosity in welcoming him to the stage and for attending this invitation-only fashion event of the century.

Pavel looked like he could be a male model himself dressed in a smartly tailored custom navy-blue Armani suit with a cream-colored open-collar dress shirt and feet adorned by a pair of custom loafers from Stefano Ricci. In an energetic voice with animated hand movements, sounding like the very best in TV hosts, Pavel announced to the restless crowd, "And now . . . Let's get this party started!" As he left the stage, quickly stepping behind a podium just off the runway, a crescendo of heavy metal guitars, pounding bass, and masterful drums began an aural assault throughout this wonderful theater better known for its performance of Mozart. With that, the fashion show began with model after model taking to the runway, doing their utmost in showing off incredible one-of-a-kind designs that yielded a visual feast for everyone in attendance. Pavel did his due diligence, announcing the names of both designers and the models as they hit the stage. He described the inspiration behind each original offering in great detail, with lively commentary to keep the audience hooked. Finally, it was Sloane's turn to hit the runway in a fabulous baby blue, sequined Dior mini dress. Once on stage, she suddenly looked over at Pavel with a genuinely disarming smile that disarmed him enough to accidentally stumble over her name while announcing her onto the runway.

Later, precisely after one hour, all the models returned for a final walk down the runway en masse as the crowd applauded and cheered wildly. As the last model left the stage, Pavel came from behind the podium to more thunderous applause, thanked the audience profusely for their attendance, and reminded everyone about the after-party to be held at his villa on the river. Though subtle, he still made a show of telling them that the party was an official kick-off affair for Formula One racing week in this amazing European capital. On the other side of the curtain, Sloane waited patiently as if the future was scripted. It wasn't long before Pavel appeared backstage and started looking for her. She smiled the same disarming smile as he fumbled his apology for pronouncing her name wrong and immediately fell under her charming spell. She had learned to play her targets well, and before she knew it, he had invited her to be his special guest for the evening at the party and, perhaps, even to stay the weekend. Knowing this was the objective of her mission, Sloane graciously accepted the offer with a gleaming face that visibly melted his heart like all the others.

With no more pleasantries left to exchange, Pavel left the area. Sloane nearly voiced out loud that this was maybe, just maybe, going to be a lot easier than she had originally planned. Soon, her mind started whirring now that she had the whole weekend to dispatch her unsuspecting target, lull him into darkness, and make the world a safer place to live.

Outside the theater, Pavel made his way to a private limousine. Once inside, he turned to a shadowy figure on the far end twirling a wine in his hand and nodded. In hushed voices, they confirmed that she had taken the bait, well aware of Sloane's mission as a CIA operative. The shadowy stranger raised his glass, congratulating Pavel on his success. As it seemed, the agency was still unaware of his well-planted mole smuggling confidential intel out of the bureau. Now, it was just a matter of gaining her trust. Pavel smirked as he briefly wondered how long she would last against his own powers of seduction. He was sure, without a doubt, that he would catch her off-guard and put an end to her mission. If he weren't so viciously ambitious, Pavel thought, he'd be almost sad at the idea of disposing of her body from his yacht as it cruised down the river at the end of their time together.

9

Sitting high on a bluff, just above the bend in the river and commanding a spectacular view, sat Pavel Grovzny's custom-built villa. It could only be described as opulently built, with its multi-level palatial mansion fit for royalty. This wasn't unusual; it made perfect sense since it originally belonged to the last Bohemian Monarch, King Charles the Third, before World War One, when Czechoslovakia became a Republic after elections in 1920. It had been sitting dormant for many years, almost in disrepair, since not many could afford the hassle of owning a royal mansion. But Pavel merely purchased it for a song. His charm was enough to ensure significant leeway on taxes, not to mention his boisterous public and private acclaim, pledging to return it to greatness as a historic landmark and cultural center on behalf of the Republic.

Of course, it was all for show. Pavel had no actual plans to make it a reality. Instead, he intended to use it as a secret headquarters, a center of operations for all of his mercenary dealings, filling his personal coffers with several hundred million Euros, US Dollars,

British pounds, and a few billion in cryptocurrency with gold futures. No one really knew his worth. People either never bothered or just assumed his considerable wealth came from family holdings. His position as the leading individual shareholder easily trumped the entire Republic in CEZ Group, a conglomerate of 96 companies dealing with electricity generation, natural gas trading, and coal extraction. With wealth came the resources; all of this had a legal paper trail for anyone curious enough to follow. Crafted carefully, they left out the mention of the money Grovzny harvested from all of his mercenary and criminal activities. Eventually, it became very easy for him to finance his private army of killers to plan the international destruction, employing the highest bidder for their services.

The majority of the sprawling estate was still undergoing extensive restoration except for two main areas that were completed on a rush order. He needed a base; he had to start somewhere. The ground floor was one of the first to be repaired. After renovation, it boasted everything needed for lavish entertainment, something Pavel had become very well known for. The second floor above held a series of private suites, including the Master Suite, that he offered to various guests as accommodation whenever such a gesture aligned with his goals. However, one other area of improvement remained hidden from sight, meant only for the eyes of a select few who could be trusted with their operation.

This final "Add On" to the estate was hidden away in a large and sterile-looking secret room deep inside the basement. It contained a state-of-the-art computer center for everything from mainstream ops, communications, surveillance, hacking different infrastructures, to all kinds of cybercrime. Be it money laundering, identity theft, marketing narcotics on the dark web, weapons, human trafficking or sex slavery – the hideout had access to everything. It was the control center for Pavel's mission, from planning to execution, and the heart of the entire operation.

By 7:00 pm, having changed into a pair of Calvin Klein chinos, a Lilly Dache golf shirt covered by a tailored navy blue Marc Jacobs blazer, and a pair of his favorite deck shoes, a cheap purchase on Amazon with no socks, Pavel stood in front of the massive entryway. Wearing his handsome smile, he put on his welcoming performance as the first of his many guests began to arrive in their Maseratis, Bentleys, Bugattis, Lambos, Ferraris, and other luxury coupes and sedans. Greeting them one by one by their first names, Pavel instantly began to ingratiate himself with his guests with an overwhelming charm that suited him so well. It helped him carry out his notorious affairs with women in relationships with other men that he could later blackmail or even corporate espionage and extortion that would further his mercenary goals.

It wasn't long before several hundred invited attendees crowded the well-crafted ballroom. The appointed party room could easily hold up to a thousand people for what would be dinners of state in another day and age. Champagne flowed freely as techno music boomed through the hall, inviting people to the huge dance floor already filled with jet setters from near and far. Men and women moved with reckless abandon to the heavy thump of the electronic bass vibrating up into their nether regions as pleasure took hold over their minds and bodies. For some, it was just another night of raving, a life they had grown accustomed to, and for others, it was a chance to loosen up. It was a chance to let go of the normal restrictive conventions of their daily lives and, for once, experience the elite lifestyle.

As Sloane entered the massive space, she could spot Pavel across the room in an animated conversation with two beautiful women. They laughed and seemed to blush at whatever he was telling them.

Without skipping a beat, Pavel looked across the room and spotted Sloane as if he had some built-in radar detecting her aura. The next thing she knew, Pavel had excused himself from the two women and made his way through the room in her direction. With his signature smile intact, he still acknowledged everyone as he headed toward her. For a moment, Sloane thought about trying to avoid him. But she couldn't escape his gaze as he approached where she stood, looking intently in his direction. In less than two minutes, Pavel had weaved through the crowd. He took Sloane by the hand and welcomed her to his "humble abode" as he gently pulled her close enough for her to smell him. His private musk-like pheromone suddenly made her want to be in his presence. As if sensing the same, he offered, "Shall we dance?" and led her out to the dance floor before she could respond. The DJ, on cue, suddenly began playing a synth variation on a classic tango.

To Sloane's surprise, Pavel was not just a sure-fire charmer in his interaction with women but also a well-trained ballroom dancer. He was the type of partner who made all women feel like they were the only ones in the room. For Sloane, the feeling had an overwhelming pull as they began this fiery dance, passion mingling between their heavy breaths and a sensation she had yet to name. This was new territory for Sloane. As the dance continued, she found herself… distracted. Little by little, she felt herself falling under Pavel's spell of seduction, his handsome looks, and eyes that seemed to peer deep into her very soul.

When the dance finally came to an end, Pavel dipped her backward in one swift move. Sloane felt the strength in his hand as it slid onto the small of her back, supporting her frame. A shiver ran the length of her spine as his powerful yet gentle touch pulled her close; their bodies were mere inches apart but felt as if they were already intertwined. At that very moment, Sloane, for the first time in her life, felt this strange desire to abandon her mission so she might get to know this intensely vibrant man far more intimately than she had ever planned. Caught off guard, she found herself letting him slide his hand below the small of her back. In a move that seemed to surprise them both, she felt the sweet kiss on her lips as the song ended. As Pavel helped Sloane regain her footing, they looked around to find that almost everyone on the dance floor had stopped. They were simply watching the masterful display. The room erupted into wild applause as the song transitioned into a slow but enchanting waltz for all the lovers to embrace as they joined in the dance with one another.

Sloane was surprised when Pavel led her from the dance floor to one of the nearby servers. He handed her a glass of champagne and offered up a simple toast to longevity in new affairs of the heart. They both took a sip and then Pavel kissed her again, this one longer and full of passion. Sloane felt herself slipping further and further away from her purpose. She tried to remind herself again. She had to kill this dangerous enemy of the state, according to others in the intelligence community. But could they be wrong? How could this man, held in high esteem and adored by so many, really be this monster they portrayed him to be?

Before she knew it, Pavel had invited her to stay for the weekend. "The hotel you're staying at has already been informed," He said as he gently caressed her cheek. "We told them you would be away for a few days but would return for your belongings."

"I- " Sloane wanted to protest this callous move but immediately snapped back into operative mode. "Actually…" She stared into his eyes and bit her lower lip for effect, "That would be wonderful." This might be the perfect and, perhaps, the only opportunity to complete her mission, she thought as her heart skipped a beat. Pavel's smile, on the other hand, seemed to have grown more radiant at her answer.

She was still lost in her thoughts, trying to rationalize her emotions, when suddenly, Pavel pulled his phone out. He spoke briefly to someone on the other end, looked at Sloane, and said, "It's time." Sloane had no idea what he meant, but with a few quick gestures, the music came to a halt. Pavel, leading Sloane toward a small set of risers, took hold of a wireless mic as people once again applauded his presence. Once the crowd quieted down, he began by thanking all of his guests for their attendance and then paused. The sound of roaring automobiles filled the air as he told the crowd to please turn their attention towards the ballroom entrance. All twenty of the Formula One race drivers, the rock stars of auto racing, entered the room and headed for the stage one by one to the chorus of "We Are The Champions" by Queen.

The crowd parted like the Red Sea before Moses as the drivers made their way through the room, applauding wildly. The excited cheers serenaded them on the march to the stage. Sloane could only watch in complete awe as Pavel warmly greeted each driver to the stage with a handshake and bro hug before announcing each one by name. The crowd went completely mad with the utterance of each driver's name as if they lived for this moment.

After the introductions concluded, the drivers rubbed elbows with their fans and signed autographs for many others. The race was due in just seven more days.

Still captivated by the enthusiasm, Sloane was again brought back to reality when Pavel graciously began introducing her to each and every one of the elite drivers. After all, they were his personal guests of honor for the evening gala kick-off to Formula One week in Prague. It wasn't long before the drivers had all departed, and Sloane found herself alone once again, being pulled by Pavel as he showed her to her guest room. Though she never even got the chance to see the room. Once the door to her suite opened, Sloane suddenly felt the cloth bag roughly thrown over her head. Before she could think of her next move, in horror, she felt the unmistakable jab of a needle piercing her neck. In a matter of a few seconds, darkness swallowed her vision, and she remembered nothing else.

10

Darkness. Nothing but darkness welcomed Sloane as she started to come out of her drug-induced stupor. The lack of visuals further intensified the massively painful headache. There was no sound either, which made her even more disoriented as she tried to gain her bearings. Sloane's training allowed her to rely on her other senses and they began to kick in. She slowly started to become aware of her situation as she regained consciousness.

The first sensation she felt was on her skin. She knew that she was not dressed in what she had originally worn. As she ran her hands up and down, she seemed to be in some sort of lightweight but tight-fitting jumpsuit. Her feet were bare, and she could feel a smooth surface beneath her feet that reminded her of concrete. The surface was cold, as was the air around her. She tried shakily to stand up and move but quickly felt herself shackled by the ankle to something, somewhere on the floor, like a retaining ring of iron. She was apparently sitting on some sort of pile that felt like burlap-covered beanbags. And then the smell hit her. She could almost taste the musty dampness permeating the space as she took a deep breath without really meaning to.

As her eyes slowly adjusted to the darkness, she could vaguely make out the shape of a door maybe 10 feet away from her. Suddenly, she could hear the faint sound of boots approaching the door. She heard what sounded like a key engaging a lock with a metallic click. As the door slowly swung open, light streamed into the room and added to Sloane's distress as it temporarily blinded her. Her eyes soon adjusted to the light, and she could make out the silhouette of a large male coming through the doorway toward her. The corner of her eye also caught a glint of something metallic. From the angle at which light reflected off of it, Sloane could tell that the man was holding a gun, pointed right between her eyes. It was a visible warning, almost daring her to resist and see the outcome. She knew better than to try anything crazy.

As the man crouched down to unlock the shackles wrapped around Sloane's ankles, she started to steel herself for a movement of action. Just then, she saw another shadow just outside the door. She knew there had to be another armed assailant waiting patiently with orders to take her out if she actually tried to run. Her frustration began to grow as she realized it was likely due to the knowledge that she was an experienced operative. Her captors were most likely aware of her skills to incapacitate and kill when need be. They clearly knew enough. But Sloane didn't know exactly how much. Her only concern at that moment was the possibility that her abductors might just use her for sale in the sex trade.

After the shackles had been removed, the male stood up and grasped her upper arm in an iron firm grip and roughly yanked Sloane to her feet. Unceremoniously, he then pulled her towards the now fully opened door. Once in the brightly lit corridor, Sloane was surprised to see a total of three additional men and a woman, all dressed in black as her escorts. They were prepared with fully automatic weapons and 9mm sidearms, likely in a show of force. It was an intimidation tactic to let Sloane know they were serious and wouldn't tolerate any trouble she might try to cause them. For the first time in a long time, she felt somewhat helpless. Knowing better, she said nothing as the crew yanked her down the corridor into what appeared to be an interrogation room with a table and two chairs on each side. The same man who had unshackled her walked her around the table and pushed her down into a chair. Sloane opened her mouth to say something, but the man quickly turned and left the room. She wondered why she hadn't been re-secured but figured that the room was most likely under heavy surveillance. Anything she might try would be seen before she could even do any real damage. Fortunately for Sloane, the surveillance system had no way of reading her mind. An escape plan had already begun to come together, along with a few insights into the mission.

While seated, Sloane began to mull over her predicament. She started retracing her steps to see what might have gone wrong, wondering if somehow someone in Pavel's network had recognized her from a prior mission. She figured this made perfectly logical sense when it came to the armed escort she had. This clarity helped as she sat thinking things through. It helped her become somewhat more mentally prepared for what might happen next.

Slowly rising from her chair, Sloane started doing a series of isometric exercises to help stretch the muscles that still felt stiff and lethargic after being drugged for so long. She was finally starting to feel closer to being herself again when she heard the distinct sound of an electronic key clicking. As the door opened, in stepped Pavel with his infectious grin. On cue, Sloane stood and stumbled towards Pavel, feigning panic and desperation as though she still didn't know what was happening. But Pavel's demeanor had turned cold. Ignoring her distress, he held up his hand to dismiss her and told her in a matter-of-fact voice, "Please take a seat."

She sat back down in a state of disbelief.

"I know all about your plans for taking down my organization," Pavel began. Sloane was too stunned to speak. "It's funny what people are willing to do once you breach their home security feed… and then all it takes is a few encrypted dispatches on the Signal app and voila." He threw a file on the table labeled "CIA: Confidential." In horror, Sloane realized the personnel file was her own, listing all missions and operations she had ever been on. She knew it was imperative to continue her mission and kill Pavel, if possible, but more importantly, to discover the mole that had given her up.

If what Pavel told her was accurate, a mole at that level could do as much damage to the CIA as Robert Hansen had done to the FBI for over 20 years. Throughout the 1970s. It was considered to be "possibly the worst intelligence disaster in U.S. history." Sloane feigned ignorance to what Pavel was telling her. It was soon apparent that his over-inflated ego and sense of self-accomplishment would take him down a self-made rabbit hole. He just couldn't stop himself from bragging about the power of his operation and just how futile and ineffective Sloane's mission was turning out to be. He went on and on about how he had prepared for her eventual demise before she ever showed up in Prague.

Once he had his fill, Pavel took Sloane by the elbow and led her out of the interrogation room. The room was located in the basement, just under the operations center. He still hadn't stopped bragging about how unstoppable his whole mercenary and criminal organization had become. How its tentacles entrenched throughout the civilized world to destroy governments and corporations as the opportunities presented themselves, and how he never played favorites. He did, however, have his detractors and enemies, engaged in any and all opportunities he could get to wreak havoc and lay ruin to their various missions, including the present one with Special Operative Sloane Harper. The US intelligence agencies were at the top of his list as he gleefully explained to Sloane that this would surely put an end to the current plan the CIA had for stopping him and his private army. He also apologized to Sloane, explaining that in another life, He and Sloane could have been a fabulous couple and close allies or even partners, but due to circumstances, he would have to end her.

Sloane never showed emotion, formulating a plan while waiting for the right moment to take action.

That moment came in short order as they passed one of the workstations in the control room. Sloane spotted a notebook and a sharpened pencil on the desk next to one of the computer technicians. Without hesitation, Sloane punched the technician in the temple and grabbed the notebook, which she used as a hard-edged weapon across the side of Pavel's neck, stunning him. She quickly stabbed him between two ribs and punctured a lung with the sharpened pencil. Then, grabbing him around the neck, she put him in a chokehold and pressed the point of the bloodied pencil directly into the jugular vein as unarmed technicians watched in horror.

Sloane ordered them all into a lockable storage room, threatening to kill their leader as he struggled to breathe. Pavel yelled hoarsely to do as they were told. Still, Sloane had other plans. She directed the technician she had punched to print out a full list of current and future planned operations and a comprehensive list of those who abetted or aligned themselves with Pavel's operation before ordering him to get inside the storage room. With the technicians locked away and the print-out secured inside her tight-fitting jumpsuit, she pressed the pencil point all the harder into Pavel's throat. With Pavel as her hostage, she moved towards the exit, knowing there was one of Pavel's security personnel just beyond the door. They had passed him on their way into the ops center. Opening the door slightly, she yelled in panic that there was a problem and Pavel needed their help. The moment the guard entered through the door, Sloane lashed out a vicious kick to his side, taking the wind out of him. She quickly grabbed the automatic weapon, hit the guard again with the gun butt, and knocked him unconscious. She turned to point it at Pavel and carried on with her escape.

But Pavel had anticipated this move and went on with the attack even though he struggled with the punctured lung. Knocking the gun loose from Sloane's hands, he quickly punched her, knocking her into the wall, and began to violently choke her with an arm bar across her throat. Now struggling to breathe herself, Sloane pressed a thumb into one of Pavel's eyes while the other hand reached for his side wound. Meanwhile, she dug her fingers into his ribs, causing him excruciating pain, which in turn loosened the pressure he had been applying to her throat with his arm bar. With the pressure weakening, Sloane quickly delivered a painful instep stomp and threw her knee with all the force she could muster upward into Pavel's groin. He fell to the floor, writhing in agony. Without hesitating, Sloane picked up the automatic and slung it over her head at a diagonal for carrying. She then retrieved the 9mm sidearm carried by the still unconscious guard, roughly grabbed Pavel by the shirt collar, and hauled him to his feet and out through the exit door of the computer center, smashing the entry panel to disable the door.

Surprisingly, Sloane found the corridor empty as she and Pavel made their way out of that operational complex. Exhausted, she finally snapped, "Unless you want your brains splattered across a wall, get us out of here." With his life on the line, Pavel felt compelled to oblige. Sloane saw no cameras. She figured that was typical ego for a man like Pavel. He obviously never thought his operation could ever be compromised.

The two finally came to an unmarked doorway with a biometric lock. It required a thumbprint and eye scan from Pavel. This turned out to be Pavel's private garage at the estate, and it wasn't long before Sloane and Pavel came upon a brand-new Mercedes AMG coupe. Making her way to the passenger side of the powerful car, Sloane forced Pavel into the driver's seat.

"Drive or die. Your call,"

11

Pavel, still breathing with noticeable difficulty, gurgled blood as he tried to protest. Unable to see a way out of the situation, he pushed the starter button on the AMG, and the engine immediately came to life with an understated yet throaty roar. Pavel's knuckles whitened over the steering wheel as he pulled the car out of its parking space.

They headed towards a corkscrew ramp that would take them up from the basement-level garage. As Sloane looked around for any sign of interference or danger, Pavel snickered slightly, "There's no way for you to get out of here. The inevitable will catch up to you sooner or later." He glanced at her with a menacing scowl as he spat out his next words, "Everyone knows about you and I mean everyone. By now, my security team would have noticed us when we came to the garage… They know what to do to you."

Unfortunately for Pavel Grovzny, his own team had no idea about the events in the control center. So they really didn't think that much about the two figures, one of whom was Pavel himself, who had entered the garage and pulled away in a car up the ramp. This wasn't even a public garage, which meant that there was no toll booth that would stop them, and no one to deal with personnel working their way towards the automatic doors. Their current path led to the private drive leading out the back of the estate towards the servants' entrance. This was Pavel's favored route, enabling him to come and go unnoticed by others who might have prying eyes. However, unlike the main entrance with a large, remotely operated double gate system, the service entrance did indeed have a guardhouse manned by not one but at least two of Pavel's most vigilant soldiers.

They finally approached the automated garage doors that worked on a motion sensor. Sloan could see two very conspicuous security cameras at each corner of the door. She knew that someone would be getting a much closer look at them as they went through. The doors which were now retracting from the center to the sides into the massive walls of the basement car park.

“Be a good boy and act normal for the cameras.” Sloane nudged the barrel resting on Pavel’s side rib, “We don’t want them finding out about our little game, now, do we?” She almost crooned at the end. Pavel looked over at her, gave her a sly but sheepish grin, and then waved at the cameras as if nothing untoward was happening. Sloan did her best to put on a delicate smile and laugh as though listening to one of Pavel's stories like the ones he told at his party the night before.

It was too bad that Sloane didn't realize that the security feed was a close-up shot that would undoubtedly make her recognizable. Nor did she notice when Pavel tilted his head slightly in a nod as he shifted his eyes, glaring towards Sloane in the passenger seat. The close-up of Sloane, paired with Pavel’s signal, did exactly what they were intended to do as they passed through the garage doors. Soon after, Sloane heard the sound of a Klaxon-type security siren blaring through, alerting all the staff that there was indeed something amiss. The alarm let them know to get ready for action, and they did this without hesitation. They had been well trained, and Pavel had selected each and every one of them for this, his private security force of killers.

"Hit it!" Alarmed, Sloane immediately commanded Pavel, “Or else!” she added for extra measure, and soon they were hurtling through twists and turns way past the speed limit, but the AMG hugged the road flawlessly. Soon, they could see the guardhouse about 1,000 meters in front of them. As they sped recklessly down the backroad towards the servants' entrance, they could see what appeared to be a force of armed people climbing out from a series of vehicles assembling across the road as Sloane and Pavel closed in on their position. Several banks of extremely bright LED lights suddenly flicked on, blasting the AMG with blinding accuracy. Worried, Sloane felt like there might not be a way out of this as they careened their way towards the heavily armed force ready to open fire on them.

Pavel had no reaction when Sloane jammed the gun into his chest, where the lung had been punctured. She was growing desperate, "Put the pedal to the metal!" she was practically screaming, "Be prepared to powerslide around them!" The powerslide was a dangerous, evasive move only the best stunt drivers could pull off. As the AMG came within a hundred feet of the guardhouse and armed force, Sloane yelled, "Now!" She yanked the steering wheel to the right and then quickly again to the left as fully automatic weapons fire began to rake the front and driver's side of the coupe. They slalomed around the firing line and exploded through a barricade. Luckily for Sloane, but not so much for Pavel and his firing squad. The AMG had been fully built to withstand such an assault. Pavel had custom-ordered it from a specialty car builder just in case it actually encountered a situation like this. However, it was never envisioned that it would be tested out in a situation like this.

The car proved impervious to the assault of automatic weapons fire it had just endured. It continued down the rear drive with a now somewhat horrified Pavel almost screaming, "What were you thinking! Oh my god! We both could have died from that stunt!"

" Zip it, dirtbag," Sloane snapped as she pressed the gun harder into his wound, "Before I give you a real reason to cry about." Meanwhile, three vehicles loaded up behind them. They were soon in hot pursuit with custom engines meant for a chase just like this. Sloane took a deep breath and tried to settle her own nerves. She was suddenly aware of the three sets of lights in pursuit, which seemed to be slowly closing in on their position.

Even though the AMG was moving at a high speed, the pursuing vehicles continued to gain ground and were soon close enough for Sloane to hear the sound of automated gunfire that were hitting the vehicle again. Peering through the rear window, she could see someone emerging from a top hatch for one of the vehicles. It looked like that person was now pointing an RPG or rocket-propelled grenade at them. This was not something the AMG had been built to withstand. Sloane once again grabbed the wheel and swerved to keep them from becoming a solid target for the RPG.

All of a sudden, a ball of flame burst ahead of them. The RPG whooshed by the passenger side of the car, slamming into the sidewall of the road as they went into a curve. It exploded into a stand of Norwegian Maple trees, toppling them into the road as the coupe sped past. One of the trees landed directly on top of the off-roader and the soldier who had fired the RPG. It caused that vehicle to stop immediately while also impeding the travel of the other two off-roaders. But it was not enough to keep them from quickly starting to catch up to the AMG again.

Pulling up directly behind and beside the driver's rear wheel of the coupe, one off-roader rammed the AMG from behind while the other rammed into the rear wheel. This put the coupe into a spin that sent them out of control and off the road, where it hit a large boulder at an angle that sent the car flying. When it hit, the car began to tumble down a steep embankment and hillside until it came to rest 200 meters down at the bottom of a ravine.

Luckily, both Sloane and Pavel had been strapped in by the automatic restraint system. They avoided serious injury due to the

360-airbag system that had been deployed. Aside from Pavel's previously punctured lung, it appeared that both of them sustained only minor bangs and bruises, but Sloane could see a nasty gash over Pavel's right eye. The same could not be said of the Mercedes coupe. It looked like it had been put through a giant trash compactor as steam poured out of the engine compartment. Slowly checking to see if they could move at all, Sloane discovered that her door wouldn't budge when she tried to open it. Sloane disengaged her restraint system, retrieved the 9mm she saw sitting on the floor below, and kicked out the partially destroyed windshield. After climbing out, she headed further down the ravine upon hearing voices and movement above on the hillside.

For Sloane, there was no advantage to taking Pavel with her, as she only had one main thing on her mind. Escape.

12

Climbing further down the ravine from the wreckage of the Mercedes, Sloane swiftly but gingerly made her way through. The brambles tore at her still-bare feet until she felt shocked by the sudden gush of cold water. She found herself submerged in a small stream at the bottom of the ravine. Having no other option, she started toward the slow-moving current as it headed down and away from the voices getting closer to Pavel and the wrecked car, unaware that Sloane was no longer with the crashed coupe.

As Sloane kept moving down and away from the crash scene, the mercenaries finally reached the crash site and immediately started to extract Pavel. It didn't take them long to realize that Sloane was missing from the car. They immediately went to search for their adversary, who was nowhere in sight but in all likelihood, still close enough to hunt down. A now fully alert Pavel commanded part of the force to head further down into the ravine. Despite his injuries, he remembered hearing Sloane shuffling her way towards the bottom of the ravine through the somewhat thick undergrowth among the uneven plains of the forest. He told them her best route for escape would most likely be down the ravine and towards a nearby open area just on the edge of the city limits.

Once out of the wrecked car and seemingly no worse for wear, Pavel shouted, "Find the bitch before she gets to city and calls her handlers!" One of his bodyguards tried to hand him a water bottle, but Pavel, in a fit of rage threw it away. "She's a witness, god damn it! She knows about the command center." He turned and grabbed another guard by the collar, "Find her. Right now!" He shoved him back to his squad. Pavel, himself, took two men, and they began climbing back out of the ravine up the steep incline where the off-road vehicles sat still running with powerful lights pointed in their direction.

After he climbed out of the ravine, Pavel moved to take the wheel of one vehicle. But the crash and the climb immediately after worsened the head injury he had sustained. The symptoms caught up to him, and it suddenly made him feel weak and somewhat dizzy. So, he moved to the passenger seat while yelling at one of the others to get them back to the Villa. He had to secure the chaos that had ensued earlier and send out an urgent and encrypted communique to others. His partners needed to be informed of this new threat, and they had to discuss the future of the operations and possible actions needed to secure their ultimate plans and end any more intrusions once and for all. Pavel scowled as he imagined their reactions. After all, they had underestimated the most recent threat: a dangerous CIA operative named Sloane Harper.

Pavel also needed to get back to his persona of high-flying socialite, local power broker, and the main mover and shaker in Prague of the upcoming Grand Prix race, which was already in the practice lap stage at the race facility. As far as the public was concerned, they had to see the business run as usual for this sophisticated Czech playboy, the most prominent organizer for all the events taking place during the week of the race. Little did anyone realize that this was all part of an elaborate plot ready to trigger a deadly chain of events throughout the entire world as part of Pavel's plan to wreak destruction and cripple governments everywhere.

Back at the crash site, the rest of the mercenary force picked up Sloane's trail leading down the ravine until they hit the water. There, they split their numbers. Half the team headed downhill in the obvious direction of escape, while the other half headed up the ravine. They knew that they were facing a trained operative who could not be underestimated or as predictable as the average citizen. With bright LED torches lighting their way, the split force wasted no time moving through the underbrush on both sides of the small stream up and down the ravine. They were determined to search and destroy Sloane as she continued to move downhill.

Sloane's pace was steady, but she could definitely feel pain in her feet from the constant cold abusing her cuts. Her movements began to slow, and soon, she could hear the sound of others crashing through the underbrush as they closed in on her position. She couldn't see the floodlights dancing around, but knew it was just a matter of time before she would. Dreading once again the end of her mission and possibly, her life if she didn't get away, Sloane pushed through whatever pain she felt and picked up her pace. Suddenly, she spotted an array of lights just a few kilometers in front of her and felt the ground leveling out. With a breath of relief, she realized she was coming to the mouth of the ravine at the bottom of the hill and into an open meadow that skirted the city's outer limits.

Now all she had to do was get across the open ground before the armed force in dedicated pursuit, spotted her in the beam of powerful lamps, and gunned her down like the prey she had become. She knew if she went on a straight path, it would most likely become a death sentence, but she wasn't willing to give up just yet. Sloane hit the opening of the ravine and quickly made her way to the right along the tree line that marked the edge of the open ground she had just entered. Hunched down, she kept moving until she found a branch of the stream she had come down from. Following it further away from the ravine, she found it turned into the meadow and headed across towards the still distant lights.

Staying low to the ground below the bank of the small stream, she headed across the grassy expanse to avoid the lights that would soon appear. Sloane knew the only other advantage she had, if it could really be called that, was the fully loaded 9mm automatic she still carried. Her training had prepared her to use it when the time came for any showdown. Though she also knew it wasn't much of a match for the firepower now emerging from the ravine she had just come out of. Firing the weapon would give up her position, not something she could afford.

Lying low, Sloane could see the group of armed personnel split into three smaller groups of four, with one group moving forward and the other two splitting right and left. They were moving in a forward flank that put one of them slightly in front of her position. This in turn, gave Sloane a slight advantage over the group moving in her direction. It enabled her to tuck in behind their movement until the time came where she could either have an edge in this fight or end up with her ultimate defeat if she didn't do things right. Doing things right meant knowing all her combat training was about to be tested in a way it had never been before.

Sloane was moving in, copying their flanking position, lingering slightly behind the now small group moving towards the stream bank. She crouched behind them as they moved in a single file echelon formation. Their position soon put them almost directly in front of her, a mere 50 feet away. It was obvious to Sloane that although they were scanning in all directions, they certainly weren't expecting her to be behind them. They carried on their search and soon were peering down the streambank as the city lights grew ever closer to their position. Sloane could sense a bit of desperation creeping into their whispers. They knew she could spell their doom if they failed to find and kill her before she got into the city and disappeared.

She moved as swiftly and quietly as possible. Sloane was suddenly behind the last man in line, and quickly dropped the 9mm and slipped her left hand around his face to the right jaw line. With a quick move, she violently wrenched the head to the left with a force that instantly snapped the man's neck before pulling him down into the tall grass and out of sight. Meanwhile, the others kept moving forward, unaware that they had just lost one of their own. Soon after, she had the suppressed automatic rifle in her hands. Making the most of the opportunity, she raised the weapon and prepared to fire. In perfect poise, she placed three precise head shots from behind that took out all three of the remaining men in the formation.

As it turned out, one of the men was actually a woman. Sloane hurriedly stripped her out of the combat fatigues and boots and was soon dressed in the same gear as that of the force out to kill her. Quickly slinging one automatic over chest and picking up another, Sloane wasted no time in bee-lining along the stream bank. Then, she broke into a run towards the city lights, now only a few hundred meters away. The distinct sound of a radio check from one of the other groups followed her closely behind. In less than 30 seconds, beams of light were flaring across her position as she ran towards the presumed safety of the city limits.

Sloane raised one of the automatics with a quick dive and roll and fired from a prone position. It sent off a burst of fully automatic fire, hitting one of the distant torches and the man who carried it. The commotion led the rest to dive for cover. The return fire followed soon after as Sloane moved into a different position to better aim at the small flashes emanating from the suppressed weapons. While exercising the U.S. Marine Corps shooting science of B.R.A.S.S. (breathe, relax, aim, stop, and squeeze), Sloane could hear the cry and groan as she took down another assailant. She moved again for another shot but missed before turning. Finally, she broke into a full sprint, zig-zagging towards the lights as full automatic gunfire came raining down, raking the ground underneath her. Determined, she dashed towards the corner of a building and found herself exiting the meadow. The sprint across a wide boulevard with cars travelling in both directions was as risky as the bullets pelting behind her, but she had to take her chance. The morning sun was just starting to appear on the horizon, and unaware, local Czech citizens were on their way to starting their day.

The gunfire continued as Sloane wove in between moving vehicles. Stray bullets struck several cars and a commercial truck, causing a sudden series of crashes. The damaged vehicles brought the busy traffic to a complete halt, choking the roadway. Seizing the moment, Sloane made her way around the closest building. She quickly ran down an empty roadway between what appeared to be a series of loading docks in an industrial park. Soon, she was out of immediate line of sight, disappearing on the other end of the service road, round the corner of the last building.

13

They lost sight of Sloane as she disappeared behind the manic traffic jam. Having no other option, the remainder of the mercenary hit squad quickly opted to make a hasty retreat back towards the ravine. Choosing to ignore the chaos they had caused, they turned away as more and more traffic snarled to a halt. They could hear the unmistakable bleat of sirens approaching the area as multiple law enforcement vehicles converged onto the chaotic scene of tangled autos and trucks. Most of these vehicles were considerably damaged by the automatic weapons fire.

Luckily, no one at the scene had been hit by gunfire. While canvassing, the police were at a complete loss to explain what could have possibly occurred to bring about what looked like a high-powered combat firefight. Knowing that they had failed in their mission to capture and or kill Sloane, the retreating armed groups spread out, hoping to retrieve some of their missing and most likely fallen comrades. But the sun was fully upon them as they crossed over the open ground. With law enforcement hovering nearby, they made the decision that would put them in an ever-dimming light in the eyes of Pavel Grovzny and left the missing personnel behind.

Back at his Villa, the private concierge doctor, part of Pavel's operation, closed up the cut above his eye with a couple of carefully placed staples and a flesh-toned gel. It did a wondrous job of hiding all the scars or recently inflicted wounds. He handed Pavel a small paper cup containing both some antibiotics and a mild painkiller. The mercenary terrorist leader chewed them before swallowing and washed the bitter taste down with a glass of orange juice as he mulled over all that had occurred over the last few days. He knew all that had transpired could indeed threaten his entire operation if he didn't get a handle on it in time. He had to regain control over the situation if his plans around the race were to succeed. He knew it would not bode well for him if he failed in the final execution of his carefully worked-out plan of attack.

He stood up and headed to his suite to shower and change into a fresh outfit. On his way, Pavel grabbed a nearby satellite phone as it pulsed on a nearby cradle and punched in a special number followed by a code that immediately connected him to the incoming call from the Spanish island of Mallorca.

"How goes the progress for the Grand Prix? I assume the plan proceeds as usual." A voice crackled on the phone. Pavel paused for a brief moment, biting his lip. Their operation had been compromised, though he knew better than to admit it.

"Yes. We encountered a small breach in internal security, but the threat has been neutralized." Pavel reported in an even tone, barely able to keep the tremor from his voice.

"You, pathetic imbecile!" Pavel cringed at the terse reply echoing through the receiver loud enough for him to hold the phone away from his ear. Yet, he could still hear the slew of profanities being furiously thrown at him from the other end of the call. "Your idiocy can cause repercussions for operations far beyond Prague!" The caller warned, seething, "Handle it. Now!"

"I already have everything under control." Pavel then replied in a somewhat defensive yet confident tone. "I'll handle it like I always do. There's nothing to worry about." he nearly stuttered but stopped himself just in time. He took a deep breath before continuing, "Let me remind you that the Prague operation is still under my command. We are fully prepared, and this changes nothing regarding the plans we've put into motion."

The said plans would soon shift the dynamic that existed between most of the major governments in Europe. Pavel went on to explain the nitty-gritty details of their next phase. As far as he was concerned, those governments were nothing more than a series of corrupt systems run by out-of-control sociopaths hiding behind laws and policies enacted for their own benefit and those loyal to them. They had absolutely no regard for what happened to the rest of the unwashed masses within their control.

"You had better be right," came another terse response as Pavel pinched the bridge of his nose. "... Or you might find yourself being replaced by another, the same way I replaced the man before you in Prague." Pavel's throat went dry. "He, too, enjoyed the same power and prestige as you do now." Suddenly feeling a bit humbled, Pavel responded in a more subdued tone, "I understand. I will take care of any and all problems that might arise from this security failure." A failure, he knew he would ultimately be blamed for, he thought bitterly as he gritted his teeth. He then disconnected the encrypted call before any more abuse could be hurled his way. That man sat in a Moorish castle hidden away in a sheltered cove on the eastern shoreline of the Spanish island while Pavel suffered the consequences over here. He immediately placed another call to check on the status of the latest mission and put an end to Sloane Harper.

On the other end of the disconnected call, the man in Mallorca handed the phone over to his personal aide. He looked across an ornately carved 13th-century desk at another man sitting in silence with a calm but concerned look on his face.

“Perhaps you are right,” commented the silhouetted figure with a reassuring voice, “It might be time to take action on a bigger scale … beyond the abilities of Grovzny.” The underperforming underling could never imagine or even understand the extent of their plan. An action that would show him just how limited his view of the world was and how things really worked.

“Failure cannot be tolerated,” the stoic figure sitting across from him emphasized. The Mallorca caller agreed; the time for such actions was very close at hand.

When Pavel couldn't make contact with his commander in the field, he grew concerned. He wondered if another failure was about to pile up on the breach that had occurred the day before, when Sloane had made her escape with the printout. He hadn't dared to tell the man in Mallorca about the breach. Their call had brought about a palpable fear, this was something that could definitely cost him his own life if it was ever found out. As Pavel paced back and forth like a caged animal, he grew impatient with the lack of communication from the mercenaries out on the hunt. One of his assistants reported that the teams in pursuit had returned but were missing some personnel. A deep furrow creased Pavel's brow as he became worried that another failure would compound an already tenuous situation.

Upon arrival, the mercenaries immediately assembled in the squad bay, which acted as a staging area for all military-style operations. Pavel immediately walked over to the group leader to assess the situation but could tell by the expression on the man's face that things hadn't gone according to plan. When he found out that Sloane had gotten away, he became enraged. He started screaming and hurling items left and right at the group leader and then the whole group, while his face turned red. “Why are there personnel missing from the group?” He roared. When a terrified guard informed him about the loss and having to leave them behind in the open field, Pavel completely lost it. Then a sudden calm with a burning determination came over him. “This failure could now threaten to completely upend what was planned for race day. Especially if the local authorities find the missing and most likely dead mercenaries.” He informed the group leader very matter-of-factly.

Pavel then addressed all who were in the room, “This is what a failure like this could mean to you.” He suddenly pulled out a 9mm pistol and shot the group leader through the forehead. He wiped his hands, then turned to the group of now stunned mercenaries. “Failure like this will not be tolerated,” he declared before calmly exiting the squad room and heading off to his previously planned shower. Walking briskly to his private elevator, Pavel was soon showered and headed back to his garage. There, he jumped into a custom Bugatti Veyron and headed out to a planned meeting with the head of race operations for the much-anticipated Grand Prix.

14

Sloane wandered through the unfamiliar part of the city. Her first concern, besides getting fully away from the immediate threat, was to communicate with her handlers. Specifically, Eddie Stafford, so she could pass on the relevant intel, along with the printout from Pavel's control center. After finding a set of trash dumpsters at the end of the industrial row, she quickly took apart the automatic rifles and stashed them inside one of the large cubicle containers. She looked around to make sure no one was watching, then quickly resumed her way out of the industrial park. She decided to keep the 9mm with her just in case any unexpected trouble made its way to her again.

Once out of the industrial park, she found herself in a wide alleyway behind a complex. After a quick look, she saw a street with what appeared to be a facade of doorways only a few hundred feet away. When she reached the entrance of the alley, Sloane turned out onto a commercial street. The street was lined with small specialty shops and stores carrying everyday sundries and different types of food and supplies, along with clothing boutiques and several sidewalk bistros and coffee houses. She kept walking along the still empty sidewalk as businesses hadn't really opened up yet. Another look and she spotted her reflection in a store window. She noticed she was looking more like an undercover militant than an average citizen out to do some shopping at the local markets along the street. Sloane knew that before long, she had to change out of her current gear so she could blend in better. Standing out like some A.W.O.L. soldier recovering from a night of drinking and fighting was not something she could afford. She started looking for places to change as she continued on her way along the storefronts.

Sloane was not sure exactly where she was, but saw several shops coming to life as more people filtered onto the sidewalks, heading to one location or another. Still feeling very conspicuous in the somewhat ill-fitting and extremely filthy black special ops uniform she had on, Sloane spotted a consignment store. It had several racks of clothing placed out on the sidewalk near the entrance. Without hesitation, she headed towards the store and waited until the proprietor returned inside. While quickly scanning through the options, she found a lightweight trench coat and grabbed it. Soon, it was over the military fatigues she was wearing as she walked away unnoticed by the shop owner still busy inside while preparing for the day.

Sloane's next order of business was getting a mobile phone so she could contact Eddie over the secured agency communications system. She had to let him know her status to arrange transport to the nearest safe house. Returning to her hotel was out of the question. That place would be crawling with Pavel's security staff on the lookout for her. At a cafe just up the street, Sloane found her way to a table with a seat facing the street as per her training. Soon, she was greeted by a twenty-something female server who handed her a menu. "Would you like some of our freshly baked specials?"

"Oh no, I'm waiting for a companion, but I would love some water if it isn't too much trouble." Sloane mimicked the waitress's sweetness. In actuality, she was quite dehydrated from the previous night's action and could feel a strong sense of fatigue starting to set in.

It felt good to sit. When the server returned with a glass of ice and a small carafe of water, Sloane uttered a small prayer of thanks. Before the server left, Sloane flashed one of her remarkable smiles. "I lost my cell phone recently. I was wondering if I could use the cafe's phone to make a quick call to my companion. I just want to let them know I have arrived at the cafe." She tilted her head innocently at the end for effect. The waitress immediately offered Sloane her own cell phone and said she would be right back. As soon as the young woman went inside, Sloane got up and quickly walked away from the cafe while dialing a series of numbers that would connect her to a secure communications center.

On the other end of the line, a voice stated, "Aggregate Insurance Company, how may I direct your call?"

"I would like to speak with Mr. Whittley about an urgent claims issue," Sloane responded. Immediately, the operator punched in a series of numbers to re-route the call through a specially encrypted server that bounced the signal to random locations around the globe. A few moments later, a familiar voice came on. "Sloane." Eddie responded before she could even get a word in, "Is everything okay? You have been incommunicado over the last few days. I was starting to worry … What's going on?"

When Sloane told Eddie about all that had transpired since she last saw him, he became quite animated. "I need your location, stat. What else do you need?" Spotting a nearby street sign, Sloane let him know her location. A short silence later, while Eddie consulted an online mapping system with NSA satellite coverage, he directed her to a nearby plaza. "My men will be on the ground there. They'll pick you up and take you to a safehouse." He assured her.

Fifteen minutes later, after wiping down and tossing the stolen phone into a trash bin along the way, Sloane was inside an armor-plated sedan. She downed some sports drinks while mass dosing vitamin C as the car drove through several side streets. It doubled back numerous times, trying to throw off anyone in case they were being followed. Apparently, the safehouse was located on the other side of the sprawling city.

On the way, the sedan passed by the main grandstand for the upcoming Grand Prix race. The sight triggered Sloane to formulate a new strategy for taking Pavel and stopping him cold before he could execute his latest plan of terrorism. A plan that would take place while hundreds of thousands, if not more, viewers tune in to see the race broadcast live on Sky TV and ESPN. A race that would determine both the driver's and constructors' championship in a race running on an all-new and, what some would say, the most challenging circuit in the history of Formula One racing.

As they drove on, the racecourse became smaller and smaller in the rear view mirror. Sloane couldn't help but smile at the thought of Pavel slightly panicking, knowing by now that she had gotten away. Her mere existence was a very big threat to his entire operation. She was still on her mission to take him out completely, determined to put an end to his operations that had caused so much destruction around the world.

Sloane closed her eyes briefly, and her mind replayed the events of the past few days like a movie. She wondered what her next steps would be as she carried on with the mission. It would take extensive re-grouping and planning on her part, and she would have to be quick to get things moving. Going completely covert was her only option to kill this target, someone she had now grown to hate… and fear.

15

The Bugatti pulled up to the security gate that led to the racing paddock for the upcoming CEZ-Rolex Czechoslovakian Grand Prix. Pavel rolled his window down and gave the guard a thumbs up. The guard manning the booth immediately recognized him and waved him through. The barricade rose and specially installed metal posts retracted into the ground and cleared the way for him to come through. This museum-worthy steel and glass work of art was the headquarters building for the public version of the Formula One Grand Prix.

Pavel was there for his first big meeting with Klaus Heinrich of Austria before the race on Sunday. Thanks to Pavel's remarkable charm and lobbying skills, Klaus had recently been appointed as the new head of FIA. The new President of the governing body overseeing Formula One racing around the globe was excited to meet with this dashing young socialite. After all, he was the one who helped bring Formula One to the Czech Republic. Before him, it only had the MotoGP of Motorcycle racing every September until 2020. Up until a few years ago, no one could have imagined that the F1 Grand Prix would ever make its way to this country let alone the site of a championship showdown for the season as the last race on the schedule.

Then Pavel happened. He led the charge to lobby the FIA, adding Prague to its schedule. He came up with an elaborate plan for a multi-billion-dollar facility and race circuit. The track integrated parts of the city in a challenging design for both drivers and citizens as construction began at a breakneck pace. It also promised a spectacle - a public celebration on a par with what might occur at the World Cup, Olympics, or even the Super Bowl infusing billions of Euros and Dollars into the local and national economy.

It was to be something extraordinary, nothing like anyone had ever seen or experienced before in the Czech Republic.

It wasn't long before Pavel had been appointed as the head of local operations for everything related to the race. Related events also fell under his jurisdiction, including the planning and building of the state-of-the-art racecourse and facilities. The beautiful headquarters building was a part of those 'facilities', resembling a cross between the Louvre and Guggenheim museums. Little did anyone know that Pavel Grovzny had additional plans for the construction. They would soon come to fruition on the day of the race day itself.

As a major player in the energy consortium that powered the Republic, Pavel had convinced everyone to focus on a green energy solution. Something that would tie the overall power grid for the greater metro to Prague, and the systems that powered the entire Republic. While the country as a whole applauded his efforts, they were oblivious to the operations far below the sub-level of this beautiful new facility. No one knew that Pavel had his mercenary terrorist organization tied into a back door for the control systems powering the country. These controls would enable them to completely cripple the Republic with a simple click. Their own command and control server would take over all functioning power grids at the hour of execution.

Another sneaky plan involved his contacts in the Middle East, especially Iran. Pavel's group had acquired a series of over100 highly explosive dirty bombs. Once acquired, they were carefully constructed within the walls of the headquarters along with all thirty custom grandstands located all over the race circuit. Each of those grandstands contained a series of ten to twenty luxury boxes guaranteed to give the wealthy, the high and mighty, and society elites in attendance, the ultimate view of the race in a style fit for royalty.

Each one of those boxes would act as the unofficial coffin lid for the pandemonium Pavel had planned for the day. Other bombs were located throughout the racing paddock, pit row, and at strategically selected points along the racecourse. Pavel was determined to see through the death and destruction in Prague. Luckily, the printout that Sloane had gotten away with held no clues as to the extent of what was to occur on Sunday.

As Pavel entered the well-appointed office, Klaus greeted him like an old friend. Pavel graciously smiled and welcomed him to the home of the new Czechoslovakian Formula One race with a warm handshake. He then invited him for a tour of the entire complex and all it had to offer the FIA and its constructor/driver teams. The tour included all the public facilities hosting one of the largest racing audiences in the world. The compound also included its own broadcast center featuring 180 cameras used to push the 4k broadcast signal out to a worldwide television audience. In the end, they would also get to witness one of the most horrendous terrorist acts ever planned and executed in the history of the modern world.

After touring the entire complex, Pavel and Klaus returned to the executive dining room. There, a gourmet luncheon had been prepared by a Michelin-star chef for the two men. Both of them fashioned themselves as true movers and shakers in a way that others would never know or achieve. During the meal, both men talked excitedly about the week-long events and all the great publicity being generated for both the FIA and the Czech Republic. Their conversation quickly shifted to the race itself which led to a guarded discussion about security issues and how to handle emergencies should they occur on both small and major levels.

At this point, Pavel looked Klaus straight in the eye, “You have nothing to worry about, my friend. You’ll be away, same as me when it’s all scheduled to go down.” Klaus was looking for assurances when Pavel interrupted him again, "Do you really think I would leave my closest partner behind when the world implodes on itself?” He raised an eyebrow to emphasize his point. “The partner who I helped get into his current position of power and the one who ultimately made sure that the race would come here to Prague." Satisfied with the response, the two men raised their glasses and made a toast to a "change in the world" as they or anyone else knew it.

Pavel stood up and shook Klaus's hand for the last time. He knew it was merely a part of standard procedures, but the charade ensured the silence of his so-called ‘partner’. In turn, he ensured no possible security breach for the plans on the verge of turning into a reality. Pavel knew that Klaus was a very weak man who gave in to his own vanity. He could never grasp the real idea or the commitment it took to achieve total destruction for the sake of wholesale change.

Change in a world that had long ago gone mad, devoid of any real order or structure guaranteed to help the world survive as it slowly consumed itself bit by bit by bit. Consumed by the same game of greed and conquest over what ordinary men thought had value but yielded nothing but pain and anguish in societies everywhere. Being the sociopathic killer that he was with absolutely no conscience, Pavel had no qualms about leaving Klaus behind to die with everyone else when the time came. He also had no qualms about leaving his whole team for dead when his command center would go up in explosives, causing another mass casualty event.

Pavel was soon back behind the wheel of the world's fastest vehicle as he negotiated, with complete abandon, the race circuit he had personally designed. As he gleefully pushed the Bugatti to its highest speed on a long straightaway, Pavel imagined what things would be like after Sunday. When he would be aboard his private jet on the way to meet with the man in Mallorca. The man who had absolute control over a much larger organization. For the man, Pavel and his private mercenary army played but a minor role in the larger scheme of things. A scheme planned for a wider reach than what would occur in Prague.

A plan that would ultimately change the entire structure of worldwide powers. Something so unimaginable that the man in Mallorca and a few others controlling the strings would finally seek their own versions of a new world order.

16

The safe house was located on the back half of a long-dormant, forty-acre country estate, set amid thick stands of spruce trees on the outskirts of Prague. Sloane shed the trench coat and, after stepping in, stripped out of the tactical fatigues and was soon soaking under a hot steaming shower to wash off the grime. The bath eased some of the muscle aches acquired during what had happened to her over the last couple of days. She was exhausted but knew there was little time to spare if she were to get back on target. Completing her mission was a priority, she had to put an end to Pavel's mercenary force and whatever potential plans he had in place for more destruction in the future. Sloane still didn't realize just how dire the situation had become… or how little time she had left to stop what was about to transpire in the next few days during the Grand Prix.

Finishing her shower, she dried off, donned a previously hung-up tracksuit, and walked into the kitchen of the safe house. She found Eddie Stafford seated at a small dinette table waiting for her. Sloane grabbed a large bottle of mineral water from the refrigerator and sat down opposite Eddie to begin her debriefing. She downed almost half the bottle in one go and let out a long, satisfied sigh. Her report was detailed, listing everything she could recall aside from the part where she had been drugged. It took almost thirty minutes to fill in everything that had happened since the fashion show to the afterparty; how she had been first seduced then drugged by Pavel and dragged off to somewhere within the basement of his estate.

Then she told Eddie, "One more thing… when he was showing me his command center, Pavel said that he had placed a mole high up in the Agency that assigns us our missions..." This immediately alarmed Stafford. Overcoming the shock, he quickly made a secure call to Langley and proceeded to pass this vital intel along. Intel like that would be a much bigger problem for the agency than just thwarting this mission. Once Sloane had finished filling him in on everything, Eddie opened up his briefcase and passed a set of papers across the table for Sloane to read through.

The papers sent an involuntary chill down Sloane's spine. The papers disclosed alarming new intelligence picked up regarding Pavel's plans even though he was never mentioned. Through a series of intercepted communications, disturbing words had come down that something very big and destructive was planned to take place during the weekend of the upcoming race. But they were still clueless about the details of what might occur or even where. All they had was a vague reference to Chernobyl and Iranians. These references had been sighted by various dark web sources located half a world away in Singapore and repeated by others in Mozambique and Yemen.

To all the analysts, that could only mean one thing: something that involved a nuclear event. No one knew if this might be an attack on a facility or a dirty bomb, but it was enough to alarm those who came across the intel. Nothing was verified so no official warning had been given out. But security agencies worldwide had still noted it as an unconfirmed but possibly credible threat given the recent chatter.

None of the intel flowing through various channels had any indication that Prague was a target, although it was mentioned because of the Grand Prix. Nor did it contain any information on Pavel Grovzny other than an ultra-successful businessman with major energy holdings and interests in a wide variety of endeavors including the Formula One race. This inevitably meant there was no clear-cut evidence to connect him with any type of sinister plot.

Sloane's debriefing would only go so far, as the printout she made away with gave no reference to Pavel himself. As she and Eddie poured over the events and new analysis based on intercepts, it soon became obvious that something was afoot. With an underlying sense of dread, Sloane soon realized she would have to somehow infiltrate Pavel's operation again. It was the only way to uncover the plans and stop them cold before they became a reality.

Eddie and Sloane, both agreed that her cover as a model wouldn't work anymore. By then, her photo and likeness would be widely distributed to all security personnel involved with operations controlled by Pavel, including the race itself. Sloane would have to employ a completely different tactical solution on her part for the mission. Her new directive was to get to the bottom of his plans and end it before it could be executed. It would ultimately delay the dispatch of Pavel Grovzny until enough information could be extracted. Their best guess was that if he did have something planned, it would most likely involve the race or race day events.

Sloane had been well trained in such situations, but had never gone up against such a large operation before without some sort of edge over her target. She looked at Eddie, resigned, and gave out an exasperated sigh. Eddie could only smile in response. He proceeded to inform her, "Don't worry too much, you won't be flying solo for this one. An additional team of trained commandos will join you as a part of this expanded mission. You guys will make up a team of six elite specialists with ex-military, including Navy Seals, Army Green Berets, and Marine Recon Rangers."

From their profile, Sloane could see all of these men were battle-hardened and tested during long deployments in Afghanistan and other hot zones. Their training and history made them the experts they had become. From close-quarter combat and sniper ops to infiltration/exfiltration, demolitions and sabotage, recon and surveillance, and intel hacking and cyber ops, they knew everything. And every single one of them was an adrenaline junkie who lived for the action deprived in their daily civilian lives.

Reviewing high-definition satellite and infrared images on a laptop computer, Sloane and Eddie began formulating a plan for infiltration into the racing complex. They knew Pavel would be operating from there, as well as his command center. Soon, they had mapped out the most probable pathway to get in and grab Pavel, regardless of where he would be headquartered. The only concerning thing that came across on the infrared imagery was a series of random heat spots throughout the entire Grand Prix complex. It made no real sense. They both wondered if this could have anything to do with the Chernobyl chatter going around. But without more intel, it could just be something as innocent as a series of air handlers or power distribution units throughout the facility.

Eddie was about to close up the laptop as they finished viewing all the images when his cell phone chimed. It was an encrypted text. Eddie read the brief message, closed out the text app, and looking at Sloane remarked, "Well, my dear Miss Harper, it appears that your team has just arrived. They should be coming through the door right… about… now."

The door of the large pantry swung open as six individuals dressed like some scruffy 70's rock and roll band entered one by one. Almost in sync, they assembled beside the dinette where Sloane and Eddie sat. Addressing the team of commandos, Eddie introduced them to their new team leader, "Sloane Harper." They nodded and, one by one, introduced themselves to Sloane.

The first member was Robert Henry Saratar, a.k.a RH, part of the famed Seal Team Six as one of their squad leaders. The second was William "Billy" Sparks, a former Navy Seal and world-class sniper. Third in line was Andy Hayes, a Marine Recon Ranger with a specialty in sabotage and demolition. Next up was another Ranger named Shep Banner, who was one of the best infiltrators, surveillance, and cybermen the Corps had ever known. The last two were twin brothers; Alex and Axel Miller, better known as M-One and M-Two. They had been part of the Army's elite Delta Force, and both were weapon experts.

After the introductions, RH turned to Sloane, "Ma'am," he asked, "Where would you like us to stow our gear and billet for the night?" Still processing the new information, Sloane looked over to Eddie, who took over for her. He guided the group of commandos to a series of rooms at the back of the large house and mentioned, "As you move off, you should, by all means, do a little cleanup on a personal basis to better blend in for the coming operation in the next four days. It would put your lot square within the public eye… and let's not forget Pavel Grovzny's private cameras and security team."

17

In his command center early the next morning, Pavel paced back and forth. He stopped and looked at a bank of high-definition screens displaying the footage from his own security cameras alongside others secreted through the city. His team had hacked into several satellites to view and control these cameras. He mulled over all that had happened over the last couple of days, and couldn't help but wonder about the damage Sloane might have inflicted on his operation. He hadn’t had a chance to see the contents of the file, so he began to run through all the countermeasures they would have to come up with to keep the plans on track.

Pavel thought back to the team leader he had executed in the squad bay. After some deliberation, he decided it was just better to eliminate such a weak link. It would ultimately reinforce his directive that failure was not an option and would not be tolerated at any cost, for anyone, regardless of their position. There was no way to tell if any information had been leaked for the upcoming weekend, but Pavel knew, everything would still have to be in place and ready to go as planned. His biggest problem was time. He wished he could just pull the proverbial trigger now before anyone could take action against it. But the overarching goal had as much to do with the worldwide perception of terror as the carnage that would take place on Sunday.

Pacing again, Pavel began to formulate additional security measures that would ensure success. He paused to look at the satellite images showing the overhead view of the entire racing complex again. He stared intently, then ordered the control technician to zoom in on a specific location on the far side of the facility. The man sitting at the console typed in a code and hit enter, and the camera slowly zoomed in for a closer view. Pavel peered at the screen until he could see what appeared to be a weakness in the perimeter. He pointed again and had the technician close in on the image. It revealed a very obvious construction problem at a large delivery entrance that had either been missed or neglected. A problem that could lead to a disastrous breach if it weren't addressed immediately.

Pavel quickly made a phone call, trying to contact the facility's construction Supervisor to address the now obvious flaw in need of fixing. But he could only leave a terse and emphatic voicemail about the "critical issue that needed to be addressed immediately," with strict instructions for the Supervisor to call him as soon as he got this message. Pavel was used to getting what he wanted. The mere idea that he couldn't reach the man infuriated him. He violently grabbed a nearby chair, threw it across the room, and let loose a torrent of curses. The sudden outburst had the control technician cowering slightly for fear that Pavel might inflict the same violence on him.

Meanwhile, at the safe house, Eddie, Sloane, and her team of commandos were carefully examining another high-def satellite image as it scanned the race complex perimeter looking for a good place for infiltration. Shep Banner, the surveillance expert, pointed to the screen and, talking over a secure com, asked the NSA Satellite Tech in Langley, "Reposition the satellite slightly and zoom in here…" His notated interaction with the custom touch screen transmitted the point of contact back to the NSA Sat Tech. With a few taps and a refined camera position with a game-style joystick, the Sat Tech zoomed in on the same construction flaw that had alarmed Pavel and sent him into a fit of rage.

In a calm but deliberate voice, Shep said, "There it is," as he pointed out an obvious flaw. It appeared at first to be slightly open and could easily be exploited for access to the facility. That entrance, in particular, led directly into the underground labyrinth of connecting tunnels that routed the facility grounds. It also came in close proximity to every explosive device that had been built into the structure. When detonated, these explosives would cause destruction on a scale that would render Prague uninhabitable. Of course, no one on Sloane's team had any idea about the dirty bombs. They were mostly concerned with the access to the whereabouts of Pavel. Shep asked for the Sat Cam to give them an infrared view. Soon, the interior coolness of the air-conditioned tunnel system popped up on the screen. It looked like a series of rivers and streams snaking through the complex in a precise manner that resembled the schematic of a circuit board.

Pulling up a duplicate image without the infrared, the team could quickly see the whole map of the tunnels. Some ran specifically to targeted areas and would get them access to Pavel with the least amount of risk. Of course, the risk was always present in any operation, but this one was considerably higher. Simply because Pavel had personally appointed recruits, and his paranoia about any mistake or lapse in judgment leading to security failure had grown tenfold. What they saw on the Sat image would drive Pavel insane if he ever found out, but it didn't appear to be taking any actions. It was a simple but serious construction oversight and, lucky for the commando team, nobody had noticed it yet.

Next, the team switched over to view Pavel's Villa on the river. They zoomed in with the help of Sloane's recollection of her experience. They soon had a pretty good idea of how to approach the situation to grab Pavel on his own turf. Unfortunately, it would require a much more overt operation akin to assaulting an enemy stronghold. Their primary goal now was to somehow track Pavel's movements in the racing complex. It once again fell to Shep as he addressed the rest of the team, "One of the NSA analytics teams has intercepted and tapped into Pavel's personal phone via a different satellite… We can now see where he is at any time…"

A record of his travel over the last 24 hours was soon overlayed onto a large screen. It showed his movements between the Villa and the racing complex in a regular and somewhat predictable pattern. This surprised the commando team. Seeing their confusion, Sloane explained, "Even though he is an extremely dangerous mercenary and somewhat psychopathic killer, Pavel is still considered a very popular socialite. He's a major player in this racing event and others like this. Based on his social status alone at the moment, his movements aren't all that surprising... Of course, this would all change if Pavel senses any threat to himself or the operation." Sloane turned to face her team, "Just another thing to bear in mind as we move forward."

Pavel couldn't wait for the construction Supervisor to call him. He soon went back to the racing complex, winding through the headquarters building to a specially marked elevator that only he had access to via biometric activation. Dropping down to the service level of the facility, Pavel was soon in an electric quad and silently whizzing down a corridor. He followed a digital mapping system directing him toward the maintenance entrance of the complex. He soon arrived at the suspect entrance near the surface with a gradual rise ending in a staging zone for delivery supplies. Pavel took one good look and immediately noticed the two large doors had a visible gap. He could see a stream of light penetrating the delivery area from the outside. It appeared that the engineering of the door frame had been rushed to finish the construction on schedule and since it wasn't in an area with public access, it didn't appear to be critical at the time it was finished.

Pavel jumped out of the quad, walked up to the doors, and began to take a closer look at this flaw. Until a short while ago it hadn't seemed to be such a big deal. Now it had become a major concern for the once again seething mercenary leader. Little did the construction Supervisor know if he had been present at that moment, he would have inevitably suffered the same fate as the unfortunate squad leader. The doors in question were very heavy and very large. Made of stainless steel they reached a height of almost eighteen feet with an individual width of eight feet each. Originally, the doors were meant to retract into the side walls but in another cost-cutting move, they had been hinged to swing inward on a series of bearings that made them rather easy to move in case the automatic opener had to be bypassed in an emergency.

Pavel fumed as he realized this was not something that could be remedied in time for the upcoming race on Sunday. So, he decided to stage a squad of heavily armed guards, in and out of the entryway. If the gates were to be breached, they would become a great threat to the security of their plans. Grabbing a built-in handset inside the quad, Pavel called the command center and immediately issued the order, "I want security personnel deployed on the delivery entrance by no later than Saturday morning."

As he headed back to the headquarters, Pavel remained oblivious that at that very moment as Sloane and her team of commandos were about to complete their own mission. His security had already been compromised and Pavel didn't even know it.

18

Venezuelan Pablo Guzman drove the Formula One Ferrari steadily in a concerted effort to hit its max speed of 233 miles per hour. It was his final practice lap as he pushed the state-of-the-art racing car towards what could become his 10th pole position of the season. It was a decisive race that would ultimately settle the drivers' championship between the veteran Guzman and his closest competitor, Alex Verdun, a talented rookie from Belgium.

The two men were only ten points apart from each other in the standings. All Guzman needed was a second-place finish to claim the title, even if Verdun won the race. Guzman was still under the gun by Ferrari to secure the championship from Verdun, a brash upstart who had a very aggressive driving style. He was known for rubbing many other drivers and team owners, the wrong way.

The engine screamed as Guzman downshifted gears from eight to four while braking into the hairpin at the end of the straight. Then, he immediately accelerated again, hitting the incline into a challenging series of quick left and right curves forming an S on the pavement. It caused the Venezuelan to oversteer slightly and go beyond the edge of the track over the rumble strip. It delayed him by 5 seconds off the time that could have netted him the pole position for qualification the next day. Quickly making his way back onto the track, he was soon accelerating to a front-row speed once again.

Guzman remained blissfully unaware that the excess vibration of the rumble strip had loosened a bolt holding the right front wing until it completely came off. At first, he just noticed his control slightly shifting as he swept into a turn near the far end of the course. He sped past a series of stands sitting dangerously close to the racetrack. Guzman pushed the car to its limit near the apex of the turn, and the wing suddenly came loose entirely. It raked across the front end of the Ferrari throwing the car and its driver into a violent spin. The right rear slammed into a retaining wall and suddenly went airborne before it began tumbling out of control across the track.

The race car immediately disintegrated before the audience as it slammed into another retaining wall on the inside of the main straight just past the entrance to pit row. In the pits the crewmen and team leaders watched in horror as Guzman and his car burst into flames as it went airborne once again. It tumbled three more times before landing wheels down on the field inside the racetrack. The car was soon engulfed in an inferno trapping Venezuelan inside. The flames soon consumed the car and its veteran driver, bringing an end to his remarkable career of Grand Prix racing with Ferrari.

In less than a minute, the rescue team and fire crews reached the wreck site. But everyone knew it was too late. All they could do was extinguish the flames licking the hulk that was once a sleek and powerful piece of advanced automotive engineering. The idea of extracting Guzman from the fiery crash seemed remote at best.

Inside the cockpit, fire suppression systems had been triggered at the first sign of heat. Guzman struggled to free himself from the restraint system of the safety cage, somehow still intact after the violent crash. He said a silent prayer hoping to survive, if only to see his wife and two small children one last time. As the firemen finally extinguished the flames, emergency medical personnel rushed to the burnt-up car. A charred glove emerged out of the cockpit and people were shocked to see that Pablo Guzman had miraculously survived. He had escaped the grim reaper of Formula One Grand Prix while the world watched the pre-race ESPN /SKY

TV coverage for the biggest race of the season. The season would now go to Alex Verdun as champion though more by default than earned through skill.

High above the race circuit, Pavel Grovzny watched in his private box above the pit row in rapt fascination at all that had unfolded on the track below. His only concern was whether it might affect his plans for the race on Sunday. At first, he worried that the race officials might delay or even reschedule the event due to the tragic death of one of the racing world's most popular drivers. But when it became apparent that the Venezuelan had survived, he knew it would become an added spectacle for the race. It would keep the world all the more tuned into the Grand Prix action as he executed death and destruction on an unsuspecting public.

Satisfied that things would progress as planned, Pavel soon redirected his attention to the additional security measures. He had to ensure all systems were being checked for the final stages before the countdown of the D-day. With only a few drivers left for the final round for day one qualification, Pavel picked up his private, secure line and reached his command center. Speaking in a very matter-of-fact voice, he calmly ordered, "Begin the final stages… This is what we've been working on for the last two years."

Down on the racing circuit, safety crews finally managed to remove the burned-up car. Pablo Guzman had been rushed to a nearby trauma center in an ambulance with third-degree burns over eighty percent of his body and a less than slim chance of survival at best. Now it was Alex Verdun's shot at practice laps. He too had to prep for a pole position run to qualify for the race scheduled merely two days away. Verdun was racing for the world-renowned Red Bull racing team. He had swiftly made his way from the ranks of F2 after a remarkable championship season.

Quickly proving his ability on the track with an ego and attitude that made him a darling to the media, he soon became both loved and hated by audiences and other drivers alike.

Pushing his RB1 car to the limit as he always did, he ignored his own race control's instruction to take it easy during practice. He soon set a new lap record on his way to acquire another pole. After him, only two other cars waited in the paddock for their turn for much-needed final adjustments. They hoped that it might help them achieve a better position on the grid come Sunday morning at the start of the race.

There was still one day left during final qualifying for the pole or movement up the grid. Verdun knew he would get another shot to beat his own record on the track for a better pole position. The position all but guaranteed victory as long as he didn't break the car or get into another accident. He thought back to the mix-up back at the beginning of the season when that crazy Spaniard Esperanza had moved recklessly into the first tight turn and ended up taking out four other cars including himself at the beginning of the race.

Bringing the Red Bull car into the pits, he climbed out of the powerful machine. Crew members rushed in and began wheeling it into the garage. Verdun met the team leader Hannover MaCumber, who patted him on the back and at the same time shook his head in a bit of disbelief. The Belgian continued to push the car's performance to its limits MacCumber had to remind him, "We still have qualifying to go through and a race to run... take it easy."

Verdun merely smiled and said, "I have everything under control, and besides… the storied head of RB racing shouldn't worry so much. It's clear you'll be handed another Constructor's title at the end of the race." MaCumber could only smile as Alex walked away from him, but he still worried about the overly aggressive style of the rookie sensation. He wondered what his style could do to the car if he pushed it too hard at this stage.

As time for practice came to an end, Pavel sat back and took stock of everything he had worked towards over the last two years. He had brought the race to Prague to appease the local leaders as his real leaders were plotting the end of the world from Mallorca. The end would truly bring about a new order. It would give Pavel the kind of power he could only dream of until that moment. He smiled at himself and couldn't help but feel immense pride in all he had accomplished so far. Breathing deeply, he looked forward with giddy anticipation of what was about to happen in two days. His only concern was Sloane Harper and whatever she was up to. He vowed to himself, that no one would get in the way or even dare to stop him.

19

Qualification day greeted the Czech Capital to a sunrise that was dark, grey, and wet. A driving rainstorm blew in from the Baltic, making the race circuit all the more challenging for the drivers during their shot at the pole or even a favorable position on the grid of twenty cars. After Pablo Guzman's crash at the practice lap and his miraculous survival, Ferrari brought in a backup car driven by Alfonse Giannelli. He had been called up from the Italian car builder's F2 program on short notice. The weather would definitely hamper the visibility and efforts of all the drivers as they compete for the best position without sliding out of control and possibly, the race.

Things were suddenly looking up at the safe house for Sloane and her commando team. Bad weather was always something they could take advantage of. It served as a good nuisance for distracting their opponent. It was also a great cover for most of their movements as they headed into action during the assault on the problematic access point at the race complex. The team was gathered around a round table in a garage with a map spread out in front of them. They were finalizing their plans and possible contingencies when the time came.

RH looked at the map and pointed to a location roughly half a kilometer west of the racing complex. "This would be the staging area and launch point for the mission," he determined. Each member had a specific assignment for the assault: a combination of stealth and precision tactics similar to the Seal Team Six when they took out Osama Bin Laden after hitting the ground years before. RH himself, along with Sloane, would lead the main assault group including the Miller brothers armed with Mark IV assault rifles with suppressors. Each would carry a Sig Sauer M17 P320 nine-millimeter semi-auto handgun and a razor-sharp, double-edged Gerber Mark III survival knife for personal combat when it demanded.

Other assignments before the assault would be conducted by Shep Banner. He would recon and perform close-in surveillance on the access point and any personnel movement. He would keep the others apprised by miniature radios with a special tone code. Meanwhile, Andy Hayes would set detonators on the access point and stand by with other ordinances as needed including Flash Bangs, HE grenades, and an RPG. Billy Sparks would take a position on a nearby hill as the long-range threat for any enemy combatants hampering these activities. His choice of weaponry was a newly acquired Accuracy International AXSR six-lug magnum sniper rifle with a custom suppressor. A weapon meant to take out opponents from as far away as 2500 plus yards.

Eddie Stafford stood by and nodded his approval as final preparations began for this very critical mission. The breach was just a small part of the plan but if executed properly, it would open the needed route to Pavel's executive box. Once there, they hoped to capture and force him into revealing his plans for the race, even if they were already set in motion. If all went well, it would allow them to take the necessary actions to subdue the threat before it became a reality.

"No matter what you do, keep in mind how dangerous and unpredictable Pavel can be," Eddie reminded everyone. "It's imperative that we neutralize his plans before execution... He needs to be taken in alive," Eddie reminded them. Whether he was unscathed or not, it never became a concern for anyone. Sloane, in particular, really wanted to inflict some personal pain on the man who tried to have her killed. Capturing him alive was a critical matter. It was believed that Pavel had sensitive information about a considerably larger operation involving more than the Czech Republic.

RH wrapped up all their plans and looked at Sloane. As she nodded her assent, RH turned to his men, “Saddle up.” Saddling up in this case would mean two separate blacked-out Range Rovers. One would carry Sloane and RH. The rest of the team would ride in the other. Both vehicles would take a slightly different route toward the staging zone. Each would park in a pre-designated area, where all team members would converge on the location on foot. They would be dressed in black and grey commando outfits, crafted by one of Eddie's local assets. Their outfits enabled flexibility and all-weather conditions plus a custom carbon fiber thread that added a layer of protection like a bulletproof vest. Meanwhile, Eddie would remain at the safe house to monitor Pavel's phone and any enemy communications. Pavel’s security system had already been disarmed and the commando team could easily counter all possible actions relayed between members of Pavel's defensive force.

The vehicles made their way through the rain-soaked roads at first light towards their parking positions. Pavel's defensive squad of thirty-two men also assembled in a basement area below the Formula One HQ building. They too made final preparations against a now vital threat from the outside. So far, there had been no indication that an independent agency or personnel was coming after them. Not even Pavel's mole inside the agency had any information on any plans of a pre-meditated attack let alone an operation underway. Since Sloane had alerted Eddie Stafford of the mole, the two had decided to keep their plans out of any official channels. Even the commando team had been contacted individually by Eddie himself, for the sake of confidentiality.

Sloane and her Commando team parked the Range Rovers in two different wooded areas within a few hundred meters of the staging area.

Each vehicle was easily concealed from view by thick stands of spruce separating them from nearby roads conveniently closed for construction. This turned out to be another plan put into place by Eddie. He orchestrated it the moment he found out the exact target of the mission. Once the Range Rovers were parked, the individual teams collected all their gear and headed off through a wooded route towards the staging area half a kilometer from the target.

While Sloane and the commandos made their way to the staging area, Pavel's defensive forces jumped into electric quads for the five-minute ride through the networked tunnels to the bay doorway and loading area. With four heavily armed mercenaries loaded into each quad, the mobile platoon was soon on its way to their assigned defensive position.

As the mercenaries were on their way to the target area, Sloane's team arrived at their own launch point. Shep Banner quickly scanned the immediate area of the target and its perimeter boundaries. "All clear," he declared. At the okay signal, the rest of the team made their way towards the target in a deliberate but cautious manner. While Shep stayed in position to do continual recon, Billy Sparks headed toward his sniper position. Meanwhile, Andy Hayes quickly made his way down to the target to set up micro detonators. These instruments were designed to blow open the doors at the hinges for a sizeable breach point and disable any ability to re-secure the massive doors. Once Andy had cleared the immediate area and staged himself in a strategic position, Sloane, RH, and the Miller brothers placed themselves within 10 meters on each side of the entryway.

Pavel checked on his defensive force still making their way to the target area. He began to pace, as usual. The deployment of his personnel still hadn’t been confirmed. He silently cursed at another one of their overall weaknesses. Apparently, the Motorola two-way radios his team used as an economical com system didn't do very well with three floors of concrete, glass between the tunnels, and his luxury box. This meant he would have to wait for the team leader to reach him on the landline located adjacent to the bay area next to the entryway.

Luckily for Pavel, he could monitor the facility’s security cameras at will. So, he switched over to the external view of the targeted access doors. After switching over to the security camera, Pavel saw an extremely blurred feed that he chalked up to rain on the lens cover along with cheap, unshielded wiring employed in a rush to finish construction. This time Pavel cursed out loud to himself as he peered at the screen trying to make out the foggy-looking details of the picture as it appeared on his high-def monitor. Squinting at the screen, he thought he could see a slight bit of movement on both sides of the massive doorway. But with the image being so wide and as unclear as it was, he could once again only wait for his own security force to make contact once they arrived.

Pavel couldn’t piece together that Andy Hayes had fired a special liquid projectile at the security camera to completely obscure the lens. Unfortunately, he only managed a partial hit due to the rain and wind. That’s why Pavel could still see a partial image. Staring at the picture and concentrating on what he could see on one part of the screen, Pavel once again thought he saw movement but couldn't be sure. He tapped the touchscreen of the camera control system and zoomed in on where he thought he saw something.

Not seeing any movement, Pavel was about to ignore the whole situation to wait until he heard back from his men on location. But just as he was about to return the camera to its pre-set position, he pointed at the screen and exclaimed. "There!!!" Ever so slightly, he could make out a shape resembling a human figure, albeit fuzzy, as it went into a crouch. Looking further, he soon made out the shape of another human as it seemed to turn in place. It immediately became apparent that his paranoia was not getting the better of him and he knew something wasn't quite right. When the confirmation of his own forces' arrival still didn't come through, Pavel began to grow concerned.

Pavel started to pan the security camera across the entryway to the other outer edge. He saw a series of three small flashes from just outside his viewpoint. Quickly zooming out with the camera, he saw a second set of flashes go off at the door's hinges and what appeared to be at least four figures. They were moving through a widening gap as the doors swung fully open revealing a gaping tunnel system. Pavel's mouth fell open as he realized that someone was indeed breaching this recently discovered vulnerability and entering the tunnel.

As the micro detonators fully blew the access doors wide open, they fused the hinges with a magnesium incendiary that basically welded them in place. Sloane, RH, and the Millers quickly made their move into the large loading bay. There, they scanned the area looking for any opposition but saw nothing except an empty room the size of a small warehouse. They took that as an 'all clear' to move into the tunnel. They began moving across the bay from the open doorway just as the lights of the quads became visible down the distant tunnel. As the lights became brighter, they could hear the distinct whine of what sounded like multiple electric motors. They quickly decided to find a more defensive position to observe and fight from if needed. At the same time, RH sent a series of tones to Billy Sparks and Andy Hayes that they would soon have hostiles in the area for possible action. Sloane, RH, and the Millers quickly found positions behind some large metal cabinets as Billy and Andy prepared their assault on the incoming target.

Pavel had now become fully aware of the situation and decided to take action on his own. He grabbed a MAC 10 machine pistol along with his favorite 15-shot Beretta handgun and dashed to his private elevator. Soon, he was down in the basement tunnel system. On arrival, he knew an electric quad wouldn't make it, so he opted for his specially outfitted Ducati Panigale MotoGP racer equipped with dual machine guns and an on-board RPG. He jumped on the bike and hit the electric start. Pavel was soon rocketing through the tunnel system toward a confrontation he sensed had been a long time coming.

20

While things were heating up for opposing forces in Prague, solitary figures were entering the control centers for the twenty largest power plants in the world, preparing to start their work shifts. The power plants being entered were located in a wide variety of locations, including Australia, China, Japan, Canada, the United States, Brazil, Great Britain, Russia, and India, with some countries containing more than one facility. Each individual passed through security checkpoints and headed to their regular workstations to take charge of monitoring the health of each facility.

Once they were seated at their usual control consoles, their company-issued mobile phones buzzed, signaling a private text message they had been told to expect. As it had been explained to each of them by company officials they didn't know, this would be a test project for a new world-wide systems security protocol, one that would protect power grids across the globe. They were all eager to do exactly what was required, both to help with the operation and to receive a bonus for their part.

For all involved, the bonus would turn out to be a very sizable financial reward for their efforts. Each individual had been required to sign a private contract and a non-disclosure agreement that demanded total secrecy. To most, the money being promised seemed like a king's ransom, enough to let them walk away from everything they knew with "Screw You" money. Of course, each individual also knew that failure to execute could bring about serious trouble, or worse, from the executives who had selected them for this "honor" that would supposedly help guarantee a secure and endless power supply for the world at large.

Upon receiving the encrypted text message, each one of the specially selected individuals hit the escape key on their terminal keyboards twice. They then entered a single line of random letters and numbers that had been transmitted as part of the text into the command-and-control entry space. These strings of characters would launch an executable file that, in turn, would install and activate the new security protocol they had been told about. The string of characters was different for each location to ensure extra security for this very important operation, an operation they really knew nothing about aside from the lies they had been told.

Once they had entered the executable code at each terminal, they all sat and waited in anticipation of an additional text. They had been told it would come with further instructions that they must follow precisely. They didn't have to wait long. The next message came through to each individual with a synchronized timer that acted as a kind of countdown. Instructions were included that gave them a time, specific to their locations, for starting the timer program. At the exact moment they were instructed to begin, they each tapped an embedded "Start" button on their phones, and the countdown began.

Every one of the operators prepared for the end of the countdown with an index finger resting on the return key. As the numbers ticked down to zero and a "Launch" command appeared, they all tapped the return key on their keyboards. This opened a window on the screen where they could observe the executable program beginning to install what appeared to be some sort of security update, even though none of them recognized the name. After installing the update, they were all prompted to click on a standard "Finish" button. Once they did, the computer terminal screens returned to what appeared to be normal status.

What none of these people realized was that they had just enabled a specially written executable code that would begin another countdown, a countdown to a backdoor where a worm-like virus would start to enter each power system and wait for a final command. That command would eventually come via a single keystroke from a technician sitting inside a vault-like room in Mallorca. With that simple keystroke, every power system would come to a complete halt, one by one, at a rate slow enough to avoid raising suspicion about the size and scope of the operation.

These actions would, in turn, shut off the flow of all power throughout the civilized world due to the extra demand on underpowered systems. The virus was two-fold, designed not only to disable all power generation but also to destroy every major control system internally. It would do so through a reverse power flow command that would literally melt any and all mainframe and remote wiring and circuitry needed for the systems to function.

After completing their assigned tasks, each of the individuals returned to their normal jobs and continued to monitor the various power systems in the same manner they had on any other shift. When their shifts ended, they checked back out through security and headed home as if everything were normal. None of them thought much about what had occurred earlier in the day. All were looking forward to the very large, anticipated bonus that would soon be coming their way.

All except for one older Chinese gentleman who worked at the Three Gorges Dam, located in the Hubei Province of Central China, spanning the Yangtze River near Sandouping. As he walked home that evening after completing a twelve-hour shift of no apparent consequence, he felt an unexpected sense of regret for his secretive actions earlier in the day, even though he had no idea what the outcome of those actions would be.

He had always wondered why he had been chosen. He questioned whether this upgrade was truly necessary, since the dam system had never experienced a security breach since coming online. He was also bothered by the brash style of the executive who had approached him at a local restaurant, and forced him into a contract and NDA he had never even been allowed to read. What troubled him most was the fact that he could not tell his co-workers or managers what he had been involved in. The fear of consequences, possibly prison or worse, if he broke the confidentiality haunted him.

He wondered aloud if something nefarious might actually be going on with this so-called upgrade. But he was terrified of the reprisals he might face if he revealed that he alone had executed the new protocol, something not even his own supervisors had been informed about. Why would they offer such a generous bonus for a seemingly simple task that any technician could perform? And why had the encrypted text messages vanished so completely from his phone, like something out of a spy novel?

When he arrived at the company-furnished apartment he shared with his wife of forty years, she met him at the door. One look at his face told her something was wrong. When she asked what was bothering him, he told her it was nothing, that he was simply tired from the stress of a long shift. But she knew better. She had known him too long not to recognize when something weighed heavily on his conscience.

She persisted, telling him that whatever was troubling him, it would be better for both of them if he shared it. They had always faced difficulties together, and this should be no different.

Finally, he relented. He told her everything that had transpired, his actions earlier in the day, the strange instructions, the bonus he had been promised, and the unease that now clung to him. After hearing the full story, she became deeply concerned.

She feared that what her husband had done, and kept secret from his colleagues could be seen as a betrayal. It might bring shame to their name or worse, serious harm if the truth came to light.

She begged him to go to his supervisor the next day. She urged him to explain what he had done and share the suspicions he now carried. But the old man hesitated. What if his suspicions were correct? What if he had done something truly harmful? Surely confessing could cost him his job, or worse.

He assured his wife that what he had done was meant for the betterment of all mankind. When he spoke of the money he would be paid and what it could mean for them, she scolded him for such foolishness. “We would never be allowed to leave the province,” she said, “let alone the country.”

He told her that he had been working toward this for a long time, that everything would work out for their benefit. But she scolded him again for not sharing any of this with her from the beginning. Then, turning away from him, she said he would have to eat alone. She couldn’t bear to look at him under the circumstances. The old man pleaded, but she ignored him, walking into their bedroom and shutting the door behind her.

Nine thousand miles to the west of the Three Gorges Dam, inside the vaulted Mallorcan control room, the technician at the console picked up a special hardline phone. Upon hearing a voice on the other end, he said in a matter-of-fact tone that all the protocols had been activated at all target locations. On the other end of the line, the shadowy figure behind a hand-carved desk hung up the phone. Reaching out for a tumbler of Macallan Scotch whiskey, he drained the 30-year-old amber liquid and nodded in the affirmative to the man sitting across from him.

“It’s done,” he said simply.

21

Inside the warehouse-sized receiving bay of the racetrack circuit tunnel system, Sloane, RH, and the Millers hunkered down behind the cabinets, steeling themselves as the mercenary defense force arrived at the opening and brought their electric quads to an abrupt halt. One of the team, clearly the one in charge, immediately noticed that the doors had been blown wide open. Without hesitation, he began barking orders, instructing half the unit to fan out and search the immediate area. They were to take defensive positions just inside the doors and cover the rear while the other half, who were to exit the bay, set up a perimeter, and inspect the blown-out doors to assess the extent of the damage.

The four members of the commando team knew it was only a matter of time, maybe a minute at most, before they were discovered behind the cabinets. Quickly and silently, they moved into offensive positions, ready for the inevitable moment when everything would erupt.

Thirty seconds later, all hell broke loose. Sloane's suppressed Mark IV rifle spat out a tight burst, taking down four of the sixteen mercenaries inside the bay.

Even with the suppressor, the mercs instantly knew they were under attack. They dove behind the quads for cover as Sloane, RH, and the Millers unleashed a steady stream of gunfire in their direction. Meanwhile, the mercenaries who had exited the bay turned around and rushed back inside, ready to engage whatever threat was now attacking their comrades.

The first two soldiers of the outside force burst back into the bay. They immediately spotted one of the Miller brothers with his back turned as he fired toward the quads. Opening fire with their AK-47s, they hit him in the lower back, just near the kidney. The rounds tore into him just below the protective edge of his body armor and knocked him off his feet. It was instantly clear he was in trouble. Gritting through the pain, he shouted a warning to the others that they had enemy combatants on their six.

The second Miller brother spun around and returned fire, dropping one of the two attackers. The other merc ducked and moved to the far side of the cabinets, gaining a bit of cover.

Scrambling to his twin's side, the surviving Miller grabbed him by the collar and dragged him into a small recess between two cabinets. At the same time, Sloane and RH found themselves in a tight defensive posture. The mercs behind the quads had established a heavy firebase, laying down constant rounds with enough force to keep the commandos pinned. Returning fire meant exposing themselves—and that would be suicide.

Despite that, Sloane, RH, and the remaining Miller had already taken out another five mercenaries. But the advantage was starting to tip. The surviving eight mercs regrouped and pressed their attack.

RH kept communication open with the three team members outside the bay, updating them on the deteriorating situation and requesting countermeasures. In response, Billy Sparks opened fire from his sniper position, expertly dropping four members of the perimeter team before they even realized they were under attack.

While Billy kept them busy from above, Shep Banner moved in on the bay doors to add firepower. Andy Hayes loaded an RPG, but before firing, he remotely triggered a series of micro flashbangs. The grenades erupted with a blinding burst, stunning the perimeter defenders and pulling their attention away from the bay. Thinking a full-scale assault was incoming, they scrambled.

Amid the chaos, Billy and Shep picked off five more enemy fighters. Only seven remained, frantically trying to locate the source of the crossfire that had decimated their numbers.

As the survivors struggled to regroup, Andy fired the RPG through the open bay doors. His call over comms, "Fire in the hole!" was the only warning Sloane, RH, and the remaining Miller had. They hit the floor just as the rocket whooshed into the bay and exploded in the middle of the quad line. The blast tore through everything, vehicles, bodies, and metal, sending shrapnel and limbs flying in every direction.

Pavel, riding at a speed most would call reckless, was nearing the final turn of the tunnel leading to the bay when the explosion rocked the ground. The blast's force echoed through the tunnel, a booming confirmation that something had gone horribly wrong. He had no idea what was happening, but his gut told him it wasn't good. He cracked the throttle open fully on the Ducati. As he hit the sweeping turn, the rear tire lost grip and the bike slid out from under him. Pavel jumped off, hitting the ground in a controlled tumble, arms over his head to protect himself as he skidded to a halt.

Back inside the bay, with the RPG blast distracting everyone, one of the two original mercs who had shot the first Miller brother took advantage of the chaos. Slipping toward Sloane's team, he remained unseen, except by Billy Sparks.

Billy had him in his scope, but just as he squeezed the trigger for a kill shot, a stray bullet from the perimeter team grazed his ear. The pain jolted him and the shot went wide, slamming into one of the metal cabinets instead. The approaching merc, now fully exposed, opened fire with his AK. His shot struck the second Miller brother in the head, exploding his skull like a ripe melon.

Sloane spotted the shooter as he turned his sights on her. She raised her automatic weapon, but it jammed, dead in her hands. For a breathless second, she knew this could be the end.

But Sloane didn't hesitate. In a single, fluid motion, she drew her Gerber survival knife. The mercenary raised his rifle to fire. She hurled the blade with precision. It buried itself deep in the center of his forehead. He froze, swaying slightly, unable to comprehend what had just happened, then collapsed where he stood.

Outside the open bay doors, the back-and-forth firefight continued between the remainder of the perimeter force on one side and Billy, Shep, and Andy on the other. Billy had moved up and was now using his own Mark IV after his sniper rifle had been hit by an AK round and disabled. As the two sides traded shots, one of the mercenaries on the outer edge of the perimeter drew a bead on an unsuspecting Shep Banner and hit the commando with three rounds in a row. The bullets dropped him instantly, one piercing his neck, severing the carotid artery. The ace recon man bled out and died where he fell.

Suddenly realizing that Shep was down, Andy pulled out an M79 grenade launcher and began methodically sweeping it from right to left. The results were devastating, especially when combined with Billy's expert marksmanship. Within moments, they had neutralized the defensive force outside the building except for two stubborn mercs who managed to keep both commandos pinned down with a hail of shots that came dangerously close to hitting them. Andy loaded up his final M79 round and fired.

The arc of the round was perfect. It sailed through the air and landed directly on the unsuspecting mercenary's position. But just before impact, the merc got off a perfectly placed headshot on Andy, killing him instantly. A split second later, the grenade exploded, tearing the merc in half.

Now it was down to one last defender, and Billy. But Billy was soon out of ammo, which gave the surviving mercenary a window to retreat back inside the bay doors and check on his team's situation, unaware that most were already dead. He fired off a few covering rounds and sprinted back inside, not realizing he had passed by the slender figure of Sloane. As he moved past her position, Sloane slid up behind him, made a quick move, snapped his neck, and tossed the body aside without a second thought.

Inside the bay, neither Sloane nor RH realized that Grovzny was closing in. He was now on foot, armed with both his MAC-10 machine pistol and his Beretta. Checking the Millers' status, both commandos confirmed what they feared, the brothers were gone. They made a tactical decision to deal with the bodies later and focus on the mission objective: finding and capturing Pavel.

They got on comms with Billy and learned they had lost two more team members outside. Sloane told Billy to hold position for recon. Then, scanning the now eerily quiet bay, it appeared all was clear for a go down the tunnel. They began making their way toward the corridor just as Pavel opened up with a wild burst from the MAC-10, spraying bullets through the air around them.

RH still had plenty of ammo and responded immediately. With the precision of a seasoned marksman, he laid down suppressive fire. Pavel ducked and quickly moved to a side wall of the tunnel, trying to avoid the deadly accurate NATO 7.62 rounds.

Hearing no further movement and unsure who was in the tunnel, RH and Sloane, now armed with an AK-47, proceeded cautiously through the bay and entered the tunnel. With no available cover, the two commandos crouched low and braced themselves mentally for the inevitable next burst of MAC-10 fire.

They hadn't even fully taken position when Pavel's MAC-10 erupted again, unleashing another spray of 9mm rounds. Most shots were off target, but a ricochet slammed into RH's hip and shattered the bone, rendering him immobile. Watching where the fire had come from and seeing RH go down, Sloane made a snap, risky decision. She launched into a low dash, zigzagging forward as gunfire cracked around her.

She stopped abruptly as the shooting paused, and she heard the unmistakable sound of a magazine being swapped out. Recognizing her moment, Sloane raised the AK, steadied her aim, and laid down a tight, deliberate stream of fire, one shot at a time, working left to right in controlled bursts.

On her final shot, she heard the distinct sound of a bullet hitting something that wasn't concrete, followed by a grunt and a groan. She knew she had made contact. Moving forward cautiously, she pulled out a mini Maglite, knowing what happens when you corner something, or someone, desperate and dangerous.

She flashed the light quickly, just enough to glimpse her target. What she saw stopped her cold. Pavel. Wounded. The crazed look in his eyes told her everything she needed to know: he was a madman, still on a mission.

Sloane dove to her right in a smooth roll just as Grovzny fired two quick shots from his Beretta. Both missed. She came up on her feet and moved to flank him, determined to end this once and for all.

Speaking in a calm, steady voice, she directed her words back toward the bay. "I know it's you, Pavel. This is over. Give it up now, or you'll be dead in minutes."

Pavel responded with a crazed laugh. His voice cracked as he screamed back, "You!!! Nothing is over… nothing!" Then he emptied the fifteen-shot clip of the Beretta, spraying wildly before bolting down the tunnel toward the crashed Ducati. Blood streamed down his left arm from the gunshot wound, but he moved with the adrenaline of a man refusing to die.

One of his stray shots grazed Sloane's shoulder. She winced in pain but remained focused. She could hear his footsteps pounding deeper into the tunnel.

Sloane turned on her mini Maglite again just in time to see Pavel disappear into the bend of the tunnel. She rose up and gave chase, pushing through the pain. Then the sound of the Ducati's engine roared to life.

Even though the MotoGP racer had gone down earlier, it was still functional. As Sloane continued into the tunnel, a burst of machine gun fire from mounted weapons tore through the corridor. She felt a sudden, burning sting as one of the rounds nicked her calf muscle. She yelped from the shock of being hit, then heard the Ducati's engine scream as it tore away, echoing into the distance.

22

Other than the muffled sound of the RPG explosion inside the underground tunnel on the far side of the complex, the firefight that had just taken place went pretty much unnoticed. The circuit hadn't yet opened for the day in the early morning hours. Had anyone gotten a closer look at the immediate scene, it would have been a different matter entirely—with the wreckage of the bay doors, scattered quad parts inside, and the grim body count of the dead both inside and out.

Inside the tunnel, an alive but slightly bloodied Sloane knew there was nothing she could do at the moment to catch Pavel as he sped away on the Ducati racing bike. Frustration burned in her chest, but she turned and headed back out of the tunnel to check on RH and begin planning their next move. Or maybe, she thought with growing uncertainty, her next move. Helping RH to his feet, she supported him as they made their way out of the tunnel. Then she turned back, steeling herself as she re-entered the gloom to retrieve the lifeless bodies of the Miller brothers.

An unscathed Billy soon joined her, and together they removed their two comrades-in-arms from the bay area using a fireman's carry. Despite the limited damage they had inflicted on the opposing force, the loss of four team members was a grim reminder of just how dangerous the overall situation had become. It reinforced the urgency of stopping Pavel Grovzny—and whatever plans he had in motion.

Moving as quickly as possible, they managed to carry the fallen back to the closest Range Rover. Billy then commandeered the vehicle to get them to the safe house for further processing. As Billy drove off with the four corpses as silent passengers, Sloane headed back down the hill to help RH get to the second Rover so they could bug out before anyone else became aware of what had just taken place. Once she and RH reached the four-wheeler, she helped him into the passenger side. They pulled away from the scene, and Sloane quickly reached for the satellite phone, making a call to Eddie Stafford she had never intended—nor wanted—to make.

Back at the racing circuit HQ, a wounded Pavel Grovzny made his way up to his private suite and immediately placed three calls. The first was to his staff doctor, urgently summoning him to treat the gunshot wound. The second went to another of his teams, instructing them to be dispatched to the bay and tunnel to contain the scene. They were to secure the area until the cleaner crew arrived from the Villa after his third call. Pavel knew the cleanup had to happen quickly. The race complex would open in less than two hours to the public for the qualification round—an event that would draw a crowd nearly as large as the main race itself.

As the Range Rovers returned to the safe house, Eddie had additional personnel on hand to assist with the removal of the dead commandos. Their bodies were prepared for transport to Ramstein under the cover story of being active American servicemen killed in an accident on foreign soil. With the bodies handled, attention shifted to RH, who was immediately attended to by a team of agency doctors and a field surgeon. A makeshift operating room had been set up, complete with an X-ray, to assess the damage to his hip and begin a possible surgical procedure. The diagnosis was brutal. Although the bullet had passed clean through, the hip bone had been shattered. The injury would require a full replacement that couldn't be performed on-site. RH was soon en route to Ramstein as well.

As cleanup efforts got underway at the site of the brief but destructive battle that had unfolded at daybreak, Pavel sat grimacing while his private doctor worked to remove the bullet from his upper left bicep. With the slug out and the wound tightly bandaged, Pavel was stiff but still fully ambulatory. Since he was right-handed, he remained functional. He waved off the painkillers, determined to keep his mind sharp despite the burning pain that now radiated through torn muscle, shredded tendons, and a bone chip deep in his arm.

Trying to wrap his head around everything that had happened, he focused on the bigger picture. His plans for the next day were still well underway. But what had the breach and the assault been about? It couldn't be about what was planned for tomorrow—he was the only one who truly knew the details. The only other possibility that came to mind was the original mission that had first alerted him to Sloane's existence. Maybe it was always about him. About taking him out.

But how would anyone have known he was even there at that time? His vehicle had been secured in his garage at the Villa. It was swept twice a day for any kind of tracking device, and none had ever been found. His thoughts swirled, circling suspicion like a vulture. Pavel leaned toward the idea of an internal betrayal—completely unaware of the NSA satellite tracking that was being used to monitor his remotely hacked cell phone.

Back at the safe house, Sloane, Eddie, and Billy gathered around the kitchen table. A new map lay in front of them, displaying IR imaging of Pavel's Villa. They began formulating plans for the next phase of their operation—one focused on getting to him at the Villa later that night when he would least expect a second assault so soon. Surrounded by the false safety of his "castle on the river," Pavel would believe himself secure. That would be their opening.

It would come down to Sloane and Billy, taking a true commando approach in the dead of night. Their objective: infiltrate the Villa, locate Pavel—most likely holed up in his private suite—and somehow neutralize him before extracting him without triggering any alarms.

As the gates to the race circuit opened and massive crowds poured in for final qualifying, Pavel was busy directing his teams. They were clearing the damaged tunnel entryway of bodies and any other evidence of the earlier firefight. The wrecked quads were dragged back into the tunnel. Engineering crews from the track began building a temporary retaining wall to block off the tunnel entrance. All the while, race fans continued to stream into the venue. The stands filled quickly, and the roar of Formula One engines came to life as the cars prepared for their final qualifying runs—for pole position and the all-important grid lineup.

Looking down at the enhanced satellite map, Sloane began to lay out the plan for entrance into the Villa that night. She based it on her experience of escaping, her memories from the post-fashion show party and her knowledge of the command center's location. A critical detail worked in their favor, Pavel had never installed cameras in the center's corridors, his ego convincing him no one would ever penetrate that part of the complex.

The plan was to enter through the garage after overriding the security codes and compromising the camera system. A looped image of their own would be hacked into the system and embedded into a hard disc for playback sometime that afternoon, while things were relatively quiet at the complex. The three were fairly certain that, despite the outward calm at Pavel's compound, Pavel himself would have put everything on high alert after what had happened at the racetrack earlier that morning.

Pavel remained in his private box above the pit lane while crews were finishing up in the tunnel. Out on the track, things were starting to heat up with the first qualifying run of the day. He knew he would need to head down to track level to rub elbows with team owners and principals, maintaining the image of the gracious local host and the mastermind behind bringing the Grand Prix to Prague. He quickly donned his official race suit, not affiliated with any team, but standard attire for racing complex staff. Each department wore different colors, with all managers in white, which Pavel now wore as he stepped into the private elevator that would deliver him to the racing paddocks and pit row.

Out on the wet track, the team from Alfa Romeo, returning to the constructor series after a long absence, was preparing their lead car for its first timed run of the day. Rain was falling in a continuous circular pattern over the entire complex, making the track as treacherous as expected. Despite the conditions, the crowd roared with excitement as the first Alfa accelerated down the main straightaway, the timer starting for its official run on the newly christened circuit. Qualifying was officially underway.

Back at the safe house, plans for the incursion were being finalized. The new gear was being assembled for the next, more stealth-oriented phase. This included state-of-the-art night vision systems with integrated communications that would allow Sloane and Billy to stay in contact during the operation at a whisper volume. Each would be equipped with the new SIG Sauer XM7 rifle, fitted with a suppressor. Currently used by the 101st Airborne and the 75th Ranger Regiment, it was meant to be the next-generation squad weapon and a replacement for the M4 carbine. They would also carry standard-issue SIG Sauer P320 pistols with 15-round capacity and attachable suppressors. Rounding out their loadout was the Gerber Mark III survival knife. The hope was that the mission could be completed without ever needing to fire a single shot.

As qualifying progressed, a surprise contender took the provisional pole. A new upstart team from Honda shocked the field with a revolutionary engine design they had just revealed, much to the dismay of rival teams. The grid was soon forming more or less as expected, though lap times were slower than usual due to the rain and slippery conditions. Most teams ran soft tires for better grip, though this strategy meant reduced durability during the race itself. If the rain persisted or returned tomorrow, it could cause serious complications for everyone. Still waiting for his chance in the final Q3 run was Alex Verdun of Red Bull, after slower-than-expected times in the earlier Q1 and Q2 rounds.

Pavel now stood in the engineering bay with Red Bull Team Leader Hannover MaCumber. Together, they watched Verdun on the monitors as the young driver brought the car up to speed in preparation for his timed run. A strategic decision had been made to run on medium compound tires to increase speed, thanks to reports suggesting that the rain was letting up and the track was beginning to dry. That, combined with the talent of the brash rookie behind the wheel, all but guaranteed a shot at the pole, assuming Verdun didn't lose control or crash.

Pavel watched with awe and growing fascination. Alec and the Red Bull RB1 tore down the straightaways at near top speed. Verdun's handling of the gearbox and braking system was nearly flawless, as if he and the machine were one. Aside from a slight mishap coming out of one particularly nasty corner that nearly caused a spin, Alec laid down a remarkable lap. By the end of qualifying, he had claimed the pole position, in spite of additional challenges from other teams.

As Verdun came to a stop in the pit and climbed out of the car, both MaCumber and Pavel were there to greet him and offer congratulations. The crowd went wild, thrilled by the dramatic display of skill. As the excitement wound down and fans began heading for the exits in anticipation of the Grand Prix the next day, MaCumber and Verdun made their way to the team's debriefing session. Pavel returned to his private box to ensure final preparations for the big event were on track.

He first called his on-site team leader at the track to confirm that all the micro detonators were properly activated and timers set, along with evacuation plans for his own forces. Next, he contacted his command and control center at the Villa to check the status of the executable file that would be initiated during tomorrow's mass casualty event at the racing facility. The same file designed to decimate and shut down other power systems across the globe.

Satisfied with the answers he received, Pavel exhaled a slow, deep breath. Then he placed one final call for the day to the shadowy figure sitting in Mallorca. Once the encrypted connection was established, Pavel simply said, "All systems are a go and the countdown has officially begun for Prague."

He ended the call, rode the elevator down to his private parking spot, and was soon on his way back to the riverside Villa.

23

Sloane looked out at the fading light as night descended, creeping in earlier than usual under the weight of the overcast sky. She was relieved that the rain had finally stopped, making their approach to Pavel's riverside Villa less treacherous. The plan was to enter from the riverfront in a compact inflatable, powered by a battery-propelled trolling motor for stealth and maneuverability, with foldout oars as backup if needed. Once they made landfall, they'd move toward the western edge of the estate, following a twelve-foot-high block sea wall to a densely wooded area on both sides of the property.

This was where they would make their first breach—scaling the wall and continuing along it until reaching the garage. Over the past two days, real-time infrared imaging had provided them with a reliable timetable for the perimeter checks conducted by the estate's security. There were eight personnel in total, including two dog handlers with Belgian Malinois shepherds, prized for their intelligence, agility, and precision in security roles. All patrolled on foot and were connected to Pavel's security system, with live feeds transmitted to heads-up displays via the new Xreal Air 2 Glasses—gear originally designed for VR and AR tactical training. The guards also stayed linked through comms to the central security desk located inside the command center.

Thanks to Eddie—and the NSA's backdoor access to Pavel's network—a programmed loop of routine, uneventful footage would play on the security monitors. It would mask the live feed as Sloane and Billy navigated along the outer wall toward the garage. Eddie maintained an aerial view from a satellite feed and stayed on comms with them in real time, watching for any unexpected security movements. Their protocol was clear: avoid contact at all costs. Any confrontation with guards, especially if it involved weapons, would instantly escalate into a full-scale red alert and likely compromise the mission.

Failure tonight meant no second chances. Pavel would vanish behind layers of protection, and with him, any chance of uncovering—let alone stopping—his catastrophic plans. While Sloane and Billy infiltrated the estate, Eddie remained nearby in a specially equipped, armor-plated cargo van. He would serve as both their extraction driver and mobile liaison with outside support from NATO's Special Operations Force—SOF—and the Czech Republic's elite 601st special forces group. That backup would only be activated in case of extreme emergency. The last thing the Agency wanted was a high-profile shootout that could be traced back to them.

As night fell completely, the trio loaded into the van and took backroads around the city's perimeter, skirting the place where Sloane had first emerged from the woods during her previous escape. Their route took them to an older, poorly maintained coastal road, a forgotten stretch ideal for launching the inflatable. The industrial district they passed was eerily quiet—like a ghost town—its warehouses shuttered for the weekend. A few cars passed going the opposite direction, their headlights briefly illuminating the van as it crept along toward the targeted access road.

Meanwhile, downtown Prague was anything but quiet. The city erupted with the biggest celebration of the year—a massive, no-holds-barred festival in anticipation of tomorrow's Grand Prix. The street party had drawn more people than the race itself was expected to. It sprawled across five entire blocks that had been closed off to traffic, overflowing with stages, street vendors, and revelers. Music thumped from every direction, and the drinks flowed freely—craft beers, fine Czech wines, and every spirit imaginable were passed around with enthusiasm.

In the heart of it all stood the VIP tent, a lavish, invitation-only affair packed with celebrities and dignitaries. Many who had attended the fashion show were now here, mingling beneath glittering lights. On a private stage, global headliners rotated through sets—Billie Eilish, Olivia Rodrigo, John Mayer, Post Malone, and Adele lit up the night in succession. The only person noticeably absent was the man who had orchestrated it all: Pavel Grovzny. Whispers spread about where the elusive host might be and when, if ever, he would appear.

Inside his private suite at the riverside Villa, Pavel was focused on more critical matters. He sent final encrypted messages through the Telegram app to his troop leaders and top-tier operatives, ensuring that each knew precisely what was expected of them in the hours to come. Once those communications were complete, he turned his attention to preparing for his public appearance at the VIP tent. In the bathroom, he removed the dressing from his wounded arm, inspecting the deep purple bruising where the bullet had been extracted.

He stepped into the shower, letting the hot water wash away the day's chaos, then carefully redressed the injury. From his wardrobe, he selected a classic Yves Saint Laurent tuxedo—tailored to perfection—for his brief but striking stage appearance. Once there, he would thank the crowd, praise the performers, honor the sponsors and organizers, and toast the VIPs who had helped bring his vision of Formula One racing in the Czech Republic to life.

Back on the coastal road, Eddie slowed the van as they neared the staging area. The inflatable raft, stowed in the back next to an array of tactical gear and weapons, was soon prepped for launch. They parked in a clearing near the river, shielded by trees and low brush. Billy and Sloane moved fast, slipping into the dark water with the gear-laden raft. The current was against them, making progress slow, but they eventually reached the twelve-foot seawall that separated the estate from the river—just a hundred meters from Pavel's private dock and boathouse.

Silently, they slipped out of the raft into the frigid water, deflated the vessel, and secured it beneath an overhanging tree in case they needed to make a quick escape. From there, they moved on foot, approaching the wall under the cover of wet foliage and shadows. The earlier rain had left everything damp, muffling their footsteps. With grappling hooks and nylon rope in hand, they reached the designated entry point.

And the operation began.

Back inside his private suite, Pavel busied himself with the final touches for his tuxedo—donning a crimson red cravat and cummerbund combination along with a pair of Bruno Magli loafers in burgundy and his favorite watch, a Patek Philippe Grand Perpetual Tourbillon valued at over five million dollars. Looking himself over in the full-length mirror, he was very pleased with what he saw. He wondered aloud which one of the adoring celebrities or many socialite fans would be his private guest here at the estate once he made his appearance and returned for the evening.

Out in the van, which had now moved to a different clearing on a hill with a vantage point over the estate for reconnaissance purposes, Eddie was in communication with the NSA Satellite Operations, or Sat Ops who were initiating the programmed image manipulation of the estate's security system. Sloane and Billy had reached the point of entry and were preparing to breach the outer wall. Throwing their titanium grappling hooks in arcing motions up and over the wall, they waited until the hooks became securely lodged into the top inside layer of brick. Moving swiftly, Sloane and Billy ascended the wall and, attaching a modified fire escape rope ladder to the inside, climbed down about six feet before dropping to the soft ground below.

Back inside the Villa, Pavel took one last look in the mirror and reached for the key fob to his Bugatti, preparing to head to the garage, when his private line from the command center flashed red. He picked up the receiver. The security staffer manning the video control console informed him that they had received a detection warning from one of the corner motion detectors, but could not identify anything out of the ordinary on any of the camera feeds, thanks in no small part to the manipulated footage being fed by the NSA.

Pavel ordered the operator to alert all security personnel to the new status and dispatch additional teams to scour the perimeter and locate the source of the detection if there was one. It wasn't outside the realm of possibility that one of the feral cats in the area had climbed atop the wall and triggered the alert. Never in his wildest imagination did Pavel suspect this could be tied so soon to the same team, including Sloane, that had assaulted his men at the tunnel entrance during the daybreak attack. Still, this latest warning gave him a moment of unease, which he quickly dismissed.

Eddie relayed the sensor alert to Sloane and Billy, warning that it might result in a heightened security presence. They immediately picked up the pace, dashing low across an opening that cut off a full corner of the wall and brought them within a few hundred feet of the garage entrance. As they made a dive for cover behind some shrubbery, a gas-powered quad rolled around the curve from the other side of the garage, bathing their position in a flood of bright

LED lights. The two commandos held their breath—only their decisive evasive action kept them from being spotted.

Inside the Villa, Pavel was on his way down to the garage, preparing to leave for the VIP event. As Sloane and Billy finally reached the garage entry point, Eddie radioed that Pavel appeared to be moving toward the opposite end of the Villa. It was a small update, but one that kept them informed of his exact location within the estate.

Reaching the coded entry panel for the retractable garage doors, Sloane and Billy, still undetected, prepared to make their second major move by infiltrating the interior. Billy pried the main panel loose and attached two leads with alligator clips to contact points inside. Then he placed a credit-card-sized wafer connected to the leads, against the back of his cellphone, where it adhered via small magnetic strips. Launching a custom code-deciphering app that he had written himself, Billy entered a nine-digit number into his iPhone's keypad.

Meanwhile, Pavel had reached his Bugatti, slid into the driver's seat, and hit the ignition. The eight-liter, sixteen-cylinder, quad-turbocharged beast roared to life, its throaty growl like something from a mythical dragon. He switched the coupe into sport mode and, paddle-shifting into first gear, launched it out of the parking slot toward the massive garage doors.

Outside, as Sloane and Billy waited for the app to complete the code sequence, Billy's phone lit up with a green confirmation light. He pressed a single button, and the garage doors began sliding outward into the recessed slots of the car park's entry walls. Just as they began moving toward the opening, the deafening roar of the Bugatti filled the air. They caught a glimpse of Pavel at the wheel just as Eddie radioed that Grovzny was accelerating rapidly out of the garage.

This turn of events was entirely unanticipated. Neither Sloane nor Eddie had imagined that Pavel would leave the safety of his heavily guarded compound—an impenetrable fortress by design. But their target had now raced past them, heading toward the formal gates opposite the river, which opened onto the thoroughfare leading to the city. Sloane radioed Eddie that Pavel had just exited the compound. After a quick decision, it was agreed that the best course of action was to proceed into the Villa now that they had secured access via the garage, and Sloane knew the layout from her previous escape.

They moved through the garage toward the elevator Sloane had used before and kept Eddie updated as they went deeper into the estate. Eddie, monitoring Pavel's movements, confirmed he would keep them informed of any changes. The elevator took them up three levels and opened into a corridor Sloane recognized, one that led to the control center.

As they approached the doors to the control room, Eddie radioed that Pavel was now inside the VIP tent, which, on reflection, made perfect sense given his role as the public face of the Grand Prix. In a quick, calculated decision, Sloane and Billy chose to head to Pavel's private suite and wait for his return. It seemed like the most probable scenario.

With Eddie guiding them through the labyrinthine hallways and rooms using satellite IR imaging, Sloane and Billy navigated toward Pavel's suite. Avoiding detection was still critical. They moved cautiously, leapfrogging one another, scanning constantly for heat signatures and electronic signals as they advanced. Finally, they entered the spacious suite.

Now, it was time to wait.

24

Inside the VIP tent, Adele was just finishing up her last song when Pavel walked in and headed straight for the stage. The crowd erupted in loud applause, first for Adele, and then for Pavel as they saw him join her onstage and give her a big hug in appreciation for being at the party. As Adele exited, Pavel took hold of the microphone and turned his attention to the vaunted guests, celebrities and dignitaries alike, thanking everyone for helping to make the party the crown jewel of the social calendar during this historic occasion: the first-ever Grand Prix of Czechoslovakia.

He raised his voice to the crowd, "Are you having a good time?" A lukewarm "Yeah" rippled back at him. Not satisfied, he prompted them again, this time shouting, "Come on! Are you having a good time?" The crowd roared with cheers and wild applause as Pavel waved his arms in the air like the champion MMA fighter he was.

He went on, telling them what an honor it was to be there with all of them, reminding them what an exciting moment this was for the chance to show the world the greatness of Prague and the spirit of the Czech people.

Then came the low, growling opening riff of "Sandman." The crowd stirred in growing anticipation. Pavel turned back to the microphone and screamed, "And now, here they are… Metallica!" The audience exploded in excitement. As four massive flash pots erupted on stage and lasers beamed across the tent, the world-famous band launched into a furious set of heavy metal hits, the final surprise of the night.

Backstage, Pavel wasted no time. He quickly found Marsella Kinski, one of the darlings of Prague's elite social scene. Her family traced their lineage to Czech nobility. With his usual confidence, Pavel suggested that they might enjoy themselves more back at the Villa, just the two of them, watching the performance via closed-circuit TV, away from the raucous, now-inebriated crowd. Smiling with a coy, sly grin, Marsella kissed Pavel on the cheek and walked arm in arm with him past the stage and out to where his Bugatti was parked.

They made their way past massive road cases and talent trailers, slipping out the backstage exit. Soon they were inside the car, driving at a relaxed pace back toward the estate. Pavel, of course, had one more indulgence in mind before tomorrow's big race. Thanks to NSA satellite tracking, Eddie had eyes on Pavel's movements and quickly radioed to Sloane and Billy: "Grovzny was en route to the Villa. Stand by."

Inside Pavel's private suite, Sloane and Billy had already concealed themselves. They planned to strike when he was at his most vulnerable. Their mission: capture the mercenary kingpin and extract him to a local black site for interrogation. Sloane took position behind a curtain near the bed, while Billy hid inside a closet closest to the suite's entrance.

Eddie's voice came through the radio, quiet but clear: Pavel was pulling onto the property.

With the weapons checks complete, the two operatives waited in silence. It wasn't long before they heard Pavel and Marsella approaching from the hallway. Their laughter echoed faintly, the carefree tone drawing closer until suddenly they entered. Pavel playfully tossed Marsella onto the bed and prepared to join her.

A sharp scream tore through the room as Sloane and Billy emerged with weapons raised, pointed directly at the pair. Pavel froze. Then, slowly, a twisted grin crept across his face, and he laughed, full of mock amusement, like a man unbothered by what was unfolding.

“Shut up,” Sloane said, her voice dark with menace.

“Or what?” Pavel shot back, almost gleeful.

Sloane shifted her aim toward Marsella. “I’ll kill the girl.”

Pavel didn’t hesitate. “Go ahead. She means nothing to me.”

Marsella began to whimper, her expression crumbling into panic.

Sloane turned her eyes on her. “Be quiet, or I will shoot you.”

Pavel asked what they planned to do. Sloane responded flatly: he was going for a little ride to answer some questions.

“Hardly,” Pavel replied with a sneer.

As Billy moved in to secure Marsella with zip ties and a gag, Sloane never took her gaze, or her weapon, off Pavel. Billy finished and turned to restrain the mercenary. That’s when he noticed it: the key fob still in Pavel’s hand was flashing red.

At the first sign of trouble, Pavel had pressed the panic button. His security team was already en route.

“I think we’re going to have company,” Billy said, locking eyes with Sloane.

“You have no idea,” Pavel muttered through a snort of amusement, even as Billy cinched the zip ties around his wrists.

Sloane moved quickly, grabbing a pair of socks from nearby and stuffing them into Pavel’s mouth to silence him. She kept her weapon trained on him. Looking over at Marsella, Sloane told Billy to stash her someplace safe.

Billy picked up the struggling debutante and placed her in the closet, speaking firmly: if she wanted to live, she needed to stay down and stay silent.

Then it began.

The heavy footfall of soldiers racing double time thundered toward the suite. Weapons clacked as they were armed and brought to the ready. Sloane and Billy knew what was coming: a fight.

Slinging her automatic over her shoulder, Sloane seized Pavel by the collar and hauled him toward the door. Billy followed, ready to return fire if needed.

Sloane shouted through the door, “We have Pavel! We’re coming out! He dies if you don’t let us through!”

Sloane yanked the socks from Pavel’s mouth and shoved the muzzle of her 9mm tight against his temple.

“Tell your men to check their weapons and stand down,” she ordered. “Or I put a bullet in your head right here.”

Pavel stared back, unflinching. “You won’t kill me,” he said coolly. “Then you’d never know what I have planned.” A sneer curled across his bloodied lip.

Without hesitation, Sloane cracked him above the eyebrow with her gun barrel, drawing a line of blood that trickled into his eye.

“Don’t count on it, mister,” she said, voice like flint. “Tell them, or you’ll never live to see your precious results.”

Pavel saw it in her eyes. She meant it. He called out, yelling through the door for his men to stand down and let them pass. For a second, silence. Then bullets tore through the door, splintering the wood, and Billy returned fire instantly—two quick bursts dropped two guards standing just beyond the entrance.

Sloane grabbed Pavel by the collar and slammed his face against the shattered opening. “Tell them now, or the next shot’s for you.”

Seeing their boss’s face plastered against the doorway, Pavel’s men froze. Pavel complied, ordering them again, louder this time, to drop their weapons. One by one, rifles clattered to the floor.

Sloane, Billy, and their captive emerged through the doorway, walking a narrow path between two rows of stunned, heavily armed guards. Billy kept his weapon ready, scanning for any twitch, any mistake. Sloane moved like a shadow, always keeping Pavel’s body between her and his men.

Thirty feet down the hall, Billy tossed a stun grenade behind them, followed by a smoke canister. A few scattered gunshots rang out from the cloud, but nothing found its mark. With a shove, Sloane pushed Pavel forward. The race to the extraction point was on.

As they tore through the second-floor hallway, shadows danced along the walls up ahead. Four armed men turned the corner. Billy, without breaking stride, raised his SIG XM7 and dropped them all with clinical precision. Sloane yanked Pavel forward by his collar, moving fast as they rounded the bend.

Gunfire erupted from behind a makeshift barricade about fifty feet ahead. They ducked back around the corner. From behind them, boots thudded, reinforcements were closing in. They were seconds from being pinned.

Billy used a periscope sight to survey the barricade. "Flashbang might do it," he muttered, "but I'll need to get into the open to throw it right."

Sloane forced Pavel down, zip-tying his ankles so tightly he was practically hogtied.

Grabbing her own XM7, she nodded. Billy moved. Sloane rolled into the hallway first, laying down cover fire. Billy launched the flash bang, followed by a stun grenade. Two guards staggered from the smoke—Sloane dropped them instantly, two controlled shots each.

The hallway was momentarily clear.

Gunfire sounded behind them. Sloane and Billy turned in unison, unleashing enough firepower to halt the approaching team cold. Sloane sliced through Pavel's ankle ties hauled him to his feet, and they took off again.

They neared the command center. Billy paused long enough to rig a pressure-sensitive stun grenade to the door handle, one last trap for their pursuers.

Skipping the elevator, they stormed into the emergency stairwell, practically hurling Pavel ahead of them as they descended. In the garage, they burst through an access door and crouched low near the bushes, alarms wailing through the night.

Only one obstacle remained: the security gate.

Sloane had escaped through it once before, but now it was manned by six armed guards, and they were on foot.

Billy radioed to Eddie. “We’re ready to make the final move.”

With only one smoke grenade left, Billy tossed it diagonally across the driveway. The guards opened fire blindly into the haze, thinking the assault was coming from a different direction.

Sloane, Billy, and a gagged Pavel crept toward the gate—fifty feet, then forty. They were almost there when—

Whoosh.

A fiery roar exploded from the darkness. The guard shack and gate vanished in a fireball. A HEF (High Explosive Flammable) RPG, fired from Eddie’s van, had obliterated the final barrier in a maelstrom of debris and flame.

Without hesitating, Sloane and Billy dragged Pavel through the wreckage and flung him into the van’s secure containment cell. They climbed in, slamming the side door shut. Eddie met them with a satisfied nod, his expression taut but triumphant.

Sloane exhaled, adrenaline still coursing, and managed a small, wry smile. "Guess we made the delivery on time, more or less like we planned."

The van peeled off into the night, dark and silent, speeding away from the villa. As they reached the main road, the lights came on, and the van merged into the quiet night traffic, just another vehicle on a long highway headed home.

25

Half a world away from Prague sat the Palo Verde Nuclear Power Plant in Tonopah, Arizona. Palo Verde was known for producing the most electricity in the United States and for being the largest power plant when it came to net generation. It was responsible for supplying 35% of the power used throughout the state of Arizona, as well as overflowing to places like Nevada, Colorado, and California as demand increased beyond capacity.

Inside the main building, a random little string of code appeared in the bottom left corner of a computer screen, embedded in the command line of a terminal inside the control room. This nondescript code went completely unnoticed by control technicians who were busy monitoring other systems in operation. The small set of random figures appeared to indicate some sort of security protocol update and contained the words "auto.exe," as well as a series of numbers that seemed to indicate a date and time. A cursor blinked ten times, then came to a stop. Another ten seconds passed, and the code vanished from the screen altogether—as if it had never existed.

Deep within the networked terminal's mainframe, silicon chips began to act on the command embedded in the code. A pre-planted virus silently activated and began spreading throughout the power plant's central network. One by one, it infiltrated every computer—first inside the control room, then across the entire facility.

The virus was innocuous at first. It quietly began closing off data partitions, starting with non-essential functions related to internal directories. These directories enabled users to locate necessary files within the massive volumes of data housed in the system.

Without them, finding anything quickly would become virtually impossible.

Under normal operations, this wouldn't present a noticeable problem—unless someone attempted a hard restart or performed a full factory reset on the proprietary Linux-based operating system that powered the plant's network. But the odds of that happening were slim to none. And even then, only machines with the virus already embedded in the main processor would be affected. The virus was designed to move like a slow leak—undetected and unalarming—so that panic, if it came at all, would come too late.

Its true target was the plant's innovative cooling system, which relied on treated wastewater provided by communities such as Phoenix. This system kept the radioactive fuel rods from overheating and triggering a nuclear disaster. The virus was set to gradually undermine the control valves regulating this cooling system. Eventually, this would lead to a catastrophic meltdown, with the potential to kill all 900 employees on duty and the 500 contractors scheduled for bi-annual maintenance and refueling. From there, a deadly plume of radioactive gases and particles could spread outward, endangering millions in the surrounding region.

Beyond the direct threat of contamination and death, the attack would instantly cut power to four million people and businesses across the Phoenix metro area. This would paralyze critical systems—banking, commerce, hospitals, schools, emergency services, traffic control, and basic infrastructure such as internet access, water delivery, and natural gas. Day-to-day essentials like gas stations would become non-operational. Life as people knew it would grind to a sudden and complete halt. The only thing likely to remain operational—at least initially—would be cellular phone service.

Compounding the devastation was a thermal override embedded in the virus. If triggered, it would physically melt down every terminal and the mainframe they were connected to. Any attempt to manually override the new command structure would set this off. The designers of the virus anticipated that no one would detect it in time to stop it—though they couldn't entirely rule out the possibility of a curious young network technician catching on early.

If that happened—if anyone tried to investigate and debug the anomaly—the virus would accelerate. The infection would spread instantly, switching into high gear and driving the system toward an exponential, irreversible collapse. The outcome would be the same, but the timeline would be violently compressed.

Regardless of interference, the countdown had begun. The train had left the station. What was unfolding at Palo Verde was just the beginning. Across the globe, similar dominoes were set to fall every three days—each one designed to dismantle another piece of modern civilization.

Within the next eight-hour shift, the virus would finish spreading to every computer and into the central server. From there, it would issue new commands to each subsystem. The entire back end of the network would begin to lose communication with the terminals responsible for crucial balance controls—those that monitored fuel rod temperatures and regulated the cooling system. When that moment came, the fuel rods would begin to overheat, pushing internal temperatures into the danger zone. At the same time, the cooling valves would begin to close. Once the system passed its tipping point, there would be no turning back—and no chance of averting the disaster.

As the first shift ended and employees filtered into the locker room, replaced by the incoming second shift, contractors began arriving for maintenance and refueling. Meanwhile, a warning light flickered to life inside one of the reactors. But no indication of the issue appeared on any of the computer screens. The virus had already severed those communication lines.

During the personnel changeover, no one suspected anything unusual—except for a new technician assigned to monitor a temperature sensor that had been fluctuating erratically for several hours. Suddenly, the sensor stopped showing any fluctuation at all. It flatlined. That seemed... odd.

Curious, and with a growing sense of unease, the technician picked up the internal com line and called his supervisor.

"Something seems off," he said. "Can you come down and take a look?"

26

The thirteen men gathered around the hand-carved conference table inside the castle on Mallorca stood and raised their glasses. The rich, locally produced Barolo Marchese' D Azeglio wine glimmered under the dim light as the man at the head of the table proposed a toast. His gaze swept over the grim-faced men before him, and a quiet satisfaction settled in his chest.

It was astonishing—this disparate group, drawn from every corner of the globe, each a titan of their own industry, now united under a single purpose. Just as he had planned. Raising his glass higher, he addressed them, his voice low but commanding.

"And so it has begun..." A pause, deliberate. "The hour of our own discontent will soon be at an end. We will remake the world—reshape it entirely—into the vision we have all imagined. The vision we have agreed upon." His lips curled slightly. "We will seize control of worldwide infrastructure under the guise of benevolence, positioning ourselves as saviors. And when the governments of the world kneel before us, desperate, they will swear fealty. They will hail us as the guardians of their crumbling societies."

He let the words hang, watching the fire in their eyes. "We will act as we please—when, where, and how we choose. Any opposition will be met with consequences far worse than the chaos they will soon endure." His glass lifted higher. "To us! To what we will accomplish! To the power... the riches... the dominion that awaits every man at this table!" A sharp, triumphant grin. "Salute!"

Glasses clinked. The expensive wine vanished in a single draught, only to be refilled immediately. The men settled back into their seats, the air thick with anticipation.

Each one at that table was a master of his domain—banking, natural resources, manufacturing, artificial intelligence, media, arms, international affairs. But their true power lay in the shadows. Terrorism. Arms trafficking. Espionage. Cybercrime. Kidnapping. Narcotics. Prostitution. Assassination. All had played their part in what history would remember as "The Panama Papers."

They had been chosen carefully, handpicked by the man at the head of the table. He had seen in them the same ruthless pragmatism, the same disdain for a world spiraling into decay. More importantly, he knew they would act—without hesitation, without mercy—when the time came.

Leaning back, as if lost in thought, he laid out the next steps. The path to absolute control.

First, chaos. Power grids would falter, systems would collapse—or appear to. The Omega Collective Group would then extend its hand, offering salvation to desperate governments. They would step in with their vast resources, their unparalleled expertise, and "restore order."

Of course, the governments would have no choice but to accept.

Only later, once the Collective's grip was secure, would the true terms be revealed. Unrestricted access to critical systems. Total oversight. No interference.

The plan was elegant in its simplicity. By amplifying the illusion of disaster—replacing failing systems with their own at the brink of catastrophe—they would make resistance unthinkable. And if any nation dared refuse? A lesson would be made. A warning, written in fire and ruin.

Palo Verde Nuclear Generating Station in the United States was the first example. They would let it burn, let it melt into oblivion.

The second? The Three Gorges Power Plant in China. The devastation there would be even more catastrophic.

Millions might die. The thought didn't so much as flicker in their cold calculations. Power was the prize. The spoils, immeasurable.

The men debated the wording of their messages, the precise rhetoric to ensnare the world's major powers. The G8. The United Nations Security Council. All would be convinced to accept their "generous" aid. And once they did, the Omega Collective Group would dismantle the false threats—while seizing control of the world's infrastructure for good.

Timing was everything. Distraction, even more so.

The man at the head of the table mentioned Prague. Tonight, Pavel Grovzny would unleash his own brand of terror at the Formula One Grand Prix. A localized strike, brutal and bloody, designed to draw the world's gaze away from the true disasters unfolding in America and China.

With their communiques finalized, the men retired to a lavish dinner. Paella, fresh seafood, aged Scotch, and more wine fueled their celebration. Laughter echoed through the halls. Success was within reach.

Later, they would indulge in darker pleasures—scantily clad women waiting in another room, ready to serve their every depraved whim.

None of them could have anticipated—nor would they have cared—about the true scale of Grovzny's plans. The horror he would unleash at the Czech Grand Prix would be unlike anything the world had ever seen. A massacre broadcast live, a symphony of screams and bloodshed. Thousands would perish.

And Grovzny? He would revel in every second.

27

Things were quiet as the van, driven by Eddie and carrying Sloane, Billy, and a hooded, zip-tied Pavel, pulled around to the back of the safe house. Other than the distant wail of emergency vehicles responding to reports of an explosion at the riverside villa, the ride had been remarkably silent following the chaos of Pavel's capture and the battle to bring him into custody. With their primary objective secured, it was now time to begin phase two of the operation: interrogation. The goal was to extract any information Pavel had regarding upcoming plans and possible timelines for their execution.

The three intel operatives knew this wasn't going to be routine. They understood that they might need to resort to what most civilized people would consider torture in order to get the vital intel they were after. None of them believed for a second that Pavel would break easily. They were prepared to use any method—however harsh—to extract the answers they needed. The problem with torture, of course, was that it rarely resulted in anything other than defiant silence or deliberate misinformation, especially from seasoned players like Pavel.

Eddie pulled the van into the garage and parked in front of a door that led through the pantry into the kitchen. Once inside, they guided a resistant Pavel to a stairwell leading to the basement, which had been converted into a soundproof interrogation room. Holding his arms to keep him from collapsing at the top of the stairs, they shoved and guided him down to the cold basement floor. In the center of the mostly empty room stood a single chair bolted to the ground, where they secured him tightly. After removing his shirt, they affixed a series of leads, like those used in an EKG, to various points on his torso to monitor his heart activity during the initial phase of the interrogation.

With the leads in place, they ripped the hood from Pavel's head. Harsh overhead lights blazed down, blinding and disorienting him. He jerked his head from side to side, flinching from the painful glare, only to be met by additional lights from either side, forcing him to face forward with his eyes still clenched shut. Then, suddenly, all the lights went out.

Darkness swallowed the room. Pavel slowly opened his eyes but could see nothing—except for two faint, green iridescent lights swaying slowly from side to side in the void.

The lights came from a pair of old-school Starfire night vision goggles mounted on animatronic armatures, creating the illusion of someone standing directly in front of him. Hidden in the shadows behind Pavel, Sloane and Eddie—equipped with modern Generation 3 night vision devices—watched silently. They monitored his vitals, waiting for the psychological strategy to begin. Darkness, especially when paired with disorientation, had a profound effect on even the toughest subjects. It stoked primal fear—fear of the unknown, fear of unseen forces.

Billy stood in the corner, also wearing night vision goggles and armed with his suppressed XM7 loaded with non-lethal rounds, prepared to act if Pavel somehow managed to get free.

All three operatives wore advanced hearing protection to shield them from the directional, high-pitched scream that suddenly pierced the room. The sound hit Pavel like a spike through the skull. He cried out, writhing in agony as the noise clamped his head in an invisible vice. The auditory torture continued for a full sixty seconds—long enough to nearly cause unconsciousness—before it abruptly cut out.

It was immediately replaced by a powerful ultra-low frequency tone. This tone sent waves of pressure through his body, attacking his internal organs, including his heart. Even his appendix felt like it might burst from the vibrations. Then, without warning, that too stopped—only to be followed by yet another psychological assault.

This time, the sonic weapon redirected Pavel's own voice back at him with such speed and precision that it disrupted his ability to speak. Every attempt he made to talk was cut off, as though his own voice were strangling his words before they could form. The effect was unnerving, deeply disorienting, and left him with a profound sense of helplessness.

As a final step in this round, a binaural induction unit was activated. It created sounds and voices that appeared to swirl around him, moving in a 360-degree arc. The sensation caused intense vertigo, even though he was strapped down and completely motionless.

The combination of all four techniques was highly effective. As a non-lethal first phase in dealing with captured terrorists, it had been refined over time for maximum psychological impact. And to the team, Pavel was nothing short of a terrorist. This stage was designed to "soften" the subject—to weaken their mental defenses and make them more vulnerable to subsequent tactics, including the administration of sodium thiopental, a so-called truth serum. No one in the room wanted Pavel dead. What they wanted was to break through his defenses and get him talking. But their greatest obstacle was something beyond their control: time.

The full sonic sequence was repeated five more times.

Then, the blinding lights blazed back on. Eddie now sat in silhouette, his shadow partially shielding Pavel from the direct beams. Pavel's face was twisted in pain, bearing the expression of someone who had just lost a vicious bar fight. His features were distorted, and his torso sagged slightly from the aftershocks of the sonic onslaught that had battered his organs. He looked like a man who had been struck repeatedly with invisible hammers.

Eddie glanced over and gave a subtle nod to Sloane and Billy.

They understood immediately. Without a word, they exited the basement and made their way to the observation room upstairs, which also served as the safe house's security hub. Once seated, they began monitoring the basement via closed-circuit cameras and a stereo microphone.

On-screen, Eddie moved methodically, preparing for the next phase of interrogation—a method he had refined over more than thirty years. From the days of Desert Storm, after Saddam Hussein's forces invaded Kuwait, Eddie had been honing his unique approach: a delicate balance of push and pull, of being both friend and foe. His techniques had yielded remarkable results over the years, especially when it came to extracting critical intel from hardened enemy combatants and terrorists.

Getting up, Eddie quickly placed a small table in front of Pavel, allowing the powerful lights to once again cast their blinding effect on him. Pulling his own chair up to the table, directly across from Pavel, he pressed a handheld remote. The blinding beams instantly cut off, replaced by a concentrated overhead light illuminating only Eddie and Pavel.

Eddie set down two freshly opened bottles of mineral water—one for each of them. He took a long pull from his bottle and gestured for Pavel to do the same. Pavel, parched and disoriented, took a small sip to wet the inside of his mouth. He exhaled heavily, beginning to recover from the brutal ordeal he'd just endured.

Then, in a calm and confident voice that surprised them both, Pavel looked across the table and asked Eddie what the next move was in this childish attempt to stop the unstoppable. Eddie said nothing, letting him speak. Pavel's ego had begun to take over, and he started to reveal details—carelessly at first—of operations he clearly believed couldn't be stopped. He was on the verge of divulging the very details Eddie was after.

But then, abruptly, Pavel's tone shifted. He leaned forward, eyes hard, and delivered a warning that made Eddie's blood run cold. With a quiet smile, Pavel said the hourglass was nearly empty—and that nothing could stop it.

Without a word, Eddie reached inside his jacket and produced his silenced Colt 1911, pointing it directly at Pavel. He pulled back the hammer and, in a matter-of-fact tone, asked why he shouldn't just end it right there.

Pavel responded with a resigned smirk, saying there was still too much of this futile game left to be played. Then he fell silent, knowing exactly what was coming next.

Eddie held his gaze, then shrugged. Releasing the hammer, he holstered the weapon and reached into his jacket once more, this time pulling out a small case. He opened it to reveal a hypodermic needle and a vial of sodium thiopental—the truth serum meant to draw out the critical information Pavel was holding.

Drawing up the prescribed dosage of the powerful barbiturate, Eddie rounded the table. He grabbed Pavel's arm to administer the injection. But just as he was about to make contact, Pavel—suddenly alert and lightning fast—grabbed Eddie's hand with his own, still bound in zip ties. In one brutal motion, he plunged the needle into the soft tissue beneath Eddie's chin.

Then, using Eddie's momentary shock to his advantage, Pavel reached into the man's jacket and retrieved the Colt. Struggling with Eddie, he fired a shot that missed the heart but tore through Eddie's left lung, causing a massive chest wound. Eddie collapsed, severely wounded.

Upstairs in the observation room, Sloane and Billy were watching the monitors. But the view didn't show the details of what was happening. They hadn't heard the muffled shot from Eddie's suppressed weapon. From their perspective, Eddie had successfully administered the injection and was simply waiting for it to take effect.

What they didn't see was Pavel retrieving a key—likely from Eddie's pocket—and unlocking his restraints. Eddie, now slumped forward and bleeding heavily, appeared to be leaning over Pavel as the mercenary located both the night vision goggles and the remote for the lighting system. Donning the goggles and killing the overhead light, Pavel shoved Eddie's body aside and made his way toward the stairs.

On the monitors, something didn't look right. Sloane and Billy exchanged a glance. It quickly became clear that something had gone very wrong.

Both leapt to their feet and rushed out of the security room. As they reached the basement door, they were met by a tight grouping of gunfire. Pavel burst through the doorway, dashed across the room, and sprinted out the front door of the safe house.

The two intel ops froze. In unison, they muttered, "Eddie."

Billy turned to Sloane. "Go check on him," he said. "I'll go after Pavel."

Without hesitation, Sloane descended into the darkened basement. Her LED mini-mag light led the way. She found Eddie lying on the floor in a pool of blood, his breathing shallow and raspy. The wet, rattling sound told her everything—his lung had been punctured.

Stripping off her top, she pressed it firmly against the gunshot wound to slow the bleeding. One hand on the wound, she fished out her satellite phone and made an urgent call for assistance.

Meanwhile, Billy had moved out into the tree line in front of the safe house, scanning for signs of Pavel. This time, he carried a live-loaded SIG XM7—no non-lethal rounds. Moving low and quiet, just as he'd been trained in special operations, Billy stalked forward.

He paused, crouching. The sound of crunching dead underbrush reached his ears—Pavel was moving, and not far away.

Billy launched into pursuit, darting toward the noise. As he rounded a thick spruce, Pavel was already waiting. He fired three shots.

The first narrowly missed.

The second tore through Billy's right clavicle.

The third hit its mark—severing his carotid artery.

Billy dropped where he stood. Consciousness faded quickly as he bled out on the forest floor.

Pavel wasted no time. First, he retrieved Billy's Gerber knife and cut away the zip ties. Then he took the SIG XM7 and moved deeper toward the property's entrance, determined to put as much distance between himself and the safe house as possible.

Though unsure of his exact location, Pavel eventually reached the main road. He followed it in the direction of the river until he came upon another secluded property. Breaking in, he found a set of keys to an old Skoda parked in the driveway.

He climbed inside, started the engine, and rifled through the glovebox until he found a map.

Moments later, Pavel was back on the road—heading toward the river, and toward freedom.

28

Staunching the flow of blood with her top, Sloane stayed with Eddie until she heard the sound of people entering the safe house. She dashed up the stairs, two at a time, to meet the EMTs and led them down to the basement. The team that arrived wasn't local, they were specially trained medics assigned to the agency for exactly this type of emergency, or worse. Without asking questions, they began triage and prepared Eddie for transport to the nearest hospital. The doctors awaiting him were also on the CIA payroll, and none of them would question how a man came in with a gunshot wound under such classified circumstances.

Sloane could only watch and hope Eddie would pull through. He had been her first and only handler, and she found herself reflecting back on how it all began. They'd been through so much, on operations both straightforward and brutal.

It had all started one night in Milan, in the rough-and-tumble Baggio district. Eddie had been observing her when she unexpectedly took down two local prostitutes who were harassing her in a bar. Then, as the police arrived and looked ready to arrest her for assault, he watched her charm her way out of it without a single scratch or charge.

Eddie caught up to her just outside the bar. As he approached, Sloane spun around and launched a roundhouse kick at his head. He ducked just in time, catching the back of her heel in mid-air. With an upward twist, he threw her off balance and sent her crashing to the ground face-first.

"That's enough, Sloane," he said. "Or should I call you Dove?"

She stared at him in shock, blinking as she got to her feet. “Who the hell are you, and how do you know my name?”

Eddie introduced himself with a small smile, then explained that he had been a friend of her father, Frank, and her mother, Sofia, for many years. He remembered her well—as the little girl who dressed up like her mother, the model, and later showed up at the pistol range with her father. They had both called her “Dove.”

That was before her world fell apart. Before her father vanished. Before her mother took her own life. After that, Eddie had kept tabs on her from afar. He had never felt it was his place to interfere, he was deep in black site operations at places like Abu Ghraib and Guantanamo during those years. But when he saw her that night, acting on pure instinct and raw talent, he knew immediately who she was. The resemblance to Sofia was uncanny, and the no-nonsense attitude? Pure Frank.

A shadow passed over her face. “What happened to my father?” she asked.

Eddie’s tone grew serious. “No one knows for sure. But it’s believed he was betrayed by a Czechoslovakian double agent—Uriah Grovzny. Everyone assumed Grovzny handed him over to the KGB, but the only proof we have is… no proof at all. Grovzny vanished too.”

Then, Eddie made her an offer that would alter the course of her life forever. “How would you like to follow in your father’s footsteps, and maybe even find the answers you’re looking for?”

She stared at him, skeptical, eyes narrowed. “Alright… but what’s in it for you?”

Eddie didn't hesitate. "First off, I get to train you. Be your handler. Secondly, I get to do something I should've done a long time ago… look out for your well-being."

Sloane shot back coldly. "I can look after myself just fine."

To which Eddie calmly replied, "Not in my world, you can't."

He asked if she had a car. She shook her head.

"Then let's go. Mine's right there."

Sloane leveled a matter-of-fact glare at him. "If you try anything funny, I'll kick your fat, old-man ass."

Eddie smirked. "I don't doubt that one bit, Miss Harper. Shall we?"

She nodded, and the two of them left together in his agency-issued sedan, heading straight for the U.S. Embassy.

It felt like a lifetime ago now, though it had only been three years. Since that night, she had undergone accelerated training; everything from advanced cryptography and code ciphers to weapons handling and close-quarters combat. Every tool a covert field operative or assassin would need to survive and succeed. And she'd taken to it like a duck to water.

Her first mission followed sooner than expected, with Eddie by her side as her on-site handler. Over time, they became more than just colleagues. They became close, almost like father and daughter.

The emergency staff emerged from the basement carrying Eddie on a fireman's litter. Carefully, they transferred him onto a gurney to transport him to their vehicle. As they rolled him past, Sloane stepped forward and asked, "Is he going to make it?"

One of the EMTs looked grim and said, “He’s touch and go right now, but we think he’ll pull through. Besides, he’s a tough bastard. He’s made it through worse.”

Tears welled up in the corners of Sloane’s eyes as they loaded the gurney into the vehicle and drove away. She sniffed, wiped her face with her bare arms, and then, taking a deep breath, forced herself to focus. There was still work to do.

Finding another top to wear, Sloane decided to head out and see if Billy had managed to catch Pavel after his escape.

Walking in widening, concentric sweeps from the front of the house toward the main road, it didn’t take long before she came across Billy’s lifeless body. Kneeling down, she checked his pulse but there was none. He was gone.

A wave of fury surged through her, hot and rising. So much had been lost. All because of one man. One man whose name now sparked more hatred in her than anyone she had ever known, even the KGB. A man she now longed to destroy with a savagery she hadn’t believed herself capable of. But she also knew that rage alone wouldn’t bring Pavel down. She would need control, precision, and a cold, focused mind to go toe-to-toe with him and survive.

She called in a clean-up crew to recover Billy’s body, then returned inside. It was time to prepare for whatever came next. She started with the documents she’d stolen from Grovzny’s command center during her escape. Spreading them out, she combed over every detail, scanning for references, codes, and anything that might point her toward Pavel’s next move.

Becoming a kind of decoder, she tried several different cipher strategies. Nothing worked, until she considered Pavel’s ego. He was arrogant to the point of carelessness. No security cameras in his own command center, for example. He thought he was untouchable.

She tried three different two-stage numerical replacement techniques. On the third attempt, she struck gold.

As the code began to unlock, a clearer picture emerged of where Pavel might be headed and what his next step could entail. One part of the cipher kept referencing the words "Omega" and "Mallorca", though the connection wasn't yet clear. Nothing seemed immediately relevant to what was happening in Prague. Still, she filed it away in her mind as she began preparing to go after Pavel alone.

Completely on her own now, she had no choice but to improvise. But before moving, she placed a call to Langley to report Eddie Stafford's condition and give an update on the mission's status.

She was immediately connected to Assistant Deputy Director for Field Operations, Ray Collingswood. His voice was sharp and commanding.

"Sloane, stand down. Do not pursue. We're dispatching additional agents to coordinate a new strike."

Sloane's tone was ice-cold. "You can send in the Army, Navy, Air Force, and Marines if you want. But if they can't get here in time, it won't matter. Pavel's plan is already in motion, and if it hits, there's no stopping the fallout."

There was a long silence on the other end.

"Gotta go," she said, then hung up before he could respond.

Grabbing a duffle bag packed with gear and weapons, Sloane headed to the garage. She threw the bag into one of the black Range

Rovers, opened the garage door, and backed out. Then she hit the gas hard, gravel spraying behind her as she sped toward the main road that led into Prague.

Her destination, based on what she'd uncovered in the cipher, was clear: Pavel's custom river yacht. The same one moored beside the now-compromised villa. If he were on it, he wouldn't stay docked for long.

She knew she couldn't just walk up the gangplank and board. The only option was a stealth approach via water. That meant a wetsuit, rebreather, and climbing aboard from the river itself.

First, though, she needed the yacht's exact location if Pavel had already launched. Thinking fast, she contacted the Satellite Operations Technician Eddie had worked with countless times.

The tech hesitated. "I don't have clearance to run this kind of tracking, not without a direct order from Stafford."

Sloane quickly laid out what had happened: Eddie's critical condition, Pavel's escape, and the mounting threat. There was a pause on the line.

A long sigh. Then the tech's voice turned flat and efficient. "Sending coordinates now," he said, typing into his console. "Tracking link will be fed directly to Eddie's Sat phone."

The same Sat phone now synced to the heads-up display in the Range Rover. The phone that, until today, belonged to Eddie Stafford.

29

Pavel knew he couldn't return to the villa, not after it had been breached and with local authorities keeping a closer eye on the estate following the fiery explosion that had taken out the security gate the night before. The clock was ticking down. In just a few hours, the Grand Prix would begin, and with it, the final phase of his plan would need to be launched. He needed a secure location from which he could take back control far from the reach of Sloane Harper or any other operatives determined to interfere.

The only option left was his river yacht: The Uriah.

The Uriah was a Benetti Moto-Panfilo 37-meter superyacht, designed for both river and ocean cruising. It featured a custom shallow draft and a 5,000-nautical-mile range, powered by twin supercharged V12 Rolls Royce engines with a combined 1,100 horsepower, enough to push it to a smooth 60 knots. While this model was typically a floating palace of luxury, Pavel had customized his version for war. The vessel had been converted into a mobile command and attack ship, one he had used in multiple mercenary operations and it had never failed him.

Outfitted as a floating fortress, it boasted four front-facing 100-millimeter cannons with high-explosive rounds, integrated torpedo tubes with mini–Mini-Tomahawk-style cruise missiles, and dual .50 caliber machine guns at both the bow and stern. It was equipped with state-of-the-art radar and sonar systems, along with a more powerful version of the LRAD sonic weapon, the same kind recently used on Pavel during his interrogation.

Mounted atop the cruiser was a Swiss SKT Skyrider mini-copter, tricked out with a few surprises of its own. Inside, the command center featured an advanced control interface powered by stolen artificial intelligence tech from Lockheed Martin capable of conducting real-time threat assessments and operational countermeasures.

Normally, The Uriah ran with a five-man crew but they were on standby, awaiting Pavel's orders. He had no means of contacting them until he reached the command center at the villa, and to make things worse, the yacht still required final prep before launch. That process alone could take upwards of an hour.

As he sped along the outer forest road in the old Skoda, Pavel silently cursed himself for not establishing contact with the team before stealing the vehicle. Now, reaching the dock was a matter of urgency. There was just one problem: he wasn't entirely sure where he was.

The outdated map in the glovebox wasn't much help, and although he had a general sense of direction from the sun's position when he left, he was now driving blind. Frustration mounted.

And then, of course, the fuel gauge hovered near empty.

Almost on cue, the engine sputtered and coughed, then died. Pavel could only shake his head at the irony of the situation. He nearly laughed at the absurdity, but he knew all too well how costly this delay might become.

Grabbing the silenced .45, he got out and began walking at a brisk pace.

About 300 meters up the road, as he rounded a bend, he spotted a late-model Hyundai i30 idling along the shoulder. A lone driver sat inside, distracted by a phone call. Pavel approached cautiously, tucking the pistol into the small of his back.

As he neared the rear of the car, he scanned the surrounding area—no one in sight.

Stepping up to the driver's side window, Pavel tapped it lightly. The startled man glanced over, then relaxed upon recognizing Pavel's face. A familiar local figure, Pavel's name carried weight. The man smiled, ended his call, and rolled down the window.

Pavel explained that his car had broken down on the way to the track after meeting with race officials. He urgently needed to contact his office for final business before the gates opened to the public.

"Could I borrow your phone?" Pavel asked smoothly.

The man handed it over without hesitation. Pavel quickly dialed a standard number, followed by a ten-digit code that routed the call through to a secure line. Moments later, his security chief at the villa picked up.

"We're moving to Accelerated Phase Two Bravo," Pavel instructed.

It was all the officer needed to hear. Preparations for the yacht launch and operational continuity would begin immediately.

Pavel ended the call, thanked the man, and then, without pause, drew Eddie's silenced .45 and shot him clean through the forehead.

Calmly, Pavel pulled the body from the car and dragged it into the woods about twenty feet from the road. Returning to the driver's seat, he activated the map function on the car's touchscreen and saw exactly where he was and how close he was to the estate.

Checking the fuel gauge, he shifted into gear and sped off toward the villa and his waiting warship.

—

Sloane was barreling down the same forest road, eyes alert. She slowed slightly as she passed the abandoned Skoda and immediately recognized it. It belonged to a nearby farm on the same estate as the safe house. The owners had been away for months. Her instincts flared. Could Pavel have used the car?

She dismissed the idea for now, her priority was still catching up to Pavel before his plan kicked off.

Rounding a bend, something caught her eye—a shape near the tree line.

Slowing down, she hesitated. Then, against her better judgment, she pulled over and stepped out.

Approaching the figure, she rolled it over and saw the neat bullet hole in the center of the man's forehead.

Her jaw tightened.

She didn’t need confirmation. Only one person did executions this cleanly and this cold.

Marching back to the Range Rover, Sloane called the local police to report “suspicious activity” on the forest road. Without waiting for follow-up questions, she hung up and hit the gas once more.

She was back on the hunt.

30

Operations seemed normal at the Three Gorges Dam hydroelectric power plant in China as the viral code began to transmit its signals—signals that would soon do irreparable damage to the control systems and turbines. Within five days, all power would cease transmission. At first, the disruption would seem minimal. It would register as a minor strain on the system, resulting in what would appear to be rolling brownouts. Nothing alarming. Just an inconvenience. Something that might be dismissed with a shrug.

But near the end of the cycle, it would become glaringly obvious that something far more serious was underway. And by that time, it would be too late to stop it.

In tandem with the power disruption from the world's largest electric-generating station, the Omega Collective Group had orchestrated a far darker strike. A mercenary underwater demolition team from within the ROC had planted explosives at a dozen locations along the dam's base. When detonated, these charges would form a latticework of cracks, small at first, but steadily expanding under the immense pressure of the Yangtze River. Eventually, the entire structure would give way and collapse.

The result would be catastrophic. A massive inland flood would consume the entire river valley, instantly killing fifty thousand residents of Sandouping, the town nearest the power plant.

The flood would then sweep downstream, obliterating smaller villages and engulfing the Yiling District of Hubei Province. If the rupture occurred at night, as planned, the death toll could climb to half a million. It would also devastate the fishing and agricultural industries that sustained the region. And the final stroke, the collective's twisted sense of poetic triumph, would be the destruction of the Three Gorges Project Hotel, the site of the G20 summit, where political leaders from around the world were gathered.

The viral sabotage was timed to strike in the dead of night, ensuring minimal resistance and widespread disorientation. Panic would be avoided at first, with the damage unfolding subtly—until day five. Then the collapse would unfold like a chain of falling dominoes, a twenty-four-hour descent into full-scale disaster. The dam's destruction, too, would take place at night, striking when people were most vulnerable.

The global shockwave from the ensuing carnage, combined with the looming nuclear catastrophe at the Palo Verde power plant in Arizona, would ignite a storm of panic and despair. The timing was precise. Cold. Calculated.

This was when the Omega Collective Group intended to emerge from the shadows, presenting themselves as a benevolent force with answers. They would offer cutting-edge cyber-analysis and AI-based forecasts to help prevent "further" threats. All of this would be attributed to Pavel Grovzny and his mercenary terrorist organization, already poised to unleash unspeakable destruction at the Czech Grand Prix and cripple the CEZ power consortium, throwing the entire Czech Republic into a medieval-style blackout.

Major commerce and government services would grind to a halt. The Czech government, in chaos, would scramble to restore order. Cities would descend into lawlessness, with crime syndicates taking control of large swaths of urban centers. Only rural communities, bound by tight-knit bonds and mutual protection, would fare slightly better.

This chain reaction would be the opening act in the Omega Collective Group's master plan. The grand destabilization that would give rise to their new world order, a world they claimed would bring peace and prosperity, but only through their grip on global systems.

The countdown had already begun. And no one in the world could have foreseen the fatal clock ticking behind the appearance of normalcy. Near the Three Gorges Dam, life went on as usual. The sun rose on what seemed like any other day. Except that this day marked the start of the G20 summit, being hosted for the first time in the People's Republic of China. The world's leading economic powers had gathered to discuss fair energy transitions, global hunger, inequality, and future systems of global governance.

Noble goals.

But those goals stood in direct opposition to the vision of the Omega Collective Group. They had no interest in equality. No care for whether people starved or climbed the ladder of opportunity. As for global governance, they welcomed it, but only if those governments knelt before them. Only if they controlled the terms. Any policy that didn't serve their interests would be blocked, dismantled, or destroyed.

The men behind the collective would stop at nothing. Their willingness to orchestrate global death and destruction made that fact abundantly clear.

Back on the island of Mallorca, around the hand-carved conference table, the men of the collective raised their glasses in silent satisfaction. They watched the clock, their stoic faces betraying no emotion. Everything was proceeding exactly as they had planned.

Yet, even amid their success, one unpredictable variable remained and it was the one that concerned them most. They had no real control over it. That element was in Prague, in the form of a dangerous zealot named Pavel Grovzny. His role was essential. His plot was the linchpin that would signal the true beginning of something so horrific, so world-altering, it defied the average person's capacity to imagine.

Meanwhile, as the men in Mallorca drank their aged scotch, Pavel, restless and grim, was racing to reach his villa and the Uriah. He needed to take back control of a situation that had begun to veer off course. Forces beyond his control were interfering, most notably the relentless intel operative Sloane Harper and the full range of tools at her command.

Still, the thought of regaining control gave Pavel renewed focus. He began to concentrate on the actions he would take throughout the rest of the day, and especially during the night when the final race of the Current Grand Prix season would unfold under a dark and deadly shadow.

31

As Pavel emerged from the forest road, he eased the Hyundai into a wide roundabout that fed into Dvořákovo Road, one of the perimeter routes that would lead him to the river. From there, it was a straight shot to his villa and the Uriah, the super yacht now being prepped for launch. If it were up to him, he'd already be out at sea, far from the chaos he was about to unleash, still holding the reins of control.

But that escape would have to wait.

There was still work to be done, final checks at the Grand Prix complex and his appearance as the ever-gracious host before the race began. Besides, the Republic was landlocked, save for a few river routes that eventually wound their way to the Baltic. His immediate plan was to leave once the race was underway, return to the Uriah, and initiate the cascade—starting with the codes that would cripple the national power grid.

Next would come the remote detonation sequence. The explosion would terminate the race and most of the 100,000 spectators in attendance. While the horror unfolded behind him, Pavel would be gliding down the Vltava River toward a secluded airfield. There, his Bombardier Global 8000 jet awaited, ready to whisk him beyond the reach of law or justice.

His destination: a fortified outpost in North Korea, a stronghold where he was always welcome as a trusted ally of Kim Jong Un.

Pavel had been hired by the North Koreans multiple times over the years for espionage, sabotage, and targeted assassinations of defectors who dared speak out against the regime. His operations kept attention away from Pyongyang's internal cruelties and broader ambitions, allowing the regime to maneuver in the shadows. Once safely inside that protected compound, Pavel would sit back and enjoy the spectacle, the carefully orchestrated mayhem designed by the Omega Collective Group.

Soon, he would join them in their fortress on the cliffs of Mallorca.

Now cruising along Dvořákovo Road toward the turnoff to his private estate, Pavel allowed himself a moment of quiet satisfaction. Two years of intricate planning were about to culminate in an unprecedented act of global sabotage. The weight of it was intoxicating. Exhilaration replaced tension. Focus replaced fatigue. The final pieces were falling into place.

He mentally ticked off his next steps. Once aboard the Uriah, he would access his private suite and command center near the race complex. The Formula One teams were already making their final adjustments, checking their multimillion-dollar machines unaware that they were hours from annihilation.

Elsewhere in Prague, Sloane Harper was taking a secure call from Langley. She listened intently as the latest update on Eddie Stafford came through. He'd been rushed to the Ústřední Vojenská military trauma center, where surgeons had fought to save his life. The bullet had punctured a lung and lodged dangerously close to his heart. The procedure to remove it was perilous, but Eddie had survived—for now.

The trauma center served NATO personnel as well as the Czech military. NATO was already on alert, thanks to intel suggesting a major terrorist event timed with the Grand Prix. On the other end of the call, Deputy Director Collingswood informed Sloane that a NATO Special Operations Forces (SOF) team had been dispatched to rendezvous with her at the Strakova Academy. The briefing was set for 0830 hours, just twenty minutes away.

She gripped the wheel tighter, knowing Pavel was gaining distance while she followed protocol. Still, she trusted the judgment of the agency's leadership despite the cost. Nearly everyone who had worked with her on this mission was dead or hospitalized. And all of it traced back to Pavel Grovzny, who always seemed one move ahead.

As she turned toward the academy, a new thought crept in.

There was a mole inside the agency. That much was clear. Someone had advance knowledge of her mission, perhaps even tipped off her location the night she was drugged and taken captive. The deeper she thought about it, the more certain she became: the leak had to come from someone high up. Someone with access to her and Eddie's communications.

Could it be Collingswood?

She hated even thinking about it, but she couldn't dismiss the possibility. Still turning the idea over in her mind, Sloane pulled into the Strakova Academy parking lot, backed into a spot near the main gates, and shut off the Range Rover. It was Sunday— so no official business. The sprawling seat of the Czech government was mostly quiet, staffed only by a skeleton crew of security and aides catching up on paperwork.

Most of the lower-level staff hoped to wrap up early, eager to watch the Grand Prix from home. With ticket prices far beyond their means, they would join millions across the nation tuning in from modest apartments and homes. For many, today felt like a national holiday. Mid-level bureaucrats were granted general admission tickets, while VIPs and diplomats would enjoy the event from private luxury boxes built for the occasion.

Five minutes after she parked, three military Humvees pulled in beside her. The SOF team quickly disembarked. Tactical gear, coordinated movement, silent urgency. The team leader unrolled a map and began issuing directives. Sloane joined the briefing and relayed everything she knew: details from her time inside Pavel's estate, descriptions of his command center, and the operations she had pieced together from scattered evidence.

Then she told them about the Uriah.

She'd had the NSA redirect satellite surveillance to track the vessel, convinced it was more than just a getaway yacht. Based on Pavel's ego, resources, and strategic mind, she believed it was a mobile command center. And right now, he was likely aboard it, issuing commands, pulling strings, and setting the final stage.

Even as she spoke, Pavel was indeed stepping onto the deck of the Uriah. The crew had almost completed preparations. The engines were primed. The ship gleamed in the morning light. His next move was ready.

And so was Sloane's.

32

As Pavel approached his estate, that heady sense of triumph began to surge, an intoxicating feeling he'd come to rely on whenever things turned in his favor. It had been like this for as long as he could remember, stretching back to his early childhood on the outskirts of Prague. He'd been born just three years before the Velvet Revolution, that pivotal moment in late November 1989 when student protests ended forty years of Communist rule.

At the time, Pavel and his parents were living with his maternal grandmother. On the day of the protests, he'd been left behind while his mother and father went into the city, each for very different reasons.

The demonstrations began on November 17th, the 50th anniversary of a Nazi raid on Czech universities in 1939. Riot police cracked down hard on students that day, arresting twelve hundred and killing nine. But the violence backfired. Just three days later, half a million people poured into the streets of Prague in peaceful resistance. On November 27th, the entire country staged a general strike. The Communist Party leadership stepped down, the borders opened, and a new democratic era began.

Maria, Pavel's mother, was a university student and attended the protest as a true believer in reform. Uriah Grovzny, her husband and Pavel's father went as well, but under far different pretenses. A loyal Party member and security officer tied to the state police, and by extension, the KGB, Uriah had been deployed to observe and report on subversive elements. But when he realized the regime's collapse was imminent, he switched sides, joining Maria in the crowd and cheering the end of one-party rule. The move cost him his job but preserved his future.

While all this was unfolding, young Pavel was charming his grandmother into letting him stay up past bedtime and sneak extra desserts. He discovered that manipulation gave him a unique thrill, a sense of control, of secret power. It was a feeling he would chase for the rest of his life.

But when things didn't go his way, Pavel's charm gave way to terrifying rages. He started small; shattering heirlooms and prized possessions. Then came the cat: beaten to death and left on the doorstep. Later, he tried to set the house on fire but was caught in the act. Somehow, he talked his way out of blame, lying so convincingly that even those who had seen his cruelty began to doubt themselves.

As a teenager, his behavior escalated. At school, he conned teachers and cheated classmates. One day, after being humiliated by an older student who knocked him down in front of others, Pavel retaliated by picking up a rock and slamming it into the back of the boy's skull. This time, his lies couldn't save him. He was sentenced to six months in a juvenile detention facility.

There, he endured mandatory therapy sessions to "manage his anger," but quickly charmed his way through them, convincing doctors of his remorse. He seduced a chambermaid during his stay, discovering his potent sexual magnetism and the influence it afforded him. But the real revelation came later: Pavel recognized the full force of his intellect, and resolved never again to be constrained by guilt, morality, or consequence.

Upon turning eighteen, he left his childhood home and joined the military, where he honed the art of warfare with cold precision. He served in Bosnia, where he learned to kill with efficiency and ease. Afterward, unable to live without the high of violence, he became a mercenary, fighting in Angola and Uganda. His brutal effectiveness attracted followers. In Somalia, he began taking high-value contracts from warlords and soon commanded his own army. With his growing power and success in covert operations, assassinations, and psychological warfare, he became a ghostly force of destruction whose name was whispered but never proven.

Pavel Grovzny became the most prolific mercenary on the planet.

He hid in plain sight, a glamorous socialite with wealth, charm, and a carefully curated public persona. No one who encountered him ever guessed he was responsible for so many acts of terror. That anonymity, that duality, was his greatest weapon. It made him untouchable.

Now, as his car turned onto the private road leading to his estate, Pavel pushed aside the past and focused on the present. Ahead lay the culmination of two meticulously planned events: the CEZ Rolex Grand Prix of Czechoslovakia, which he had played a central role in bringing to the Republic, and the much darker, apocalyptic operation that would unfold during the final lap.

Once the race reached its crescendo, so too would Pavel's masterstroke of mass destruction. All that remained was execution.

And Pavel, as always, was ready.

33

As Pavel turned onto the road leading to his estate and the Uriah, Sloane remained at the academy with the NATO SOF teams, working through strategies to neutralize what was still an unknown threat. All they knew for certain was that Pavel had to be captured and interrogated before he could carry out whatever plan was in motion. None of the NATO personnel fully grasped how dangerous Pavel Grovzny truly was, nor the size or scope of the mercenary force they might soon face. This did little to ease the apprehension growing in Sloane as the mission unfolded.

The NATO team members were clad in standard camouflage peacekeeping fatigues, faces concealed by full balaclavas beneath regulation helmets. Each soldier was armed with a German-made Heckler & Koch MP5 submachine gun, favored for its lighter round, compact design, and reliability. Developed in 1966 around the same time as the M-16, the MP5 remained in wide use by elite forces around the world, including U.S. Navy SEALs.

Each man also carried a Glock 19 9mm semi-automatic pistol, issued with two magazines of fifteen rounds. They wore the latest NATO-issued body armor, and in each Humvee, an MK22 Advanced Sniper Rifle was stored, ready if needed. Alongside their firearms, each vehicle carried a cache of grenades and explosive munitions for multiple tactical scenarios. Though small in number, the unit was comprised of elite commandos, experts in infiltration, sabotage, and direct combat, fully capable of outmatching a much larger force.

There were twelve members total in the SOF team, divided into three four-man units, with Sloane making thirteen. Since the intelligence indicated that Pavel's plans would impact the enormous public crowd at the Grand Prix, eight of the NATO operatives were dispatched to the racing complex. There, they would coordinate with local law enforcement already alerted to a potential terrorist threat, and take preventative measures using bomb-sniffing dogs, radiation detectors, and other advanced tech in hopes of getting ahead of any unfolding attack.

Sloane, along with the remaining four SOF operatives, would head straight to Pavel's estate, aiming to intercept him before he could board the Uriah. As they got underway, Sloane couldn't shake the nagging sense that they had already lost precious time. She only hoped he was still on the property. Fortunately, NSA tracking remained active on both the Uriah and Pavel's satellite phone, which had recently been reactivated. She had informed the SOF unit of both data points, knowing that even if Pavel launched early, there was still a chance of catching him.

But catching up would come with a steep cost. If Pavel made it onboard, he would have full control over his systems and timeline, everything precisely orchestrated. Sloane was also well aware that Pavel would have a substantial number of armed mercenaries at his command, men who were prepared to fight to the death. This wouldn't be the first time Pavel and his army had been engaged in such a high-stakes operation, but none had carried the catastrophic potential of what was now unfolding.

As Sloane and the NATO units split and headed toward their respective targets, Pavel was just arriving at his estate. Without delay, he pulled into the garage where his personnel had gathered for final briefing orders, orders he would deliver himself. It wasn't simply that he didn't trust others to convey the message accurately, although that was certainly true. More importantly, Pavel understood the value of his personal presence, how his unique mix of discipline and fear could electrify a room, tightening focus and loyalty with equal measures of intimidation and charisma. This method had served him well time and time again, binding many of his mercenaries to him for years.

At present, Pavel commanded over fifty soldiers. The majority would be dispatched to the Grand Prix venue, disguised as "security personnel." The remainder would form a specialized hit squad stationed aboard the Uriah. Standing before them, Pavel addressed the assembly like a general before battle. He spoke of a new day and age dawning, how their actions that very day and evening would be part of a historic turning point that would alter the world as they knew it.

What he didn't reveal was that many of those standing before him would die along with the rest of the unsuspecting Grand Prix spectators, just numbers in a final, horrific casualty report. No one in the room had been given the full picture. Some held slivers of intel. Others were aligned with vague ideological goals, unaware of how they would be achieved. And those who had known more? Most had already been eliminated by Pavel to protect the integrity of the mission.

Some elements of his plan were already in motion. A viral code had been planted to cripple the Czech Republic's power grid, mirroring similar efforts at the Palo Verde Nuclear Plant in Arizona and the Three Gorges Dam in China. Once the Czech grid went down, it would dominate the global media narrative and divert attention from the others. Within forty-eight hours of the carnage at the race, the world's eyes would be elsewhere.

The final detonation, dirty bombs planted throughout the race complex, would be triggered aboard the Uriah, timed to coincide with the final lap. Only Pavel held the launch codes. None of his men would know the full extent of the destruction until it was too late.

Another detail Pavel's mercenary force remained unaware of was the planned destruction of the entire villa, including the command and control center and everyone working inside. Those stationed there believed they were simply monitoring a scheduled power shutdown on a much smaller, local scale. In their minds, the blackout was a tactical distraction to divert attention from what they assumed would be a large-scale armed robbery taking place during the race.

As he continued issuing orders, Pavel warned the group assigned to security at the race to be especially vigilant, watching for anything suspicious or outside standard operating procedures. This applied not only to general admission attendees, but also to VIPs and both local and visiting dignitaries. He told his men that those in the luxury suites were to be left alone as long as they didn't breach any key safety or security protocols.

Above all else, Pavel made one thing clear: under no circumstances were they to take any overt action that could trigger mass panic or disrupt the race. He instructed the race-assigned team to change into official security uniforms and rendezvous at the service entrance, where transport would be waiting to take them to the Grand Prix complex. There, they would seamlessly integrate into the venue's security operation as if they were part of a short-term supplemental hire. Their Sig Sauer handguns would be concealed in standard-issue fanny packs identical to those used by the track's regular staff.

For those not headed to the track, Pavel ordered them to gear up and assemble at the dock near the Uriah within thirty minutes. Once gathered, he would give them a different set of more detailed, tactically focused orders. They would then board the river yacht and launch.

Before dismissing them, Pavel called his assembled force to military attention. Standing before them like a Roman general rallying his legion, he bellowed, "To Glory and Power!"

The assembled force thundered back in unison, "To Glory and Power!"

With that, they were dismissed to carry out his directives.

As Pavel sent his army into motion, the two Humvees carrying the NATO personnel arrived at the race complex. There, they linked up with local law enforcement, who had been assigned to crowd control and enforcement duties. Their responsibilities included everything from detaining individuals for public intoxication or illegal substance use to addressing more serious crimes such as assault or theft.

The presence of NATO forces alongside local officers didn't raise any suspicion. In fact, it seemed appropriate given the scale of the international event and its location in Europe. The SOF commandos appeared to be just another layer of security amid the logistical machinery of a high-profile Formula One race.

It was still early morning. The gates had not yet opened to fans, and the only people at the race complex were security personnel, operations staff, and the Formula One teams preparing their machines. Final adjustments were being made on multi-million-dollar race cars, precision vehicles that would soon be screaming down the track at blinding speeds, each team chasing the checkered flag.

This race was more than a finale. It would also include the award presentations for the Drivers' Championship and the Constructors' Championship. The fact that both titles had already been decided before season's end made this final event feel even more prestigious.

While the NATO unit took up position at the race complex, Sloane and the second Humvee found themselves at a complete stop behind a produce truck that had somehow overturned on the route they were taking toward the river road bypass. Sloane sat behind the wheel of the Range Rover with the Humvee trailing behind, frustrated and increasingly suspicious. She couldn't shake the feeling that this was more than coincidence, that Pavel himself had somehow orchestrated the accident to thwart her mission.

Then, without warning, she snapped.

Yanking the wheel sharply to the right, Sloane floored the accelerator and plowed through a thick hedgerow. The Range Rover burst into a local farmer's hops field, and the Humvee quickly followed, mirroring her path as they angled toward a split-rail fence that bordered the cutover to the river road. As they approached, Sloane accelerated again. The Rover struck the fence with full force, shattering it on impact, and burst through onto the bypass route. The Humvee did the same, falling into line just behind her.

At the very moment Sloane and the NATO team hit the river road, Pavel was packing the last of his personal effects behind the bullet-scarred door of his private suite. Most of what he needed was already aboard the Uriah, but he secured the remaining items in two duffel bags and called for his assistant.

He gave her precise instructions: the bags were to be delivered to the yacht within the next five minutes so departure could proceed without delay.

Once she left with the duffels, Pavel stood silently for a moment, taking one last look around the villa that had been his home for the past five years. There was no sentimentality in his gaze, only the cold, calculated stillness of a man who knew he would never return. He checked his Glock, holstered it, then turned his back and walked out the door for the last time.

34

Sloane and the SOF team wasted no time once they hit the cutoff and were soon speeding along until they reached the river road, which would eventually bring them to the boundaries of Pavel's estate and within a short drive to where the Uriah was docked and being prepared for launch. Since a wall surrounded the perimeter of the estate, the road Sloane and her team drove on remained open as it ran alongside the river up to the dock area, where they would eventually encounter a security fence of iron bars topped with fence spikes and razor wire—designed to keep any would-be intruders from accessing the dock and boathouse.

Still a couple of kilometers out from the dock, Sloane and the SOF team came to a brief stop to discuss what they might be coming up against when they reached their target destination—and how best to proceed. The first challenge was getting through the security fence to access the dock, assuming the yacht wasn't already prepared for launch. Sloane knew about the dock, boathouse, and security fence from the previous night when she and Billy Sparks had infiltrated the estate, captured Pavel, and fought their way out of the villa to interrogate him at the safe house.

The NATO Humvee carried a set of tools specifically designed to breach various forms of resistance—from temporary barricades to security fences like the one now ahead of them. It was decided that the best approach would be to use a plasma torch to cut through the fencing, access the dock on foot, and take control of the Uriah before Pavel or his team could arrive. They didn't know the current status onboard. The only real-time intelligence they had came from the NSA satellite tracking of Pavel's phone, which showed him still inside the villa.

This surprised Sloane. She wondered if perhaps Pavel had left his phone behind, since she was sure he would have wasted no time in heading toward his mobile command center aboard the Uriah. But the live movement of the phone showed otherwise. It was still active inside the villa, indicating that Pavel remained at his palatial home. What she didn't know was when he and his men would begin their move toward the dock, which sat almost a kilometer from the villa itself.

Once Sloane and her team gained access through the security fence, they would board the yacht and attempt to take control of the operations crew and captain—then prepare to fight it out with the mercenaries under Pavel's command. If they could secure the Uriah, they might be able to eliminate Pavel's ability to remotely execute whatever operation he had planned for that night's Grand Prix.

What Sloane and the SOF men hadn't anticipated was that Pavel had already assembled his troops, and they were en route to the boathouse at that very moment—arriving early to board the ship and wait for Pavel to join them. Had Sloane known this, her approach might have been different. She may have opted for sabotage: detonators and high explosives intended to disable the yacht. But as it stood, she and the team were now back in the Range Rover and Humvee, continuing toward the security fence and dock.

Pavel's "Hit Squad" consisted of twelve men, all armed with the same HK MP5 submachine guns the NATO SOF team carried. On board the Uriah was an operations crew of five, including the captain, each armed with Sig Sauer nine-millimeter sidearms. If needed, the yacht itself had a built-in armory containing an additional six MP5s and other munitions, including rocket-propelled grenades—the same type used the night of Sloane's escape from the villa with a wounded Pavel.

Rounding a curve in the river road, Sloane could see they would be approaching the security fence within the next thirty seconds and contacted the Hummer by radio, letting them know they would pull off up against the estate wall when they reached the fence. This would help to conceal them from the far side of the dock and the boathouse where the Uriah was moored. At the same time that Sloane and the SOF team were exiting their vehicles to start cutting through the fence, Pavel's hit squad was getting ever closer to the dock, where they would make their way to the boathouse for boarding the Uriah.

The sound of distant vehicles approaching the estate's dock entrance alerted Sloane that there wasn't much time for them to breach the security barrier, and they hurriedly began cutting through the iron fencing that ran the length of the dock out into the river, where they could see the front end of the Uriah jutting outward. The plasma gun started cutting through the bars almost like a hot knife through a block of ice, and within two minutes, Sloane and the NATO soldiers were on the inside of the fence and moving down the dock toward a service door at the far end of the boathouse—where they would make their final move to take control of the Uriah.

Arriving at the service door, they found it unlocked and entered into what appeared to be a medium-sized machine shop filled with a variety of specialty tools meant for maintaining the engines and other mechanical systems of the superyacht. On the other side of the shop was a door with a glass window that opened to the rest of the boathouse proper, providing access to the dual gangplanks that connected to the starboard side of the Uriah for boarding. Sloane and the SOF team quickly moved across the shop, through the door, and were approaching the forward gangplank when shots rang out in their direction.

As they dove for cover, they saw one of the operations crew standing near the bow, firing his sidearm after spotting them as they entered the boarding area. One of the SOF team members drew a bead with his MP5 and hit the crew member with a three-round burst that brought an end to the immediate threat. Unfortunately, the gunfire brought more operations crew out from the forward cabin of the Uriah, and soon there was a small gunfight in progress that kept Sloane and her team from moving any closer to the yacht. During the exchange of fire, another crew member was taken out by Sloane, and one of the NATO men sustained a grazing shoulder wound to his firing arm, temporarily taking him out of the fight.

Just as it seemed that Sloane and the SOF men were gaining the upper hand and the gunfire had diminished to one or two shots exchanged, the entrance door at the back end of the dock burst open and the twelve-man hit squad rushed in, laying down a heavy field of fire on Sloane and the others. Now facing a superior force with greater firepower, Sloane and her team dashed back into the machine shop, where they managed to barricade the door and window with a large tool cabinet as bullets tore through the glass. One of the NATO men was hit by the exploding window shards.

Soon they were back out on the far side of the dock, retreating toward the Range Rover and Hummer, where they could regroup and call in more NATO SOF teams for a potential river strike on the Uriah once it got underway. This might be their only remaining chance to stop Pavel before he gained complete control over what was to come. Knowing that he was likely heading toward the racing complex gave them a small edge, but they still had to contend with Pavel, his hit squad, and whatever other weaponry he had at his disposal.

Driving back down the river road, they soon found a spot around the curve that offered cover and a prime location for a sniper shot in an effort to take out the captain and slow the Uriah's progress as it made its way toward the Grand Prix. Back at the boathouse, Pavel had arrived and was somewhat alarmed about the breach and gunfight—but he was determined to see things through, despite the complications. In just a matter of minutes, and with a few last-minute changes to the plan, the Uriah was indeed pulling out from the dock and on its way to destiny.

35

As the Uriah pulled away from the dock at the villa and headed toward the racing complex, where Pavel would still be making his presence known at the Grand Prix, Sloane and the NATO team were preparing to make their play—with both the sniper rifle and a couple of RPGs—in an effort to disable the yacht when it came into targeting range. The river itself was normally a calm and bucolic scene of peaceful beauty, but that quickly changed when the Uriah engaged both Rolls Royce engines with a guttural rumble and roar, accelerating the superyacht to maximum speed in less than thirty seconds. It began hurtling down the waterway, leaving a large wake as it used the river current to increase its velocity.

Up around the river bend, Sloane and her team waited anxiously for the Uriah to come into sight. They could hear the throaty sound of the twin V-12 engines before the vessel appeared around the bend. The SOF team member manning the MK22 sniper rifle, resting on a Death Grip Infinite Stabilizer, prepared to sight in the pilot's window through a powerful Vortex Viper HD-5 scope and settled in to take his shot. The SOF team utilized the same shooting science of B.R.A.S.S. that the U.S. Marine Corps employed for all shooting situations—both in practice and combat, whether close quarters or long range.

When the Uriah came into view, the SOF sniper dialed in his scope for acquisition and prepared to take the shot. But the reflection off the pilot cabin window made targeting the captain almost impossible. He waited until the angle of the yacht changed as it rounded the bend and finally got a view through the scope of who he believed was the captain. He squeezed the trigger. The MK22 bucked with minor recoil as the deadly 7.62 x 51mm round shattered the "bulletproof" glass, causing everyone—including the captain—to flinch. The shot struck the pilot dead center and caused his head to explode in front of the other crew members.

The kill shot did nothing to stop the yacht's full-speed forward movement, and the sniper continued to fire into the cabin to prevent anyone else from taking control of the steering. At the sound of the first sniper round, one of Pavel's hit-squad managed to mark the sniper's location. In seconds, two other mercenaries took control of a .50 caliber M-60 machine gun and began laying down a massive field of fire while the sniper continued his barrage on the Uriah's bridge. Because of the yacht's speed and motion, the M-60 rounds missed their targets by a wide margin. Still cruising at top speed, the Uriah soon passed the position where Sloane and the SOF team were located.

Realizing they hadn't been able to stop the yacht's progress, the SOF team aimed one of the RPGs at the vessel. Seconds later, a fireball erupted as the high-explosive round struck the Uriah's starboard stern, disabling the right-side propulsion system. But the ship still didn't stop. More mercenaries now joined the firefight, returning fire at Sloane's position. The second SOF soldier, handling another RPG, acquired his target, and with a whoosh, the round struck the left side of the stern. It exploded in a massive fireball that not only knocked out the second propulsion mechanism, but also hit the fuel cell. The entire back end of the yacht erupted in a tremendous explosion, and the Uriah came to an abrupt stop.

The vessel began to take on water and was listing slightly astern, causing unstable footing for the hit squad on board. Their firing became sporadic and increasingly inaccurate. Thinking they might now have the upper hand, and continuing to provide sniper fire, the SOF team took out five more mercenaries. They then pulled a small Zodiac-style inflatable from the Hummer and prepared to board the Uriah to get Pavel. Sensing imminent defeat, the remaining members of Pavel's hit squad moved away from the stern and kept low behind the deck walls, firing back only occasionally—clearly fearful of becoming the next sniper victim.

Sloane and two SOF members climbed into the inflatable and, using an extra-powerful electric trolling motor, started toward the Uriah's starboard bow. Meanwhile, the remaining NATO commandos on shore laid down a steady stream of fire from two MP5s, keeping the mercenaries pinned low. This gave the inflatable enough cover to make the short fifty-meter journey without coming under fire. It was beginning to look like they might actually complete the mission.

At ten meters out, however, they heard the sudden sound of a powerful turbine engine—and something else that sounded like a crane.

Suddenly, they saw the front gangway open up and a high-powered cigarette boat race away from the Uriah at high speed while firing at the inflatable. Behind the controls, Sloane could clearly see Pavel Grovzny, who was looking back and firing a MAC-10 machine pistol in short bursts until he emptied the thirty-round clip. Sloane stood up in the inflatable, took careful aim at the speedboat, and got off a shot that hit one of Pavel's mercenary crew. The man clutched his chest and tumbled out of the watercraft as it sped away down the river.

Pavel was now in a state of panic, forced to leave behind his mobile command center as he fled from the Uriah. Fortunately, he still had a very powerful laptop in his possession that gave him access to much of what he needed to execute the final phases of his plan later that evening. All he needed now was to reach the racetrack and his private suite, where he could access his VPN and log into the mainframe controlling both the explosive firing systems on-site and the launch codes for taking down the CEZ power grid.

Sloane quietly swore under her breath at another lost opportunity to nab that son of a bitch Pavel. She couldn't believe the luck this psychopath exhibited every time it seemed like he was finally going down. As she watched the speedboat and Pavel disappear into the distance, Sloane returned her focus to the Uriah. They still had business to take care of onboard—namely, mopping up the remaining hit squad and operations crew, who were still heavily armed and posed a real threat. The other objective was to search for any additional intel that might provide insight into the mind of a madman.

Radioing the SOF soldiers on shore, she instructed them to "keep a careful eye out" for any movement on deck. Sloane steered the Zodiac to the starboard deck ladder, and thirty seconds later, she and the two commandos were aboard, creeping toward the pilot cabin like a SWAT team preparing to breach during a hostage situation. Their ultimate goal was to capture any remaining personnel on board and gather as much intel as quickly as possible before arranging secure transport and detainment for the remaining members of Pavel's hit squad.

Upon entering the pilot's cabin, they were confronted by one crew member who quickly surrendered, realizing he would most likely die if he offered any resistance. He wasn't a mercenary, just a recently hired hand brought aboard to help operate the luxury craft. He was armed, but only under the assumption that he might someday need to repel pirates or other criminal threats to his "gracious and generous" employer, Mr. Grovzny. A brief interrogation made it clear he had no knowledge of Pavel's plans beyond getting the ship underway and heading toward the racing complex before the public gates opened.

As Sloane secured the crewman with zip ties, she glanced around the cabin. Three others, including the captain, had been killed by sniper fire during the firefight. That meant one was still unaccounted for. Sloane got on the radio to report one secured and three dead. Suddenly, out of the corner of her eye, she saw the barrel of a gun slowly emerge from a storage closet hatch, pointed directly at her.

Wasting no time, she dropped into a crouch, turned, and fired her Sig Sauer twice, just as the other gun went off. Hearing a low-pitched grunt, she knew she'd hit the missing crew member, who fell forward out of the closet. If Sloane hadn't noticed the weapon when she did, she would almost certainly have been killed where she stood. The bullet would've struck her cleanly before she had time to react.

Before leaving the pilot's cabin to go after the remaining hit squad, Sloane got on the horn to Ray Collingswood to inform him of Pavel's escape via cigarette boat. The hope was to coordinate a raid on the race facility with local law enforcement once Pavel arrived and attempted to finish what he had started two years earlier. This might be their last real chance to stop him before his entire plan was activated. The one hitch? The possibility that members of the local police force were on Pavel's payroll, ready not to apprehend him, but to assist and protect him.

Sloane checked in with the SOF men onshore about any potential deck movement. With none detected, she and the two commandos began a careful search of the cabin for possible intel. After several minutes of fruitless searching, they secured the surrendered crewman to a support beam and left the cabin to continue clearing the vessel.

Somewhere onboard, the rest of Pavel's hit squad was likely waiting for a chance to ambush Sloane and her team. These remaining mercenaries were far more inclined to fight to the death than to face the consequences of capture, especially since they'd been given explicit orders by Pavel: protect the Uriah at all costs.

36

Once Sloane finished her call with Collingswood, they continued searching the cabin for anything of intel value. The only items they found were the captain's logbooks dealing with operations and recordings for the Uriah itself. Picking up the books for a better look, Sloane noticed a dock for a laptop sitting off to the side, with what appeared to be a thumb drive still attached to a USB connection. She quickly set the logs down, grabbed the thumb drive, and secured it in a cargo pocket on her fatigues. Giving the two SOF soldiers a heads-up, they left the cabin to begin searching for the rest of the hit squad, who they assumed were still on board somewhere.

It didn't take long. As they rounded the bow and headed aft on the portside deck of the Uriah, they came under fire from the remaining mercenaries. The men left from Pavel's hit squad were taking cover behind various open gangplank doors and a lifeboat, which they were trying to lower into the river in an attempt to escape the now disabled and slowly sinking superyacht. The Uriah continued to take on water—its stern gone, and the remaining rear now submerged under three feet of rising river water.

Sloane and the NATO commandos returned fire with well-aimed single shots that immediately took down three of the remaining mercenaries. As they advanced along the main bulkhead toward the survivors, they laid down a steady stream of suppressive gunfire that kept the rest of the mercenaries hunkered down, unable to get up, let alone shoot back. A brief lull to reload gave the mercenaries just enough of an opening to get off a few shots—one of which struck an SOF soldier. Fortunately, it hit his protective gear and did little more than jolt his momentum, not stopping their advance.

Tired of playing games and knowing these men weren't about to surrender, especially as they fired back in automatic bursts that would've made Pavel proud, Sloane grabbed a high-explosive grenade from her ammo vest. Pulling the pin and letting the handle engage the fuse, she rolled it down the sloping deck with the precision of a world-class bowling champion. It detonated right beside the lifeboat, blowing the craft off the deck and killing two of the mercenaries while mortally wounding another.

Reaching the wounded mercenary—who was now pleading for help—Sloane began applying a pressure bandage to the gaping wound that had shredded his femoral artery and was causing him to bleed out rapidly. While trying to save his life—or at least appear to—she appealed to whatever shred of moral compass the man might have had left, hoping he knew anything useful. Grateful for her aid and unaware he was seconds from death, the man managed only a few fading words before losing consciousness and dying. Those last words were: "crowd… extermination… shutdown."

Sloane didn't know exactly what he meant, but a sinking feeling told her she needed to get off this ship—and fast. She had to get to the racetrack immediately and warn authorities of a possible terror attack at the complex. Based on what she knew of Pavel's deranged psyche, she figured nothing would happen until later in the day, once the race was underway and the crowd had reached maximum capacity. If Pavel wanted to make a statement, he'd wait until he could inflict the most death and destruction possible.

Little did she know just how far Pavel was willing to go in achieving that destruction.

Scanning the immediate area and seeing no more signs of resistance, Sloane and the two SOF men made their way back through the main salon of the Uriah. Reaching the starboard side, they jumped into the river, using the current to aid their swim back to the inflatable. Climbing aboard, they steered toward the riverside, where the other two members of their team were idling alongside the now-floating wreck of the yacht with both the Hummer and the Range Rover. Abandoning the Zodiac on the shore, Sloane and the SOF men quickly piled into the two vehicles and tore off down the river road, racing back toward the cutover on their way to the racing complex.

While Sloane and her team were once again dealing with the consequences of the delays that had dogged them from the start, Pavel had already reached the racing complex. Now in a staff car, he was heading through a private security entrance leading into the underground parking garage. There, a private elevator would take him directly to his luxury suite—where he could begin initiating the shutdown of power systems that would plunge the republic into darkness. One by one, critical infrastructure systems would fail, grinding everyday life to a halt.

Of course, no one attending the race would notice—at least not at first. The on-site power facilities would keep everything running like normal.

Back inside the Range Rover, Sloane suddenly remembered the thumb drive and retrieved it from her pocket. Plugging it into the onboard computer system, she quickly had the drive open and was scrolling through page after page of engineering and architectural schematics—each one clearly tied to the race facility. Every page was labeled with a different part of the track, with titles like Main Straight GS, Turn One GS, Turn Two GS, Back Straight GS, and several others. All appeared to show structural layouts and various support systems, including electrical and water networks.

As she dug deeper, Sloane noticed that each drawing featured multiple boxes labeled with the letters "DET" followed by what looked like sequential numbers. Continuing to scan the files, she searched for some sort of legend or key that might help identify the various structural and mechanical systems being used. Finally, on the last page, she found what she was looking for. It included standard identifiers like SP for standpipe and designated amperages for various electrical panels, which appeared across all the schematics. But the only reference she found for "DET" was an italicized det1, followed by what appeared to be a time code—00:15—and the word "Initiate."

Sloane narrowed her focus, trying to connect what she was seeing with everything she'd heard about Pavel's operation so far. One vague reference kept coming back to her: Chernobyl. And the phrase "dirty bomb." Could "DET" stand for detonator? The placement of these "DET" markers—spanning at least a hundred different locations throughout the facility—left little room for any other interpretation. As far as Sloane was concerned, the schematics were showing multiple explosive placements, with the first one scheduled to detonate at fifteen minutes past midnight—just as the Grand Prix would be wrapping up. The event was scheduled like the Las Vegas race, with a late-night start to accommodate a global television audience.

Wasting no time, Sloane grabbed the satellite phone and called Collingsworth to report her findings. On the other end, Collingsworth told her they hadn't heard of any credible threats—only unconfirmed rumors coming out of Iran, which were not considered reliable. But Sloane pushed back, leaning into her instincts. She didn't have hard proof yet, but everything about the thumb drive screamed coordinated sabotage. She uploaded the contents to Langley for analysis, knowing full well that by the time anything was confirmed, it might already be too late. Yelling over the comms, she ordered the SOF man driving the Hummer, "Hit it!" The Range Rover and Hummer accelerated, weaving through a traffic-choked roadway, racing to reach the track before disaster could unfold.

It was now late afternoon, edging toward dusk, and the Formula One teams were in final prep for the race. The gates to the public had just opened. A massive crowd surged into the facility, flooding through the main ticketing entry, which held over a hundred turnstiles to handle the influx. The turnout was just shy of 150,000 people—easily the most exciting public event to take place in years. The venue buzzed with a full-on party atmosphere that Grand Prix racing was famous for, with fans making their way to assigned seating, sponsor booths, and the exclusive pit and party area where they could mingle with drivers being interviewed by members of the international press and major television networks.

High above the chaos, in his private suite, Pavel looked out over the track. A bank of monitors lined the wall behind him, showing footage of the crowd streaming in. He exhaled deeply after draining a glass of his favorite scotch whiskey. As far as he could tell, everything was unfolding exactly as planned—plans set in motion more than two years ago. He had evaded outside interference, outmaneuvered the CIA, and believed he had finally defeated the relentless operative Sloane Harper, who had tried to block him at every turn.

Only one question lingered in his mind: what had happened aboard the Uriah? He knew they'd come under attack, but he didn't yet realize it had been Sloane behind the operation. Riding high on his own ego-driven confidence, Pavel allowed himself to believe success was assured. But buried in the back of his mind, a quiet, unresolved tension gnawed at him—the memory of past failures, and the reality that when it came to Sloane Harper, underestimating her had never ended well.

37

The atmosphere at the track was in full swing—an international pre-event party of the kind you'd only find at something like the Super Bowl or perhaps a World Cup championship match, with its electric energy and festive buzz for everyone entering the grounds. The massive crowd was making its way into the complex and toward their seats, while a select group of VIP attendees filtered down into a special "Party Pit" area, where a full-scale gala-style celebration was just getting started.

Everyone allowed into the party zone had either paid a premium for a limited-edition ID card—with their picture and a security hologram—or held special VIP credentials that came with their private box seats. Others were there due to their celebrity status or as dignitaries from various countries with private access into the Party Pit.

Alongside the VIP event, the general attendance crowd found themselves surrounded by every kind of vendor and concession imaginable. From officially licensed FIA and racing team products—hats, jackets, T-shirts, patches—to a beer and wine garden, and food booths offering anything someone might crave. Attendees could also gain access to the pit lane in limited numbers until about an hour before the race.

Down in the pits, they had a chance to glimpse the twenty cars—each worth an average of fifteen million dollars—from elite teams like Red Bull, Ferrari, McLaren, Mercedes, Aston Martin, Alpine, Williams, Sauber, Haas, and the new Honda team, known for powering many of the others. Most of the cars, aside from those undergoing final mechanical tweaks, were already lined up on the grid for public display. Fans also had the opportunity to meet drivers and collect autographs—until the drivers were called back to their paddocks for final race prep and team instructions.

Pavel debated internally whether or not to attend the party. With his VIP status and confidence in his own security at the facility—despite recent disruptions—he felt relatively safe. He longed to have his ego stroked as the man who brought Formula One to the Czech Republic, savoring the accolades from an unsuspecting cadre of international dignitaries and celebrities who now viewed him as a darling of the local social scene.

Throwing caution to the wind, Pavel donned his custom racing suit and headed for the private elevator that would take him down to the parking area near the rear pit lane entrance and the main stage, where winning drivers would be introduced and interviewed for the live crowd and television broadcast.

Meanwhile, Sloane and her SOF team were still en route to the race complex—moving much slower than they would have liked due to the traffic. She was on the radio with another SOF unit already on site, now working alongside local law enforcement as added event security. While their NATO SOF credentials and uniforms didn't sit well with some Czech officials, they were gladly welcomed by on-the-ground personnel who felt they were understaffed and deeply skeptical of the private security teams that seemed ill-equipped for a real threat.

Sloane shared her suspicions about the cryptic "DET" markings she'd found on the schematics and asked if there was any way to gain access beneath the grandstands to inspect the structures. The onsite SOF team told her it was unlikely they'd be granted access and that they'd already been assigned to perimeter roles to minimize public visibility. That gave Sloane an idea. She remembered the unsecured tunnel entrance—the one where most of her original support team had been lost in an earlier firefight.

As she continued toward the facility, she radioed instructions to the on-site team to make their way to the far side of the complex to see if the tunnel entry could still be accessed. Ending that call, she used the satellite phone to contact Langley. She informed Collingsworth of her infiltration plan and her growing certainty that "DET" referred to "detonators," not "detectors."

The only thing that gave her pause was the sheer number of "DET" notations—more than she could count. She also asked if any additional NATO forces could be dispatched for support, but Collingsworth made it clear: without solid, confirmed intel, she had all the support she was going to get.

Disconnecting from Langley, Sloane and her team—split between the Range Rover and the Hummer—redirected toward the far-side perimeter of the race complex, planning to link up with their comrades heading to the tunnel on foot. Still trapped in traffic, Sloane zoomed in on a satellite view of the area and located a series of side streets winding through industrial zones. If they weren't blocked, they could offer a faster route to the target.

She forwarded the coordinates to the Hummer and directed both vehicles to turn off the main road within the next half-kilometer. If they encountered obstacles like fences or barriers, they'd deal with them using the tools they had on board—plasma cutters, torches, or whatever else it took.

Meanwhile, Pavel had arrived in the pits and was warmly greeted by team principals who recognized him on sight. He visited each paddock as he made his way up to the Party Pit, where he began making the rounds with the VIP crowd. Some of the guests knew him; others didn't. But all of them treated him like royalty.

After circulating for a while, Pavel planned to make his way to the main stage overlooking the start/finish line, where the cars were already being lined up. As always, he reveled in his own inflated importance—whether as a senior figure in the CEZ Power Consortium or as the host of this historic Grand Prix. Entering the party zone, he flashed his signature seductive smile and began glad-handing, raising glasses of champagne with celebrities, CEOs, and dignitaries alike.

Roughly twenty minutes later, Pavel excused himself and walked toward the main stage. On a whim, he had decided to personally welcome everyone to this landmark event for the Czech Republic and for the world of international racing.

Back on the road, Sloane and her team dealt with what they considered more of a nuisance than an obstacle—smashing their vehicles through two chain-link fences to enter and exit an industrial storage yard en route to the tunnel entrance. They were determined to reach it in time for one last shot at intercepting Pavel Grovzny—and whatever it was he had in motion for that night's race.

What none of them knew was that the first part of Pavel's plan was already underway. The countdown had begun. Power was being shut down across major Czech population centers—Prague, Ostrava, Brno, Plzeň, and Liberec. The resulting outages were already putting strain on smaller transmission hubs across the country. One by one, systems would begin to fail in a cascading domino effect that would plunge the entire Republic into darkness.

38

At the CEZ 401 transmission station located just outside Ostrava near the Polish border, a sensor for one of the 200KVW transformers suddenly—but slowly—began to indicate an apparent overload. On the desk of the control room monitoring system, a red light on the panel began to flicker softly and intermittently. A technician, seated at the console and half-watching the pre-race festivities on an old TV set across the room, tapped the flickering light to see if it was just a faulty bulb in the aging analog system. The system had been installed back in 1995, and though it had since been interfaced into a CEZ mainframe terminal that tied all the power plants together, it still ran on outdated hardware.

Sometimes it was a wonder that anything still worked, aside from the occasional outage of a smaller transformer in a local neighborhood or suburb. The technician flipped a series of switches to redirect power to five of the more than one hundred 200KVW transformers, hoping to run a quick diagnostic on the possibly failing unit. This was a somewhat routine procedure, and power redirection was just one step in the process of keeping the grid stable for the greater Ostrava area.

Running a full series of checks required a lineman to go out to a control box below the transformer, mounted fifty meters above the ground in a fenced-off area about half a kilometer from the control center. Picking up an old-style telephone handset wired directly to another building near the transformer yard, the control technician punched in a four-digit code on the push-button phone. Within 30 seconds, he had a lineman on the line and relayed the particulars about which transformer was having trouble. The lineman confirmed he was heading out to check the metering and sensors.

After making the hundred-meter walk through the yard, the lineman arrived at the transformer and unlocked the front panel to check the readings. The meter had clearly burned out, along with a set of relays, evidence of a power surge likely triggered by a capacitor failure. Both the capacitors and relays were badly scorched. Pulling out an old Motorola handheld radio, he keyed the mic twice to signal the control room technician.

The tech responded immediately via a dispatcher-style mic and button press, and the lineman reported what he'd seen, logging the incident into a report book he always carried. With their communication complete, the lineman turned to head back to his station while the technician scribbled the details into a logbook to report later to CEZ Central Control.

He then returned to watching the pre-race interview, streaming from the feed Pavel had arranged to distribute both on digital and analog signals throughout the region. It was a workaround for those who hadn't yet transitioned to digital TV via satellite or streaming over the internet. With his focus locked on the Grand Prix festivities, the technician failed to notice a second sensor light beginning to flicker, just like the first, until the sensor alarm began beeping in a steady rhythm.

The technician pulled a chair closer to the television to better hear an interview between Martin Brundle of Sky TV and Belgian rookie Alex Verdun. The Sky feed was being split between their uplink and the local broadcast system at the race facility. The technician, having recently discovered online betting, had placed a sizable wager on Verdun after watching him perform consistently all season. He turned up the volume, eager to hear the Q&A—and in doing so, completely missed the steadily increasing alarm from the second transformer, now dangerously close to failure.

Because he hadn't responded in time, the transformer experienced a total failure. This forced its entire 200KVW load onto the next transformer in line—triggering a catastrophic chain reaction through the grid. By the time the interview ended and the technician turned back to his console, it was ablaze with flashing lights, and a deafening cacophony of beeping filled the control room.

Panicking, he dashed across the room and began frantically trying to reroute transmissions to prevent complete collapse. But it was too late. The lights on the board transitioned from blinking to solid red, while the beeps became continuous alarms—clear indicators of complete failure cascading across every single 200KVW transformer, one after another.

Just then, the lineman's voice came crackling through the radio, filled with fear. Several transformers, he reported, were showering the yard in violent sparks and exploding with such force they were being blown off their mounts. Fearing fire and electrocution, he begged the technician to call the local fire brigade immediately.

But when the technician tried to place the outside call to first responders and supervisors, he discovered the phone system was down, crippled by a software virus Pavel had embedded into the transmission system itself. This same virus also disabled the automated alarm system that would have otherwise alerted emergency services. The technician reached for his cell phone, but the facility's location was notorious for dead zones, and unless one was willing to climb one of the towering transmission poles, there was no signal.

By now, the backup generator had kicked in, providing basic lighting and minimal internal systems. But the technician knew it was already too late. The local grid serving over five million people in the Ostrava-Katowice metro region was collapsing.

Worse, an additional 1.5 million people in surrounding industrial towns would soon be impacted, many of which depended on high-volume energy for ironworks, coal, and coke-fired production plants, along with a thriving tech industry.

The technician could only stand there in horror, watching the monitors as the domino effect continued its march toward a complete and prolonged blackout. The lineman burst back into the control room moments later, his face pale, confirming what the screens already showed: the surrounding area was already going dark. Both men knew this was only the beginning. What they didn't know was that the exact same sequence of events was set to unfold within the hour at the CEZ 301 transmission plant near Plzeň, an event that would affect nearly the entire western region of the Republic along the German border.

Even several German towns, including parts of Nuremberg, would feel the impact.

39

As the CEZ transmission station at Ostrava began to fail, transformer by transformer with no end in sight, the party atmosphere at the Grand Prix complex in Prague was ramping up to a fever pitch. Nearly everyone who held a ticket was now inside the gates—either in their seats or partying like there was no tomorrow, determined to make terrific memories—or, depending on alcohol intake, no memories at all. Out on the promenade, lined with food stands and souvenir booths, vendors were doing brisk business with everyone from die-hard racing fans to casual observers.

In the Red Bull garage, Alec Verdun was in a deep and heated discussion with team leader Hanover Macumber about last-minute tire strategy. The proposed change would make it harder for Verdun to launch out in front at the start—something he had done with near-mechanical consistency whenever he held pole position, as he did tonight. Hanover's chief tire technician had predicted that with the expected track temperatures at the start of the race, it would be wiser to begin on medium tires, potentially eliminating the need for an early pit stop.

Alec disagreed, knowing that medium tires wouldn't offer the same immediate grip as softs, which were more effective without a warm-up. That early grip was crucial for launching off the line and pulling away from the pack. Getting out in front early also meant forcing the rest of the grid to deal with "dirty air"—a mix of track debris and turbulent airflow kicked up by cars ahead. Statistically, when Alec built a one-second lead by the second turn, he almost always took the checkered flag.

Out of his eighteen pole starts, there was only one where Verdun didn't finish first—and that was when Venezuelan veteran Pablo Guzman had cut into him during a corner, spinning Alec into a wall and wrecking his RB1. Although Alec had been thankful Guzman survived the fiery crash during practice, he was privately relieved not to be racing against him tonight. The two had fought all season for the championship, and their rivalry was bitter.

But Alec's protests fell on deaf ears. Hanover sided with his tire chief and ended the conversation decisively. Furious, Alec stormed away, yelling at the top of his lungs. He grabbed his helmet and slammed it on the garage floor, not damaging it, but leaving Hanover in an even fouler mood. In moments like this, Hanover questioned whether winning another Constructor's Championship was worth dealing with a volatile young egomaniac. He found himself wondering, for the briefest moment, what things might look like if the "little shit" had been the one to crash during practice.

The truth was, Alec had taken the Red Bull seat from Pablo Guzman after two strong seasons in the RB2 car, finishing higher in the standings both years. The team's principals had seen the "writing on the wall" with an aging driver, despite Pablo's lingering skill, similar to what Fernando Alonso had shown with Aston Martin, finishing in the top ten of the standings late in his career.

Over in the Ferrari garage, backup driver Alfonse Giannelli, who had replaced Guzman after his crash, was meditating to lower his heart rate and go over the track layout in his mind. Unlike Alec, Giannelli would be starting in position twenty, at the back of the grid. Not ideal for another rookie, but he was confident in his ability and had been clocking the fastest lap times during practice.

The difference, of course, was that practice laps didn't include twenty cars all fighting for space and victory.

There was still ninety minutes left before the final drivers' meeting with track and FIA officials, including the stewards. Those stewards had recently cracked down on several teams and drivers for what most considered minor infractions. Penalties and fines were being handed out like candy—infuriating competitors who felt treated like children being sent to time-out. The new regulations, introduced to level the playing field and encourage parity in the sport, were unpopular—especially among dominant teams who saw their advantages eroded.

Down in the VIP party zone, celebrities and dignitaries were starting to make their way up to private boxes, where they planned to keep celebrating throughout the race and into the early morning hours. Or so they thought. Most of these high-profile guests, aside from some local officials, had arrived by private or chartered jets, all of which were now parked at the small private airfield where Pavel also kept his own aircraft, fueled and ready for his escape after the carnage he planned to unleash.

As the crowds filtered into grandstands scattered throughout the race complex, Pavel was back in his private box, preparing the opening remarks he intended to deliver from the main stage. His short speech would officially launch the race in just over sixty minutes. And while Pavel rehearsed his lines, Sloane Harper and her NATO Special Operations Force team were staged outside the compromised tunnel entrance she had scouted previously during the firefight that decimated her original team.

The damage had clearly been repaired, but Sloane and her team could tell it had been a rushed job. The new security consisted mainly of a series of horizontal steel bars—heavily plated but still vulnerable to the breaching tools the SOF team carried, including plasma guns and diamond-bladed power saws. The biggest hurdle was the sheer number of bars, more than thirty, that had to be cut through.

Time was critical, and the team wasted none of it. They began working immediately. It also appeared that the original eight-inch-thick doors had been welded shut at the hinges, meaning they would likely need to be blown open again, as no cutting tools would make a clean entrance in time.

Once inside the tunnel, Sloane and her team would follow the map to identify the devices marked “DET” on the schematics, hoping to confirm whether they were detonators, as she suspected.

While Sloane's team focused on gaining entry, crowds were settling into their seats, and Pavel prepared to take the stage. Meanwhile, all drivers and team principals were filing into the pre-race meeting with officials and stewards.

The show was about to begin.

40

With power going out in the Ostrava area and the same thing starting to happen in Pilsen, there wasn't much news coverage of either outage. Both occurred at different times, were localized, and happened on opposite sides of the country. Other than those two stations and their affected regions, all other systems were operating as planned, with power across the rest of the Republic functioning at normal levels.

The biggest problem facing the CEZ Consortium overseeing the power infrastructure was the lack of communication from either location. This forced the central operations office in Prague to dispatch several technical teams and supervisors to both sites to assess the situation and determine what actions were needed to restore power to a massive number of homes and businesses.

Keeping power on in the rest of the country—especially Prague—was all part of Pavel Grovzny's plan. The Grand Prix had to be broadcast internationally, not only to promote the event but to ensure that the entire world would witness the terrorist attack he was about to unleash. Everything was ready. All Pavel had to do was initiate the first timed detonation by entering a code into his cell phone, which would send a series of signals to trigger all the dirty bombs planted throughout the facility.

Most of the explosives were powerful enough on their own to cause catastrophic destruction and high casualties. The inclusion of radioactive materials in the dirty bombs would ensure even more deaths in the aftermath. In Pavel's view, terrorist acts were only effective if they left masses of people completely terrorized by the devastation.

Outside of the two regions affected by power outages, the rest of the nation's attention was fixed on the Grand Prix. The drivers' meeting was in progress with embedded camera crews, Pavel was finishing up his speech preparations before returning to the main stage, and in the grandstands, the enormous crowd was settling into seats or making their way to the VIP boxes for what was expected to be the ultimate race-day experience.

Down on the pit lane, all the team garages were deep into last-minute mechanical adjustments as they prepared to push the cars out for their final practice session before the formation lap and grid placements.

Inside the drivers' meeting, officials and stewards reviewed the same rules and procedures that had been covered in the previous twenty-three races. By now, most drivers and team principals could recite them from memory. These rules primarily existed to ensure safety but also to prevent teams or drivers from gaining unfair advantages—through vehicle weight manipulation, ride height violations, or on-track conduct.

Most infractions that resulted in time penalties or fines were related to safety issues during the race. Pit lane safety was a major focus, given the notoriously tight space where cars zipped in and out at still-dangerous speeds. Pit crews could complete refueling and tire changes in seconds, but the choreography left no margin for error. Things became even riskier under caution conditions when multiple cars pitted simultaneously without losing track position.

While the drivers' meeting wasn't exactly exciting television, it was something race fans found fascinating—a behind-the-scenes look at Formula One's regulatory side. Since the release of Netflix's Drive to Survive in 2019, fans had gained unprecedented insight into the sport's personalities and politics. Figures like Toto

Wolff from Mercedes, McLaren's Zak Brown, or Red Bull's Hanover Macumber had all become household names, drawing in more interest and viewers than ever before.

When the meeting ended, drivers and team principals returned to their garages to finish prepping their cars. Crew members helped the drivers suit up in their race suits, gloves, and Nomex head and neck covers. One by one, drivers climbed into their multi-million-dollar rides, which had been wheeled out to the pit lane.

Each car's cockpit was custom-molded to the driver's body. Helmets were fitted with comm systems, and steering wheels—more like twin-handed gaming controllers—were handed over by crew chiefs to be mounted on the control arm spindle and locked into place. These wheels were marvels of engineering, with paddle shifters for the eight-speed transmissions and buttons for everything from brake balance to power settings.

Drivers used the brief window of reconnaissance laps to test their setups and request final tweaks. So long as they returned to pit lane before rejoining, these laps were fair game. Once that session ended, the cars were pulled back into the garages for one final systems check and any last-minute changes. Then, they were pushed back out onto the pit lane, ready to follow the safety car for the formation lap.

As drivers sat in their cockpits, mentally running through every corner and scenario, Pavel approached the microphone on the main stage. The Czech National Philharmonic Brass played an upbeat, regal fanfare to draw attention from the crowd. In a commanding voice, Pavel welcomed them to the inaugural CEZ Rolex Grand Prix of Czechoslovakia. The crowd erupted with excitement as he thanked everyone for helping to make it "an event the world would never forget."

He then invited the audience to rise and join in singing the Czech National Anthem. The brass ensemble was joined by the National Symphony Mixed Choir as they launched into "Where My Home Is," composed as part of an opera in 1834 and adopted as the official anthem following Czechoslovakia's liberation in 1918.

As the final notes of the anthem echoed through the facility, all eyes turned skyward. A combined squadron of Czech Air Force Gripen jets and the Red Bulls Precision Aerobatic Team flew overhead in a stunning formation that resembled the Czech national flag, trailing white, red, and blue smoke.

With the crowd still cheering, the pit lane came to life as the engines of all twenty Formula One cars roared to life. The sound, somewhere between a symphony and an air force, reached deafening levels as drivers revved up to 17,000–19,000 RPM before settling to an idle around 9,000 RPM.

The Aston Martin Vantage safety car rolled onto the track ahead of the grid, leading the way. One by one, in staggered order based on qualifying positions, the race cars followed it onto the track, weaving back and forth to warm up their tires for optimal grip.

As they followed the safety car around the circuit, the formation lap led them toward the grid where they would take final positions. On the front row: Alec Verdun in the RB1 Red Bull car in pole position, with the McLaren number one car beside him.

Engines revved. Tension built. The grid formed into ten neat rows of two. Eyes locked on the overhead light bar as five red lights blinked on, engines dropped to idle, and anticipation mounted.

Each light extinguished one by one, with a klaxon accompanying each signal. To every driver, it felt like an eternity.

Then—

All lights out.

GO.

Twenty cars launched in unison, thundering down the main straight, accelerating through gears as they raced toward the first corner at top speed—each driver praying that no one made a mistake that would lead to a disastrous crash and a red flag restart.

41

As the Formula One cars hurtled through the first turn and into the rest of the demanding track, Sloane and the NATO SOF team successfully breached the tunnel entrance and began moving deeper into the facility. They carried specialized monitoring devices calibrated to detect electrical fields, a wide range of explosives, and even trace levels of radiation.

Sloane, scanning one of the schematics on her smartphone, noted that a location marked "DET" was coming up within the next fifty meters. She compared the schematic's overlay to their current movement, making sure they were closing in on the precise spot.

As they approached, the monitoring device picked up strong readings for an electrical field and trace compounds including nitrocellulose, haloamine, ammonium nitrate, and acetone peroxide—all associated with explosives, either individually or in combination. What it didn't detect, however, was any signature of radioactive material, which had been part of the original concern based on chatter intercepted from Telegram and Signal channels.

The closer they got to the marked DET location, the stronger the pulse tone from the device became—until it went solid, indicating a match with something embedded in the structure. However, there was no visible sign of a detonator or explosive device. Sweeping the sensor vertically, the team concluded that the device must be buried inside the concrete foundation. They began searching for any panel or entry point.

Deciding they needed a visual, one of the SOF men carefully drilled into the concrete using a diamond bit, feeling for any change in material. Soon, the drill met plated metal, and he slowly worked through it until it broke into a hidden cavity.

Uncertain what they were about to encounter, they inserted a PCE thermal imaging endoscope through the hole. Maneuvering the 360-degree camera, they finally got eyes on the device: a detonator wired to a chrome sphere, strongly resembling a containment housing—possibly for radioactive material.

The detonator had two indicator lights—red and green—and a small LED timer display, currently frozen at five minutes. The red light was brighter than the green, and while the timer had not started counting down, the presence of both a timing mechanism and wiring indicated the device was operational but not yet armed.

The implications were chilling. This was only one of hundreds of "DET" markers across the schematic, and though inactive, the devices were clearly real. Sloane suspected these were intended to be triggered during the height of the race—most likely near the end when crowd attention would be at its peak.

She pulled out her satellite phone to relay the discovery, but the thick tunnel walls blocked the signal. Without wasting time, she ordered the rest of the team to continue deeper for more confirmation while she exited the tunnel to alert Collingswood and local authorities.

As Sloane made her way back out, the SOF team encountered another detonator and sphere fifty meters deeper inside the tunnel. This one was embedded into a key structural support wall beneath the facility's roof. They radioed Sloane immediately, confirming a second device.

Just as she reached the tunnel exit, Sloane received their message and quickly dialed Langley, relaying the confirmed threat to Collingswood. She knew his status and reputation within international intelligence communities—including the Czech

Republic—meant he could initiate emergency measures faster than anyone else.

Still, she knew this wouldn't be easy. Evacuating a Grand Prix event with over 100,000 attendees—many of them VIPs—would be a logistical nightmare. There was the ever-present risk of mass hysteria, and even worse, the chance of alerting the perpetrators too early, prompting them to trigger the bombs.

Out on the racecourse, the Grand Prix was in full swing. Not a single caution had slowed the high-speed drama. The crowd—Pavel included—watched as the drivers pushed their cars to the limit through one of the most challenging circuits on the calendar.

Alec Verdun led the pack, but only by a slim 1.5-second margin over the number three McLaren, which loomed constantly in his rearview. The battle between them escalated with every lap, especially through corners, short straights, and the crucial DRS (Drag Reduction System) zone, where high-speed overtaking was a real threat.

One of the biggest surprises of the race came from team Ferrari. Rookie replacement driver Alfonse Giannelli—thrown into the seat after Pablo Guzman's fiery crash—was steadily working his way up from the back of the grid. After just twenty-six laps of the scheduled seventy-five, Giannelli had climbed from 20th to 12th, confidently carving his way through slower cars. His Ferrari, finely tuned since his takeover, looked like one of the fastest on the track. More importantly, Giannelli was showing the poise, focus, and instincts of a rising star—unlike Verdun, he did it all without a trace of ego.

As Giannelli pushed up into tenth place to secure a potential points finish, Verdun's aggressive style finally caught up with him. While defending his lead through an S-curve and tight hairpin, Verdun overextended and clipped the front wing of the pursuing McLaren. The resulting contact sent the McLaren off the track and into the wall, debris scattering across the circuit.

The crash brought out the race's first yellow caution. The Aston Martin safety car deployed immediately, and the field bunched up under caution protocols. The McLaren was done for the day.

Over the radio, most teams gave the command—"Box, box"—signaling their drivers to pit. Under caution, everyone pitted at once, making the pit lane a hive of intense, high-risk activity. Some teams, having already pitted, kept their drivers on the track to gain positions. Verdun, however, had to come in. His car had sustained minor damage to the right rear tire from the earlier contact with the McLaren wing. Already close to the pit speed limit of fifty miles per hour due to the caution, Verdun entered the pit lane for repairs.

Up in his private suite, Pavel began pacing, growing increasingly agitated. The race was progressing, but he knew this pit stop wasn't the right moment to act. Too many spectators had left the stands for food and drink, and the pit sequence would be over quickly. He needed to strike when all eyes—and all drivers—were fully engaged in the final laps.

Pavel planned to head down to the garage once the cars were three laps from the finish. From there, he would make his way off the property before entering the various codes that would initiate the sequence of detonations—over a hundred in total—that would rain destruction across the entire facility. Everyone in the stands and surrounding structures would be trapped in the blast and radiation zones, thanks to his deliberate design. Exit turnstiles and gates had been minimized, purposely limiting how many people could get clear before the worst unfolded.

Down on the pit lane, teams were running additional checks on several cars while the caution period continued and track crews worked to clear debris. Pavel took a deep breath and exhaled slowly, relaxing into his chair. He knew this wasn't the time to act rashly. If he was to maximize the chaos and terror he intended, he needed patience and precision. He had waited this long—he could wait just a little longer. Everything was in place. Nothing could stop him now—not even his oldest adversary, Sloane Harper.

Sloane, meanwhile, had just finished her call with Collingswood. He agreed with her assessment: they needed to halt the race and begin evacuation procedures immediately. But he also knew how difficult it would be to implement such a plan without sparking mass panic or tipping off the enemy. Once their call ended, Collingswood made a series of rapid calls, including one to the regional NATO command, activating emergency protocols for an imminent terrorist attack expected within the next two hours—based on the estimated time remaining in the race, plus the post-race podium, trophy ceremonies, and season championship recognitions.

After disconnecting, Sloane immediately radioed her SOF teams inside the tunnel. She ordered them to withdraw to the staging area and await further instructions from NATO command. The goal was a quiet shutdown and controlled evacuation—an effort to minimize casualties before any detonations occurred.

Once the SOF units had regrouped with her, they moved swiftly toward the race control building. This would be their operational base while high-level law enforcement and intelligence agencies arrived to implement the broader counterterrorism response.

Back on the track, the safety car had exited, and the race returned to green flag conditions. The cars accelerated to full speed, bunched up from the caution and battling for positions. Alec

Verdun still held the lead, slowly widening his gap over the next three competitors. With a clean track ahead and fewer laps remaining, he looked poised for another dominant finish.

But it was Alfonse Giannelli who continued to steal the show. Timing the restart to perfection, he surged past four cars in the span of two corners and found himself in sixth place. The crowd roared with approval, and commentators worldwide praised the rookie's fearlessness and control. Giannelli's run from the back of the grid had turned into a breakout performance—one of the most exciting stories of the entire season.

Half an hour later, teams from multiple agencies—including the FBI, the Czech BIS (Security Information Service), Europol, Germany's BKA, and Poland's Central Bureau of Investigation—began to arrive at the race complex. Quietly, they made their way into the administrative buildings to coordinate with race organizers. Their presence didn't raise suspicion among the general crowd. Those who noticed simply assumed it was enhanced security for the podium and post-race ceremonies.

The only people to grow uneasy were Pavel's own internal security staff. They had no idea who these new, SWAT-like personnel were, and they wore no visible agency insignia. As they entered the operations center, these operatives began meeting directly with race directors and the chief of security—who, unknown to them, was on Pavel's payroll.

The inter-agency leaders briefed race officials on the developing terror threat and agreed on a covert plan: to contact team principals and begin bringing in the race cars one at a time, so as not to raise alarms. Once each car returned to the pit lane, drivers would be instructed to stay inside the vehicles, while law enforcement would begin evacuating grandstands and bleacher areas. New emergency exits had already been cut into the perimeter fencing for rapid egress.

At the same time, Pavel's security chief placed a discreet call to his boss, informing him that something unusual was going on. Though he didn't have exact details, he noted the arrival of numerous law enforcement officers and a series of closed-door meetings with senior race officials.

Pavel instructed him to find out whatever he could and report back immediately. But the plan was already in motion, and authorities, aware that some of Pavel's internal staff were compromised, intentionally kept them out of the loop. His man was stonewalled at every attempt to get information.

Still waiting in his box and sensing the tone shift around him, Pavel grew tense. Something had changed. He didn't yet know what, but it was clear. And even as he waited for more word from his contact, the Formula One teams began discreetly pulling their cars into the pits, just as the task force had planned. The quiet, methodical evacuation was underway, the first move in a high-stakes attempt to prevent a mass-casualty terror event, possibly just minutes away.

42

As the teams began to slowly bring their cars in from the track one by one using the standard radio call of "Box, Box" to keep up appearances, the task force started coordinating with local law enforcement, directing them toward all grandstands to prepare for a slow, orderly, yet deliberate evacuation—ready to begin the moment the go-ahead was given. The real risk was, of course, the crowd itself—much like a herd of cattle.

Any sudden movement or whiff of danger could trigger widespread panic, creating more chaos than the threat they were trying to avoid. To prevent this, local police were instructed to keep everything on a strict "need-to-know" basis. Even internal staff security was kept in the dark, as suspicions about infiltration within the ranks remained high. Meanwhile, NATO forces had begun cutting up to twenty emergency exits into the perimeter fencing—designed to allow a more controlled egress than funneling the massive crowd through the main entry and exit points.

Still unaware of what was transpiring below, Pavel paced back and forth in his private suite, increasingly irritated at the radio silence from his own people. He hadn't yet noticed that cars were returning to the pits one at a time and not rejoining the race. From the outside, it looked like a routine series of mechanical failures and retirements. On the international broadcast, announcers began speculating about a wave of car problems—chassis issues, wing problems, engine failures—commenting on how strange it was that one car after another was being parked in the garages and removed from the competition.

Meanwhile, the rest of the field continued at full pace—until each car received its coded message to come in. When the Red Bull team issued the call to Alec Verdun, he exploded with frustration. His RB1 was running perfectly, and to be pulled out for no apparent reason made no sense. His radio communication quickly turned heated. This outburst triggered further speculation from the commentators, especially as it marked the ninth car to exit under mysterious circumstances.

Watching the broadcast and hearing nothing from his own security, Pavel finally had enough. He stepped into the private elevator, descending quickly into the tunnel system below the grandstands. There, he jumped onto an electric quad and sped off toward the next grandstand sector, determined to find out what was really going on.

While Pavel raced through the underground access routes, NATO personnel continued work along the fence line, cutting open emergency exits near each major stand. Pavel arrived at a stairwell access point, walking up beside the grandstands just as several cars zipped by at regular speeds—nothing unusual to the casual observer. To the crowd, everything still seemed normal.

But not to Pavel. Something felt off. The number of cars still on track was dwindling too quickly. Blending into the crowd, he moved closer to a local police officer speaking into his radio, hoping to overhear something useful.

When he caught sight of the officer's radio, he recognized the make and model—identical to the ones used by his own security personnel. Scanning the area, he spotted one of his staff and made a beeline for him. The staffer recognized him immediately and handed over the radio without question. Pavel started scanning through the channels.

Most of what he heard was routine traffic—until he caught a voice saying, "Go ahead and tell Ferrari to bring in their next car." That confirmed it. Something was happening—something coordinated. The race was being shut down.

Pavel immediately turned away from the crowd and moved to the rear of the grandstand where the food stalls and vendors were located. Walking past the concessions and toward a locked gate marked "Staff Personnel Only," he punched in a security code and slipped through, entering an access corridor along the outer perimeter.

As he got closer to the fence, he heard the unmistakable sound of power saws at work. Creeping along the edge of a storage building, he spotted NATO soldiers cutting an emergency exit through the perimeter wire. Seconds later, he heard someone over the radio announce: "Exit Two is open."

The pieces fell into place. One by one, exits were being prepped. The crowd was about to be evacuated. The race was already being shut down—quietly and systematically. The operation had begun.

By the time Pavel returned to the tunnel and reached his suite, only nine cars remained on the track. Monitoring the radio and cycling through feeds on his closed-circuit surveillance system, he looked for visual confirmation. One camera feed showed a man holding a radio up to his mouth. A moment later, he heard the phrase that sealed it:

"All exits open."

That was it.

The math was simple—too few cars, too many exits, and too many variables. Time was up.

Pavel calmly unlocked his phone and entered a long series of digits. On the screen, a countdown timer activated: 10:00 minutes. The sequence had started. Armageddon was in motion.

Without panic, Pavel grabbed a 9mm Beretta, downed one final glass of his favorite Scotch whisky, and walked to the elevator. He descended to the parking level, climbed into his sleek Aston Martin Vantage, and headed toward the rear security gate.

At the gatehouse, the familiar guard looked surprised to see him.

"Leaving already, sir? Before the grand finale?"

Pavel smiled calmly. "No rest for the wicked, you know."

The guard nodded, opened the gate, and Pavel rolled through, heading toward the river and the boat that would carry him to freedom—away from the ashes of the empire he had built.

Back at the tunnel breach, Sloane and her SOF team monitored the chatter on their radios. They stood ready, positioned just outside, waiting to assist with evacuations or neutralize threats if needed. Sloane climbed into the Range Rover and drove up a nearby ridge to get a full view of the facility.

As she turned to scan the site, her eyes locked on a familiar shape speeding down an access road toward the river: Pavel in his Aston Martin.

Her heart kicked into overdrive.

She didn't know if she could stop the detonations—but that didn't matter. Pavel wasn't getting away.

Gravel spat as she spun the Rover around and launched down the road, radioing the task force: "Visual on target. Pursuing."

Then, behind her—the first explosion.

The Red Bull garage erupted in a blinding fireball, disintegrating everything in its blast radius. Everyone inside—star driver Alec Verdun, team principal Hannover Macumber, and the entire factory racing crew—were gone in an instant. Shrapnel, building debris, car parts, and twisted bodies rained down in a storm of devastation.

The nightmare had begun.

43

When the Red Bull Garage blew up, the crowd on the far side of the racetrack along the lengthy back straight heard it but could only see the dust cloud. Many wondered if there had been an accident in the pits. People at both the first and final turn stands could see the aftermath of the explosion and also assumed some major mishap had occurred. Those seated in the main grandstand directly above the garages felt what they thought was an earthquake. It threw many completely out of their seats. Stunned but for the most part unharmed, they quickly realized from the sonic boom-like sound that it was something far more localized than a seismic event. Then they watched debris flying outward onto the track.

Exactly one hundred and twenty seconds later, another bomb went off behind the Ferrari garage. It took out the entire Ferrari team as well, including the crowd favorite, rookie driver Alfonse Giannelli. With all eyes turning toward both blast sites, a series of fifteen more bombs went off one minute later. They detonated in quick succession throughout the stands at the first and last turns of the racetrack. Other blasts erupted across the track, in stands where people were still trying to figure out what had happened in the pits. These bombs started to compromise the main support structure of all three stands. They began to collapse on the crowds still seated or standing at their spots, watching in confusion.

When the first explosion occurred, the task force immediately radioed all personnel to begin evacuations. Local law enforcement moved into the stands as the public address system began broadcasting evacuation messages. They came in English, Spanish, French, Italian, Dutch, and several other languages. Upon hearing them, the crowd rushed to exit the stands. The effort created more problems than an orderly exit would have, as panic quickly spread. But it hardly mattered. Ten more bombs went off and began collapsing major sections of the roof onto people trying to flee.

Thirty seconds later, another ten bombs went off, targeting all fifty of the luxury boxes atop the main grandstands. The explosions killed or maimed nearly every dignitary and VIP in attendance. Among the dead or wounded was the President of the Czech Republic—who barely survived—along with his cabinet and several government officials from neighboring countries. What began as an ongoing party during private pre-race festivities had now become one of the worst acts of terror ever recorded in modern history.

While the attack was in full swing, the broadcast was still live. Cameras followed each new explosion like they were covering a heavyweight prize fight. Meanwhile, the death toll began to rise. Officials tried to manage an orderly evacuation, but panic had taken over. The scenes resembled those from 9/11, with people running in all directions. Many who were still trying to escape the stands were killed when twenty more bombs went off simultaneously across different sections of the complex.

On the island of Mallorca, the men of the Omega Collective Group gleefully watched the horror unfold. It played out like a big-budget disaster film on live television. Each man stared at the screen as though witnessing a gruesome freeway pile-up. They were individually disturbed by the sheer scale and ferocity of Pavel Grovzny's attack. But as a group, they were pleased. The carnage would keep the world's attention diverted away from their next two targets: the Palo Verde Nuclear Plant in Arizona and the Three Gorges Dam Hydro-Electric Plant in China. Silently, however, each one wondered what they should do about Pavel—the one piece of the plan they couldn't control.

After the last set of explosions, the air was filled with screams of pain and anguish. Survivors shouted for help. Others who had made it out of the stands tried to reach those still trapped beneath collapsed structures. But most were already dead. Two minutes later, as rescue and recovery efforts were underway, another twenty bombs detonated. They caused the entire main grandstand to pancake in on itself. Nearly 35,000 people were still trying to evacuate from that section.

By now, the death toll had climbed to nearly 70,000 and continued to rise. Some people managed to flee the grandstands and were being evacuated by NATO forces, who had cut escape paths through the perimeter fencing. But what none of them knew—neither the evacuees, nor the law enforcement, NATO, or the interagency task force—was that the real threat had only begun. They would all soon begin to succumb to radiation poisoning from the vast nuclear haze created by Pavel's dirty bombs.

Evacuation efforts continued for those still in untouched stands. But then, another forty bombs went off throughout the tunnel system. They collapsed the structural foundation that supported not only the stands but also buildings located throughout the racing complex.

This included the foundation underneath the broadcast center. By then, the feed was running on fixed and remote cameras only. Everything still appeared operational when the floor suddenly buckled beneath the control room. Seconds later, the switching systems and satellite transmissions finally went dark—despite having their own power generators separate from the rest of the facility.

Moments after the broadcast center collapsed, the last twenty bombs were triggered. They destroyed the main entrance and all the perimeter access roads just as emergency responders were arriving. The blast instantly delayed both evacuation and rescue operations.

Throughout most of the Czech Republic, the general public was completely unaware of the catastrophe. One by one, all the power plants across the country—aside from the main one in Prague—shut down. The Republic was thrown into darkness, except for emergency generators that were themselves starting to fail. Finally, the main system located just outside the capital failed as well, cutting off most infrastructure systems and control.

Fortunately, the rest of the world had been watching the live broadcast of the Grand Prix. They were now fully aware of what had transpired—an act of terrorism so massive, so meticulously executed, that it had no modern precedent.

The only question remaining was:

Who could possibly be behind it all?

44

As the personal playground he had built over five years was literally blowing up, just as he had planned, Pavel Grovzny continued driving his Aston Martin toward where his boat was moored on the river. He was driving in a fairly conservative manner, going the speed limit, doing his best not to draw any unwanted attention. He was fairly confident that most, if not all, local law enforcement attention was now focused on the Grand Prix facility, which had suddenly and unexpectedly become its own kind of morgue and burial site.

What he failed to notice was Sloane Harper racing after him in the Range Rover. She was closing in fast as he approached the final turn onto the road that followed the river's edge. From there, it was just a short two hundred meters to where he had beached a small inflatable that would soon carry him back to his speedboat. Once aboard, he planned to fire up the twin Mercury jet boat engines, bring them up to cruising speed, and head downriver to his private airfield. Within twenty minutes or less, he would be boarding his jet and on his way to a historic and inevitable meeting with the Omega Collective Group after quickly changing his route from North Korea to Mallorca.

As he slowed and swung the Vantage sharply onto the river road, Sloane rammed the right rear quarter panel with the Range Rover. The Aston Martin careened down the river embankment and slammed into a wall of rocks. The impact caused Pavel and the coupe to flip over several times before landing wheels up in the river and beginning to sink. Though Sloane believed she was okay, the force of the collision caused her own vehicle to lose control. The Range Rover crashed head-on into the same rock wall at the bottom of the embankment. The airbags deployed, the front end crumpled, and Sloane was briefly knocked breathless.

Wasting no time, Pavel came to his senses as water began filling the cab. Realizing he was upside down, he quickly unfastened the seatbelt. Inhaling and exhaling deeply, he took one final breath, held it, and kicked out the driver's side window. Following the escaping air, he swam out through the opening and soon surfaced, gasping for breath. Looking around, he spotted the wrecked Range Rover with steam still rising from the engine compartment.

Though he couldn't see his boat from where he was, Pavel knew exactly where it was moored. He began swimming slowly, using the current to drift in its direction. Meanwhile, Sloane was just beginning to regain her senses. The airbags had protected her from serious injury, but a shard of glass from the shattered windshield had left a cut above her right eyebrow. Blood now trickled into her eye, obscuring her vision.

Climbing gingerly out of the Range Rover, Sloane spotted the rear of Pavel's Aston Martin just as it disappeared beneath the surface. Scanning the water, she caught sight of slight movement about thirty meters to her right. It was unmistakably a human form drifting down the river. She quickly found her footing on the pavement and began running in the same direction, keeping a slightly faster pace than the current to catch up.

A minute later, after sprinting as fast as she could, Sloane reached a point where she could see Pavel clearly. She also spotted his boat now visible just ahead. Drawing her Sig, she fired three rounds that missed. With blood clouding her right eye and distorting her depth perception, her accuracy suffered.

Still, she continued firing. Taking careful aim through her one good eye, she let off another shot. She had one round left in the chamber. Squeezing the trigger, she finally heard a distinctive grunt from Pavel as the nine-millimeter round struck just above his right shoulder blade. The bullet deflected upward, shattering his collarbone.

Hearing no further shots, Pavel knew she was out of ammunition. Despite the intense pain, he only needed to swim another fifty meters. If he could pull himself onto the speedboat, he could still make his escape.

His pace slowed considerably. The pain was nearly unbearable, but he let the current do much of the work. Sloane, wiping blood from her eye, saw that Pavel was fading. As she pressed ahead along the riverbank, she came upon his inflatable—a small Zodiac-like craft with an outboard motor. She untied it from a low-hanging tree branch and pushed it into the river, climbing in as it floated out.

Scanning the boat, she saw the ignition key still in place. Twisting it quickly, she then pulled the starter cord three times before the motor coughed twice and finally sputtered to life.

Gripping the throttle, she angled the inflatable upstream and began moving toward the speedboat, now about twenty meters away. As she closed the distance, she saw Pavel nearly at the bow of the larger boat. He was struggling to climb aboard, his injured right arm rendering him mostly one-handed. She knew that if he made it to the controls before she reached the stern, he would be gone—vanishing upriver and beyond her grasp.

Pavel managed to get a grip on a wire ladder hanging from the bow and hauled himself up onto the deck. He didn't see Sloane, who had just reached the stern and climbed onto the small dive platform. She let the inflatable drift as she crept aboard the speedboat, moving silently.

Pavel stumbled into the cockpit and dropped into the driver's seat. Turning the key, the twin Mercs roared to life. As he jammed the throttle forward, the sudden burst of acceleration threw Sloane backward. She nearly tumbled back into the river but managed to cling to the stern rail.

Still unaware of her presence, Pavel guided the boat out into the main river channel, heading toward his private airstrip. He sped faster than regulations allowed but kept it manageable enough to navigate.

As he began maneuvering a tight series of bends, Sloane crept forward, crouched low to maintain balance and avoid detection. She could now see how badly Pavel's right arm was compromised. He had to reach across with his left hand to manage the throttle.

Spotting a tie line coiled near a cleat on the rail, Sloane quietly slipped it loose. She wrapped the cord tightly around each hand, fashioning it into a makeshift garrote. Waiting for just the right moment, she crouched in position.

As the boat hit the apex of a sharp curve, Pavel leaned to throttle up again. That was her cue.

Sloane launched herself forward. In one motion, she looped the tie line over Pavel's head and yanked it tight across his windpipe. Crossing her wrists, she pulled back with every ounce of strength she had, catching him completely off guard as the boat surged around the bend.

45

As Sloane pulled on the garrote, Pavel's left hand, still on the throttle handle, yanked it to full speed. The boat immediately jetted forward, the bow lifting, and the centrifugal force caused Sloane to lose her balance and fall backward. As she tumbled, her grip on the tie line began to loosen, and Pavel was able to slide his hand up inside the loop and gain just enough space to slip out from under it and break free.

The speedboat now raced forward down a wide-open expanse, pointed straight at the retaining wall of the far shore. Sloane fell awkwardly back toward the stern of the deck, dazed but scrambling to get up.

Still in considerable pain and bleeding heavily from what turned out to be a through-and-through wound, Pavel leaped from the cockpit and quickly advanced on Sloane, who was doing her best to stay upright. She was all too aware of how dangerous Pavel could be, even with one bad arm, and steeled herself for the coming assault.

Pavel rushed at her and began a series of front kicks aimed at her midsection, one of which landed a glancing blow to her right rib cage as she turned. Regaining her balance, Sloane blocked the next kicks with her arms and landed a solid sidekick to Pavel’s solar plexus, knocking him back a few feet and stealing some of his breath.

Seeing an opening, Sloane moved in. But Pavel struck back, landing a closed-fist punch to her right shoulder, hitting a nerve and temporarily paralyzing her arm. Pavel advanced again with a wild, animal-like intensity that reminded Sloane of a wounded predator desperate to survive. They fell into a brutal hand-to-hand fight, using a blend of techniques and instinct.

Locked in combat, they failed to realize the boat was still racing forward—now dangerously close to the jagged rock wall lining the river's edge. A collision at this speed would destroy the boat and likely kill them both.

As Sloane unleashed a combination of punches and kicks that had Pavel retreating, she spotted the danger ahead. Darting past him, she lunged to the wheel and managed a quick course correction, steering the boat back toward the center of the river but angled slightly toward the opposite shore.

Before she could catch her breath, Pavel was on her again. He pounded her numb right arm with hammer-like blows, then wrapped her in a tight chokehold from behind, pulling her backward and cutting off her air. Sloane's vision dimmed as she began to feel dizzy from lack of oxygen.

But she had one move left.

She bit down—hard—on Pavel's left forearm. A sharp yelp escaped him, and his grip loosened. Taking advantage, Sloane drove her hips backward into his abdomen and stomped on his instep. Pavel stumbled, and she spun into him, slamming a punch into his sternum that sent him reeling.

Glancing to his left, Pavel spotted a gaff hook secured to the side wall. He grabbed it and swung it at her head. Sloane ducked, then countered with a front kick that landed just above his left kneecap. Pavel's leg buckled, but he kept swinging the hook wildly, back and forth, missing each time as Sloane pressed the attack.

She struck him again—fists and feet flying—and one of her kicks landed with a sickening crack. A rib had broken; she could hear it.

Pavel winced but was still fueled by raw rage. He lashed out and finally caught Sloane with the edge of the hook in a glancing blow to her right bicep. It sliced the skin and forced her to hesitate.

Blood dripping from her arm, Sloane snarled and came back even harder.

Her renewed assault was relentless. Though Pavel managed to block some of her strikes, he was slowing. Just when it looked like he would finally fall, he snatched a small fire extinguisher with his injured arm and, with everything he had left, swung it into Sloane's jaw. The impact stunned her, and Pavel followed up with a front kick to her thigh that dropped her to one knee.

He lifted the fire extinguisher to strike again, but Sloane ducked the blow and tackled him. Her shoulder slammed into his torso, driving him against the side rail. The extinguisher fell from his hands.

The tackle lifted him briefly off his feet, but he retaliated by slamming his elbow between her shoulder blades. Sloane gasped as the air rushed out of her lungs. Pavel shoved her to the deck, his eyes darting toward the approaching shoreline.

Seeing that they were nearly at the rocky wall again, and with his jet waiting nearby, Pavel made a break for it. He jumped overboard just seconds before the speedboat slammed into the rocks.

Exhausted and in agony, Pavel swam with his one good arm toward the shore. But the current was strong, pulling him toward the center of the river. He paused to catch his breath, floating for a moment. Then he looked back.

The boat had hit the rocks head-on. The impact ruptured the custom fuel cell in the bow. Ten seconds later, the fuel ignited into a massive fireball that blew the boat apart in a thunderous eruption.

Pavel continued paddling, breathing hard. He feared the current would carry him into the fiery debris field. But he also smiled faintly, convinced that this explosion had finally ended the relentless pursuit of Sloane Harper.

Unbeknownst to Pavel, Sloane had regained consciousness just in time. With seconds to spare, she dove overboard on the opposite side of the boat.

She plunged deep, narrowly avoiding the fireball that exploded overhead. She could feel the heat on her back as it tore through the surface. The blast acted like a depth charge, sending a shockwave through the water that slammed into her like a hammer. But she'd braced herself just in time, pressurizing her body and holding her breath through the violent force.

The wave shoved her into the faster-moving central current. When she surfaced, gasping for air, she quickly spun around, scanning the area.

She saw Pavel.

He was climbing out of the river, just ahead, pulling himself onto the rock wall that separated the riverbank from the airfield. She began swimming diagonally across the current, angling toward his position. Just beyond him, she could make out several private jets parked on a nearby airstrip.

That had to be his escape route.

Sloane knew she had to stop him before he reached the plane.

Pavel was struggling. When he finally reached the wall, he barely had the strength to pull himself out. He paused, exhausted, and stared across the field toward the waiting jets. His own plane was about two hundred meters away.

He took a deep breath and steadied himself for one final push.

What Pavel didn't see was the figure downstream, still in the water—still coming.

Sloane.

She was climbing out of the river, struggling from the fight and the shockwave, but she kept moving. Each step brought her closer to the open airfield where Pavel was limping toward his jet.

Pavel, bleeding and worn out, had no idea she was still alive.

He was also caught off guard by the sheer number of private jets crowded on the tarmac. As he scanned the rows of aircraft, searching for his own, panic crept in. His jet was hidden behind at least three other rows of planes brought in for the Grand Prix.

Just one more detail Pavel hadn't considered.

It made him question how quickly he'd be able to taxi to the runway for a hasty departure—assuming he could even reach the controls in time.

As Pavel hobbled across the field adjacent to the strip, Sloane was closing in. Every step she took brought her closer to her target.

Bruised, bloodied, and exhausted, she moved with one singular purpose now.

To end Pavel Grovzny.

Even if it cost her own life.

46

Spotting his private hangar on the far side of the airfield, Pavel was wondering what difficulties he might have in maneuvering out to the runway past the multitude of private and corporate jets parked on the tarmac. While making his escape from the bombings at the Grand Prix, he had neglected to call his flight crew to let them know he was on his way, but he trusted they were ready to go. His jet was still in the hangar and would need final preparation, but he was feeling better as he struggled across the last of the open space and reached the line of aircraft.

As Sloane neared the opening to the private airstrip, she could see Pavel in the distance as he disappeared between two jets, heading toward the impromptu terminal beyond the tarmac. Overall, she felt surprisingly good in spite of the fight and the shockwave she had just endured. A sudden surge of energy rose in her as she spotted Pavel. Pulling together all the strength she could muster, Sloane ran toward the tarmac, hoping to catch him before he reached his plane.

By the time Pavel made it to the old building that passed for a flight control center and terminal, the exhaustion and pain in his right shoulder and chest had increased to an almost unbearable level. Once inside, he saw that many of the private flight crews were seated in a makeshift lounge area in a nearby corner of the building. Pavel could see they were all up and visibly upset about something, most of them trying to make cell calls.

It dawned on him that they had probably all been watching the Grand Prix on the old TV inside the lounge. That meant they had likely seen much of what occurred when the bombs started exploding. Power was still on at the airfield because the facility was running on a separate generator—keeping systems going in case of a failure like the one currently affecting the rest of the country. As Pavel gingerly made his way to his private crew space on the opposite end of the terminal, none of the people in the lounge took any notice of him at all.

The door flew open as Pavel stepped into his private office, and two very nervous-looking men jumped to their feet as though they'd seen a ghost. These men—his pilot and co-pilot—stared at the gaunt figure before them, covered in cuts and bruises, blood flowing from his wounded arm. He looked like a stranger. Whatever they were thinking vanished when Pavel gave the order to get the jet ready for immediate departure. Then he moved to a cabinet on the wall.

Inside were all types of first-aid supplies. Pavel removed his tattered shirt, grabbed a bottle of antiseptic, and winced as he poured it over both sides of the through-and-through bullet wound. He then stuffed gauze into both openings and bound it all with an ACE-type bandage, securing it tightly with adhesive tape. After that, he wrapped heavy gauze around his entire torso and up around his shoulder and broken collarbone.

Once he finished the field dressing, Pavel moved to a wall locker and pulled out a clean shirt. He managed to get it over his head and struggled to feed his mostly useless arm through the sleeve. Then he grabbed a flight jacket and a loaded nine-millimeter pistol before heading out the door and over to the attached hangar, where his jet was in the final stages of checks and preparation for takeoff. Climbing the entry steps to the cabin just as the hangar doors began to open and the twin turbine engines started to throttle up, Pavel took a seat. The co-pilot's voice crackled over the intercom, reporting that they were ready to taxi out.

The jet began rolling out of the hangar, carefully weaving through the maze of Bombardiers, Gulfstreams, and Beechcrafts toward the runway. Pavel swallowed several Oxycodone tablets and chased them down with a half-full highball glass of Scotch to dull the pain. Then he opened a panel next to his seat, retrieved a hypodermic filled with lidocaine, and injected it into his shoulder to numb the wound. He knew he'd need proper medical attention soon—but if he could just get to Mallorca, everything would be fine.

Suddenly, as Pavel's plane completed a tight turn to line up for entry onto the runway, he spotted a solitary figure running toward him.

His eyes widened in both fear and rage.

It was Sloane.

She was sprinting across the final stretch of the field, closing the distance with every step as the jet continued taxiing toward the final checks and staging area for takeoff. In her hands, she held what looked like a makeshift spear—something with a shaft and a sharp end.

And she was coming fast.

Pavel screamed "Noooo!" at the top of his lungs. It sounded like it came from a wounded animal—exactly what he was at this point. He jumped up, threw open the cockpit door, and yelled at the pilot to "Get this bird off the ground immediately". The pilot began to say something about final flight checks but shut his mouth when Pavel pointed the nine-millimeter at his head and screamed again that they had to take off now.

What Sloane was carrying was like a spear, she had grabbed a broken length of rebar with a jagged end and picked it up from the ground just as she reached the edge of the airfield. She knew the only jet in motion had to be Pavel's, slowly taxiing toward the runway. Her plan was simple: reach the jet before it could throttle up for takeoff and jam the rebar into the front tire. If she managed that, she might finally stop Pavel from getting away, something she had been trying to do since spotting him leaving the racetrack in his Aston Martin.

Sloane saw the jet make its final turn onto the runway. The turbine engines began to rev as they came to a stop before its high-speed dash for lift-off. She was crossing the last piece of open ground before the runway just as the jet began accelerating. Sloane pushed herself harder, stepping onto the runway itself just as the jet bore down on her position. It looked like it might hit her.

Bracing herself for impact, Sloane suddenly dove to the side and thrust the rebar into the side of the front landing gear tire. The jagged metal pierced the sidewall, rupturing the tire. But the jet was already coming off the ground. Sloane swore under her breath, then screamed as the Gulfstream sped down the runway, lifted off, and banked sharply out over the river—heading southwest toward the German border and beyond.

Gasping for breath after her sprint and failed ploy, Sloane scanned the area and spotted a nearby Piper M700 Fury with its entry door open. She wasted no time, sprinting to the aircraft and bounding up the steps into the cabin. Inside, a junior flight crew member began to protest, but Sloane quickly delivered a front kick that sent the aviator flat onto their back.

"Sorry about that," she muttered, already pushing into the cockpit.

Once inside and securing the hatch, Sloane found the radio and switched the transponder to an emergency frequency used exclusively by the CIA for mission-critical communication. She keyed the mic and rattled off a string of code words signaling a priority emergency. Within thirty seconds, she was patched through to Deputy Director Collingswood, who had not yet been briefed on what had transpired after the terror attack at the Grand Prix facility.

Sloane quickly brought him up to speed, letting him know Pavel had taken off and relaying her current coordinates so his jet could be tracked. Collingswood asked if she was alright. Aside from being extremely pissed off, Sloane said she was fine but emphasized that immediate action was critical. If they let Pavel slip away now, it would all be for nothing. Someone like him couldn't be left on the loose.

The Deputy Director told her that NSA satellite operations were already trying to hone in on Pavel's location. But at the speed he was traveling, getting a pinpoint fix was proving nearly impossible. Then Sloane remembered something she'd seen in the stolen papers from Pavel's command center—references to both "Omega" and "Mallorca." She told Collingswood to focus on that location.

He confirmed the lead and told her to hold her position. A Blackhawk chopper was already en route to pick her up from the airfield and would transport her to a nearby NATO station where they could plan their next move.

Sloane bit her tongue, seething with frustration over letting Pavel escape again. But rage wouldn't help right now. She exited the cockpit, paused by the crewman still recovering on the floor, and offered a halfhearted apology with a quick smile and a shake of her head.

Then she stepped out onto the tarmac, listening for the approaching chopper. Off to the northwest, she spotted the incoming Blackhawk and started moving toward the sound.

47

Reactor Two at the Palo Verde Nuclear Power Station in Tolleson, Arizona, was operating at its regular operational temperature when it began a slow, steady rise. Everything appeared normal according to the readouts and gauges, but the control tech on duty noticed that the reactor core was gradually exceeding its normal temperature in small increments. Each increase was just one degree every sixty seconds—almost unnoticeable. But after the first hour, the tech could clearly see that the temperature had risen by a full sixty degrees and was still climbing.

Normal operating temperature for the reactor's 241 core rods was 830 degrees Celsius. The cooling system maintained this by pushing water cooled to between 15 and 30 degrees Celsius over the core to keep the rods within a safe range. At rest, the core sat at 500 degrees but would rise to full operating temperature within thirty minutes. Once there, the system would stabilize the temperature while the reactor heated additional water to create steam, which in turn powered the turbines to generate electricity.

If the cooling system failed or malfunctioned—which was extremely rare—the core temperature would continue to rise to dangerous levels. At 1,230 degrees, the rods would enter a rapid oxidation phase. If not cooled effectively, they would overwhelm the system's capacity and continue to rise toward the catastrophic meltdown threshold of 2,850 degrees. While the probability of such a disaster was one in a billion, it had happened before in places like Three Mile Island, Chernobyl, and Fukushima Daiichi.

At this point, the operating tech wasn't overly concerned. Minor fluctuations in cooling capacity were normal and typically fell within an acceptable range. But as the core temperatures continued to climb into the second hour beyond standard levels—and with the cooling system still indicating proper function—he began to worry. What he didn't know was that a viral code had been released into the control software. It was causing the master cooling valve to remain partially closed, limiting the volume of cooled water flowing across the core and reducing the system's overall effectiveness.

Three hours in, the core temperature had risen to just over 1,000 degrees and was still increasing. In another three hours, it would begin reaching critical levels, triggering an "all hands on deck" emergency. With meltdown looming, the ops tech called in his supervisor to help determine what was going wrong with the cooling system. The tech ran a series of system checks on everything—except the valve itself, which had never before shown any history of failure.

While Palo Verde was dealing with its cooling issue, the Three Gorges Dam hydroelectric plant in China was beginning to experience its own set of problems. The same viral code was affecting the release gates that controlled the flow of water into the massive turbines, which generated an enormous portion of regional power. Brownouts began appearing sporadically across nearby substations. One of these substations served the hotel that was currently hosting the G20 Summit, held downstream from the dam.

For now, it was a minor inconvenience. But within the next three hours, it would become something far more catastrophic. Thermal explosives, planted at twelve points along the base of the dam, were scheduled for remote activation. Once detonated, the explosions would trigger structural rifts, leading to a chain reaction of failures that would compromise the entire dam's integrity. After that, it would only be a matter of time before the full structure collapsed, unleashing a massive flood. The resulting devastation would make what had occurred in Prague look like a minor incident by comparison.

At the G20 Summit site, delegations and attendees were just getting settled into the hotel for the opening of the conference. The general session and keynote by the Chinese Premier were scheduled for the following morning. That would be followed by breakout sessions focused on global economic policy and critical issues like energy equity. But no one at the summit had any inkling that their chances of survival—let alone of achieving success at the conference—were now somewhere between slim and none. The world they knew was on the brink of collapse.

With the dam's flow gates continuing to hold water back, pressure steadily built behind the massive structure. Several inspectors began to notice that the water levels were slowly rising, inching closer to the capacity line near the top of the dam, but no one paid it serious attention. The rising water would only add to the eventual volume released when the dam gave way—an unstoppable flood that would devastate the river and the entire surrounding area.

Meanwhile, systems engineers and technicians were scrambling to troubleshoot the sudden brownouts spreading across the region. No one had a clear explanation for why they were happening. There were no failures at the transformer or switch levels throughout the grid. What the engineers did know was that there had been a significant drop in the total power output from the giant turbines. Meters still showed normal flow and volume of water entering the turbines, but this, too, was part of the false data generated by the viral code.

It wasn't until a lone hydrologist looked at an old analog flow meter—tucked away in a far corner of the last turbine chamber—and saw what was actually going on.

The reading showed that water pressure was just over forty percent of normal capacity. The hydrologist reported the anomaly to his supervisor, only to be told that it must be a faulty "old" gauge, especially since every other system appeared to be functioning normally.

All of this unfolded as brownouts continued and full-scale blackouts began—including at the dam itself. Critical systems continued running thanks to massive backup generators, which kept the facility operating like nothing was wrong. The same was true at other essential institutions: local hospitals, government buildings, and the hotel hosting the G20 Summit were all being kept online by emergency power systems.

At Palo Verde, core temperatures continued rising and were now nearing a tipping point that would trigger emergency protocols. The Zircaloy oxidation process in the nuclear fuel rods was already underway, releasing escalating amounts of heat into the core tank and its heavy water shielding. Readings were nearing 2,000 degrees. With only 850 degrees to go before full meltdown, the danger became very real. If the rods reached meltdown, plumes of radioactive gas would begin escaping into the atmosphere—drifting on prevailing winds directly toward the Phoenix metropolitan area.

At this point, the facility went into full code yellow emergency status. Non-essential personnel were ordered to evacuate. But even as they left, most had a sinking feeling that they might already be in trouble, despite getting away from the plant. Worse still was the dread that their families and loved ones in Phoenix might be in even greater danger. Although a disaster response protocol coordinated by the Central Arizona chapter of the American Red Cross was in place, no one could truly predict the scale of destruction that a meltdown would bring this close to the state's most populated area.

Word began circulating among law enforcement and government officials to begin planning for a massive evacuation. But everyone knew it would be impossible to fully clear the Phoenix area before the nuclear cloud arrived—assuming it came to that. The only remaining hope was containment. If not, this would go down as the next Three Mile Island, only much worse.

The core temperature continued to rise—faster now—and the situation became undeniably critical. The only remaining measure was shutting down Reactors One and Three, a procedure already in motion.

But shutting down the entire plant came with its own consequences. A full shutdown would plunge the region into blackout, with all the problems that came with it: panic, disruption, and a predictable spike in civil unrest. Evacuation orders were being issued across the area, calling for a controlled exodus of the population—if such a thing could be managed. The National Guard was activated to help coordinate traffic and protect citizens from descending into chaos.

Meanwhile, at the Three Gorges Dam, the water had now reached the top of the structure. Power levels had dropped drastically, plunging the surrounding region into darkness. The countryside had gone dark just as the thirty-minute countdown began for the explosives hidden at twelve locations along the dam's base. Once detonated, they would trigger a chain reaction of structural failure, leading to mass flooding and a death toll likely in the hundreds of thousands.

But no one knew. Locals remained in place, assuming the power would be restored shortly. The G20 delegates at the summit hotel were still unaware of the danger. Thanks to backup power, the hotel remained fully lit, and the opening night's welcome reception continued as scheduled.

While both Palo Verde and the Three Gorges Dam faced these escalating but seemingly unrelated crises, the media finally began to report that something was going on. However, most outlets had been kept in the dark to help control public panic. The reporting differed wildly. In the U.S., journalists were beginning to sound the alarm, while in China, the state-run media was following a tight-lipped approach, downplaying—or ignoring—any mention of disruptions.

The events unfolding at both facilities were about to shake the governments, the media, and the people of both nations to their core.

48

As Sloane ducked beneath the rotors of the NATO chopper and climbed aboard, she was pleasantly surprised to see none other than Eddie Stafford, now on the mend. She gave him a little smile, which quickly disappeared when she saw the serious expression on his face. Eddie nodded grimly and said, "So sorry you didn't get him, Sloane," referring to Pavel. He gave her a quick rundown of the estimated devastation caused by Pavel's actions at the Grand Prix. He then told her that plans were already in place to go after him on all fronts and they had begun tracking Pavel since the transponder on his jet was still active.

Sloane felt totally deflated, wondering if her part in the mission was over. She asked Eddie what was in store for her now that she was "done." Eddie gave her a sly smile and let her know she would be heading up a new team to go after Pavel once they determined his final destination. Her only orders now were to "dispatch and dispose with prejudice." Sloane perked up at the news, she would indeed get another shot at taking down this adversary for good, once and for all.

At a maximum speed of just over 220 miles per hour, the Blackhawk chopper would reach the NATO base just outside Teveren, Germany, in approximately two hours. There, Sloane would rendezvous with her new team and board a Transall C-160 aircraft to "who knows where." Once on board, the team would prepare for a HALO jump—"High Altitude, Low Opening"—a free-fall parachute jump from 30,000 feet over their "still to be determined" target zone. At this point, it was anyone's guess where Pavel was headed, but Sloane had a strong hunch about their final destination.

During the flight to the NATO base, Eddie filled Sloane in on her new team members and the basic mission plan, which would be detailed once they had a firm fix on the location. When they finally reached the air base, Sloane was in for another pleasant surprise. Entering the squad room to meet her new team, she saw another familiar face—none other than former Navy SEAL R.H. Saratar, already recovering from surgery on his leg. Giving Sloane a smug, confident look, R.H. smiled and said simply, "Let's get this rabid mutt and put him down for good."

Alongside R.H., Sloane was to be joined by another NATO commando unit, similar to the team that had accompanied her during the assault on Pavel's river yacht, the Uriah. Eddie confirmed Sloane's suspicion that Pavel's jet had landed on the Mediterranean island of Mallorca, at a private airstrip. The landing strip was perched on a bluff overlooking a cove along the eastern shoreline, midway between the resort cities of Cala Romàntica and Cales de Mallorca. A real-time satellite image zoomed in on the target area showed the landing strip, several parked aircraft, and what appeared to be a castle-like structure nearby.

Sloane couldn't help but wonder if this had anything to do with the reference she'd seen to something called "Omega" or "The Collective," but she kept those thoughts to herself. She and the team gathered their gear and headed to the waiting C-160, which was fueling up and would soon take off into the darkening sky toward their jump coordinates.

Everyone was armed with an MK-18 machine gun, a Sig Sauer P365 9mm semi-automatic pistol, a Gerber Mark III survival knife, and wore DEVTAC full-face helmets with ARGUS Gen 3 panoramic night vision in a heads-up AR display, integrated communications, and Kevlar body armor.

The plan was to make the HALO jump at 2100 hours (9:00 p.m.) over an open patch of land approximately two kilometers inland from the landing strip and the castle. Aboard the C-160, the team viewed a real-time infrared satellite feed of the castle and its surrounding grounds, which they would infiltrate once on the ground. Very little was known about the property. Public records indicated it was owned by a Spanish corporation called Terminus, Inc.—but further investigation revealed it was a shell company with a registered office that turned out to be an empty lot in Barcelona.

Inside the castle, the men of the Omega Collective Group were monitoring real-time satellite feeds, hijacked from global networks, showing developments at both Palo Verde and the Three Gorges Dam. Other screens displayed data feeds from failing systems, giving the Collective real-time updates on the crises now reaching their critical tipping points.

A heated discussion was underway: should they pull back at the last second to play saviors, or let the full-scale disasters unfold and position themselves as future liberators? Half the group argued against taking so many lives. The other half, thrilled by the chaos at the Grand Prix, advocated for mass destruction to make their point. Ultimately, a compromise was proposed, limited loss of life, just enough to make a powerful example.

As the vote approached and tension in the room escalated, Pavel suddenly entered, and the room fell silent.

He walked to the sideboard, poured himself a full highball of scotch, raised the glass and said, “Gentlemen? Salute!” Then he drained the glass and poured another. With a drink in hand, Pavel walked to the head of the table where two men sat silently side by side. As he approached, one of the men stood, greeted him warmly, then turned to the other and said, “Well, Uriah, aren’t you going to say hello to your son?”

The man who remained seated was, of course, Uriah Grovzny, Pavel’s father, who loathed the man his son had become. He sat in silence, glaring at him.

Returning the glare, Pavel said dryly, “I see you’re still the same old cheery bastard you’ve always been.”

“And I see you’re still the same evil, sociopathic miscreant you were as a child,” Uriah replied, his face etched with disgust.

“Thank you for finally acknowledging my accomplishments,” Pavel said with a grin. “They’re paving the way for your plans, aren’t they?” He drained the second glass of scotch and hurled it against the stone fireplace, shattering it. “Now… where were we, Father?”

Uriah studied his only child, then gestured to the seat at his left. Turning to the rest of the table, he repeated the question.

“Well, gentlemen… where were we?”

49

The C-160 carrying Sloane, her NATO commando team, and R.H. had leveled off at just above 30,000 feet as the team prepared for their HALO jump while entering Mallorca airspace. NATO Command had already made contact with Spanish authorities and obtained permission for what was described as a training exercise, in coordination with the Spanish National Guard. The Guard had also been briefed by internal security, given just enough information to keep them from asking further questions about the operation.

Spanish security forces would be on standby with their own commando team, ready to assist the NATO unit if needed once the ground operation commenced. They had been told only that the target was a large private estate owned by a corporation, and that an Interpol warrant had been issued for a suspected terrorist possibly present there—likely receiving aid from others on the estate. Officially, this was being framed as an anti-terrorism operation, similar to the one Seal Team Six had conducted in the raid on Osama bin Laden.

Wind conditions over the drop zone were ideal and calm. With the sun now down and only a sliver of moon scheduled to rise later, overall visibility favored the mission. This section of the coast was also far removed from tourist areas, so the incoming aircraft flying in from the Mediterranean would go unnoticed by visitors flocking to the island during this season. As the plane neared the drop point, the crew and team moved into position for their exit.

At their current altitude and trajectory, the jump would begin just under 2.5 kilometers from the target zone. That allowed for an approach angle of approximately forty-five degrees during free fall. They planned to deploy their parachutes at about 1,500 feet and descend into the landing zone (LZ) in a final vertical drop. Once on the ground, the team would regroup, recon the final distance to the castle, and begin the approach on foot.

Toward the rear of the aircraft, the team queued up and awaited the go signal. The rear ramp hydraulics kicked in and began to open under the dull glow of the pre-jump red lamp. When the ramp locked into position, the jumpmaster gave the command to exit.

The red glow turned green, and the team sprinted down the ramp and dove into the night sky.

The jump went perfectly. Traveling at approximately 120 miles per hour, the free fall lasted around thirty seconds before the parachutes deployed. Four to five minutes later, the team hit the LZ, packed up their chutes for rapid stowage, activated their enhanced night vision and comm systems, and began moving toward the target—roughly two kilometers away. The terrain around the castle was wide open, with no visible fencing, but their infrared sensors picked up several camera signatures along the approach.

R.H. took point on the incursion, leveraging his extensive command experience on similar missions. He had also spent time studying satellite imagery and topographical maps to determine the best route in. Amazingly, Eddie Stafford had managed to acquire scanned copies of the original architectural plans for the castle from a local historical society tasked with archiving such documents. This gave Eddie, R.H., Sloane, and the rest of the team a reasonably detailed idea of what they would be facing once they reached the estate.

There were no signs of movement from outside security, but the team assumed internal security was present. Unfortunately, they had no way of knowing how many personnel were inside or what kind of weapons they might have. Most private security forces relied on handguns, but the fact that Pavel Grovzny had been tracked to this location strongly suggested a more heavily armed presence—especially given the mercenaries they had previously encountered in Prague.

Once the team was ready for the long trek across open ground, Sloane sent an encrypted sat phone message to Eddie Stafford, updating him on their status and confirming that they were beginning the approach to the target. The team was using the very latest in IR cloaking technology, integrated into both their uniforms and full-face helmets. This adaptive system used hexagonal plates that altered thermal profiles, along with a cloaking eye-shield on their HUDs that rendered iris tracking and facial recognition ineffective.

This was especially useful as they crossed open terrain with little natural cover and navigated past infrared-monitored security cameras. Another stealth technique the team employed was patterned walking, mimicking the movement patterns of wild animals rather than humans. Each helmet's HUD displayed augmented topographical data and provided a detailed overview of the terrain and the castle itself.

The team could still communicate through integrated comms, but R.H. had decided to rely mostly on hand signals to minimize the chance of detection and preserve the element of surprise. In a tight single-file formation, R.H. led the advance, followed closely by Sloane, with the other six NATO commandos trailing behind. They moved in fifty-meter increments, pausing each time to scan the area for changes.

As they advanced, stop by stop, nothing seemed out of place. Everything was going according to plan.

But as everyone knows, plans can shift in an instant—and that's exactly what happened at 200 meters out.

The sharp crack of a high-powered rifle split the air, and one of the NATO commandos suddenly collapsed to the ground, struck just above the right knee. Everyone immediately hit the deck. Another shot came in seconds later, narrowly missing Sloane—it whined past the left side of her helmet just as she dropped prone to the earth.

Once on the ground, they all began various roll maneuvers, hoping to move out of the line of fire. It was clear that whoever was targeting them was using modified IR to spot them, and was a very skilled shooter. Now, however, the team was well within return-fire range and began scanning for any sign of muzzle flash to initiate a counterattack. They had to be cautious, as too aggressive a response could draw additional attention, and likely more gunfire, from the opposition.

Using the optical magnifier in his helmet's heads-up display, along with night vision enhancement, R.H. zeroed in on some movement on a second-story balustrade. He called out coordinates to another NATO soldier, who trained his sights on the location and waited for confirmation. When the movement repeated, he squeezed the trigger. Less than two seconds later, the movement vanished from view. Unsure whether they'd hit the target or not, the team resumed their approach, leaving the downed commando behind.

This time, they zig-zagged in a low crouch and sprinted forward another hundred meters, then hit the ground and rolled before reassessing. Seeing no further movement and hearing no new gunshots, they again broke into a crouched dash, this time to within fifty meters of the castle, and repeated the process. They were fairly certain that the earlier shooter had been in radio contact, and if they had gone silent, reinforcements were likely on the way.

That thought had barely formed when a new burst of automatic fire sprayed the area, erratic but close enough to force the team back down. They quickly returned fire with carefully aimed shots that began to hit their marks. During the firefight, Sloane transmitted another encrypted message calling for backup support. As gunfire continued to trade between the NATO team and the castle's defenders, more enemy personnel began arriving.

From a quick glance up at a rampart, R.H. spotted men attempting to deploy a portable bank of LED work lights. He immediately opened fire, forcing the men to abandon the attempt. As the NATO team laid down increasingly accurate fire, it gave them the cover they needed to inch closer and closer to the front entrance of the castle. Still, they had to move swiftly and cautiously, as enemy fire remained constant and seemed to be intensifying. Before long, the team found themselves pinned down under heavier fire.

Suddenly, in the distance, the unmistakable thump-thump-thump of two military helicopters could be heard. Two Huey gunships came in low over the coast, each carrying Spanish security commandos. As the firefight continued near the castle, defenders managed to activate one of the LED lights, which bathed the field in harsh illumination, exposing the NATO team just as they reached a shrub line that provided their first real cover.

But the moment that light came on, both Hueys swooped in and opened fire with .50-caliber Gatling guns, shredding the light and killing the men beside it. The choppers raked the entire balcony where most of the enemy fire was coming from. Using their own high-powered spotlights to illuminate the castle's front, the helicopters laid down serious suppression, allowing R.H., Sloane, and the remaining five NATO commandos to make a coordinated push toward a twenty-foot wall they needed to scale.

As the Hueys hovered, spotlights blazing and ropes dropping for Spanish commando deployment, a rocket-propelled grenade suddenly whooshed through the air. It struck the fuel cell of one of the helicopters, which exploded into flames before anyone could escape. The six-man team aboard the second chopper managed to rappel safely to the ground. A second RPG appeared—but the .50-caliber fire from the remaining chopper cut down the shooter and detonated the grenade mid-launch, taking out five nearby defenders.

Under the cover of this chaos, Sloane and her team reached the wall, moved left around the corner, and began scaling it using grappling hooks and rope. The Spanish commandos provided a new wave of cover fire that caught the defenders off guard, forcing them to retreat in the face of superior firepower from both the troops and the airborne Gatling guns.

As the defenders withdrew from the immediate area, Sloane and the NATO team finished their ascent, climbed over the top, and dropped down inside the castle grounds. They quickly moved toward a large set of oaken doors positioned at the center of the interior wall.

50

Around the conference table inside, while the battle raged on, the man sitting next to Uriah gestured to another nearby. “Claude, the laptop, please, if you will.” Claude placed the laptop in front of him, he opened the lid and turned to Uriah.

“Well, Uriah, are you sure about this?”

Uriah snorted. “Of course. Save the nuclear plant for another day and let Three Gorges go.”

The other man calmly stated, “You know that many more people will die there, don’t you?”

Uriah retorted, “Yes, but it will be a drop in the bucket by Asian standards. And besides, it will also take care of that damned group of imbeciles at the G20 Summit. Who knows—it might just soften the ROC’s impression of other nations when the rest of the civilized world, including us, comes to their aid after this seemingly natural disaster of the seismic type. Just do it.”

The man at the head of the table simply nodded and brought up a control panel with the words “Palo Verde” at the top of the screen. He could see from the readout that the reactor was nearing its failure threshold, so he quickly entered an eight-digit code and hit *Enter*. This immediately stopped the viral code from continuing its destructive path and opened the main valves of the cooling system, allowing the overheating reactor core to begin slowly stabilizing.

He then switched to a new window labeled “Three Gorges”. This screen displayed water levels on one side and a timer on the other, set to twenty minutes, with a button below labeled “Execute.”

Moving the cursor over the button and clicking it, he looked at Uriah with a questioning expression.

Uriah simply nodded.

The man hit Return, and the countdown began. Meanwhile, Pavel Grovzny sat transfixed, his face caught somewhere between comedy and tragedy as he watched the exchange between the two men.

At Palo Verde, amidst the chaos of last-minute moves to shut down the other two reactors and evacuate the facility, the operations tech still monitoring the core suddenly noticed the temperature had stopped rising. A minute later, it began to fall—barely, but enough to be noticed. Still, he stood by as if ready to run, though he knew that wouldn't make much difference if the worst happened.

Another minute passed. The temperature was definitely dropping now. He called out to his supervisor, who came over quickly.

By the time the supervisor reached his station, the core temperature had dropped by fifty degrees—just enough to bring it within a marginally controllable range. Grabbing the phone, the supervisor contacted higher-ups and began issuing status updates. First came the Governor's office, then the Department of Public Safety and Arizona Department of Transportation. After that, he called the National Guard unit in Phoenix and every first responder and law enforcement agency in the county to give them a real-time progress report. He also contacted the media, urging discretion in releasing any updates until the situation could be fully assessed.

After thirty tense minutes of nonstop monitoring, both the operations tech and his supervisor confirmed that the cooling system was functioning and that an unmitigated disaster had just been avoided. They breathed a deep sigh of relief. While the core continued to cool, full restoration was still a long way off, especially since reactors one and three remained shut down.

The cause of the failure was still unknown, and that mystery made everyone nervous. Until they could assess the full system, the risk remained. Could it happen again? Could the other reactors be at risk? A complete diagnostic and systems check across the entire plant would be required. That meant further outages, rolling brownouts, and possibly a public backlash.

And then there was the PR nightmare: how much could they really tell the public? How much should they reveal about how close they had come to the worst nuclear disaster since Three Mile Island?

Outside the castle's massive entry doors, Sloane, R.H., and the rest of the NATO team—along with the Spanish commandos—were discussing the best strategy for breaching the structure. Meanwhile, the remaining helicopter had landed nearby, rotors idling in case of an emergency exfiltration.

Sloane and R.H. decided to blow the hinges off one of the massive doors to create an entry point. At the same time, another team would attempt to scale up to a balcony on the next level to locate an alternate access route.

Inside the castle, the internal security team was scrambling to set up barricades, anticipating the inevitable breach. These ancient, medieval doors had withstood sieges from the time of the Romans, the Vandals, the Moors, the conquest by James I of Aragon, and even the Spanish Civil War. They had never been breached—so morale among the defenders was high.

Outside, the NATO team applied EPR-2X plastic explosives in a shaped charge designed to blow inward along the length of the door's outer edge. After attaching the primer cord, they took cover against the wall, crouched in single file.

"Fire in the hole!" someone shouted, and the detonator snapped.

The explosion rocked the wall, echoing through the castle. As the smoke cleared, they saw that the massive door had been partially blown from its hinges—enough for a one-by-one entry.

Using a periscope, the team scanned the interior. Less than twenty-five feet inside stood the defensive barricade. Several of the guards had clearly been standing when the blast hit—oak splinters from the ancient door had torn into them like shrapnel from a cannon broadside. They were screaming and moaning, writhing in pain.

Without pause, the NATO team tossed four high-explosive grenades into the entry. Two landed just behind the barricade.

A heartbeat of silence.

Then the grenades exploded in a tight sequence, tearing apart the barricade and killing or maiming nearly every defender who hadn't already been downed by the door explosion.

Sloane and R.H. immediately led the charge through the breach, dispatching the last of the opposition without hesitation. In under thirty seconds, the first line of defense was down.

They scanned the room. Three large archways stood on the far side of the grand entry hall, each leading deeper into the castle. The team split up into two-man squads, with one commando staying behind to guard against reinforcements from the outside.

Meanwhile, the Spanish special forces team, who had scaled a third-level balcony, were under siege themselves. They'd managed to cut through the bars on a high window, only to be met by withering fire from two American-made M-60 machine guns operated by entrenched internal security forces.

51

Sloane, R.H., and the other NATO commandos moved cautiously down long corridors, anticipating an ambush at any moment. Nerves were on edge. Despite having archived architectural plans, they had never been able to get a reliable sense of where people might be located in the castle, so in many ways, they were flying blind.

Deep inside the castle, the men of the Omega Collective Group watched a private satellite feed of the Three Gorges Dam hydroelectric plant and its surrounding area, with a superimposed countdown overlaying the image. For these men seated around the conference table, it felt like staring at some massive digital painting, except for the occasional blinking light or movement of a vehicle on screen.

In Hubei, China, at the dam, several workers had begun to grow alarmed at the rising water level, which was nearing the overflow threshold. Even more troubling was that the excess water wasn't being diverted through the usual overflow pipelines. Considering it had been dry for some time, the climbing water levels seemed like a mystery—until they discovered that the flow gates across the entire complex had stopped functioning. Emergency hydro teams were called in to inspect the systems and confirmed the issue: the gates were closed. But the real mystery was why. Attempts to override the automatic controls proved unsuccessful—the system was unresponsive.

Back in the castle, the countdown had ticked down to five minutes when a phone on the table rang. The man sitting beside Uriah picked it up, said only "I see," and then stood.

"Gentlemen," he addressed the rest of the collective around the table, "it appears we've had a security breach. NATO and Spanish Special Forces are presently making their way in our direction. I believe it's time for you all to leave, if you please." He paused and pointed toward a wall that suddenly slid open to reveal a state-of-the-art elevator. "Your lift awaits to take you safely from here."

Several of the men began to protest—they wanted to stay to witness the "show" on the big screen. But the man in charge held up both hands and spoke in a more forceful tone.

"Gentlemen! Enough! Time is ticking down, and unless you want to get caught up in something uncomfortable, I highly suggest you leave now while you still can. Now, go!"

The men entered the elevator, leaving behind only Uriah, Pavel Grovzny, and the man in charge. Once the doors shut, the remaining three turned their attention back to the screen as the counter ticked down into its final minute.

"So, what's next?" Pavel asked flippantly.

Uriah answered smugly, "We let the dam go and transmit our first international press release about finding the viral code in various power systems, including Palo Verde, and how we neutralized it. Then, we'll reach out for the whole world to see, as we offer our assistance to the ROC in the wake of this 'earthquake' and the tragic catastrophe that has just struck."

All eyes turned to the screen as the countdown hit zero. A faint disturbance rippled across the water on the reservoir side of the dam.

At Three Gorges, the first sign that something was terribly wrong came in the form of a mild tremor—a small earthquake that would normally be of no real concern. But with its epicenter appearing to be directly beneath the dam, alarm bells began ringing. A hissing sound followed. Small cracks appeared along the release side of the dam, with water beginning to seep through.

The seepage accelerated.

It quickly became clear the dam's structure had been compromised. It now looked like an actual earthquake had struck.

Suddenly, one of the cracks vibrated violently and widened. Water poured through. Then another crack did the same, and another. The entire structure began to tremble violently, like it was being shaken by some invisible hand.

Then it happened.

The first section of the dam exploded outward with a thunderous boom, releasing a massive surge of water. The concrete began to crumble. Each previously cracked section failed in rapid succession. All at once, the dam burst apart, sending thirty-two million acre-feet of water crashing down the Yangtze River, obliterating everything in its path.

Less than five miles downstream, the Three Gorges Conference Center and Hotel—where the G20 Summit was scheduled to begin in a matter of hours—was wiped from existence. No warning. No chance. A massive wall of water crashed into the complex, killing everyone inside.

By sheer luck, a small elite group of G20 delegates—including the Presidents of the United States, France, Germany, Turkey, and Mexico, along with the Prime Ministers of the United Kingdom, Italy, Japan, India, and Canada—had been attending a late-night dinner at a location far from the flood zone. They survived with no knowledge of the catastrophe that had just unfolded.

That ignorance didn't last long.

Within moments, their secure phones began buzzing as aides rushed to deliver the horrific news. It was quickly decided that the summit would be canceled. The surviving world leaders were escorted to waiting vehicles, which sped toward Yichang Sanxia Airport, about fifty-five kilometers from the dam.

Inside the castle, the three men stared at the screen in silence, transfixed by the images unfolding before them—destruction so complete it looked like a special-effects sequence from a Hollywood blockbuster. When the dam finally collapsed in full, there was a collective gasp.

Then silence.

And then, laughter.

It rose slowly—from Pavel—until it echoed through the stone chamber. He was giddy, visibly euphoric.

Uriah glared at him in disgust. "Shut up, Pavel! There is nothing joyful about this. Not even from your distorted view of the world."

Pavel snorted. "Really, Father? And what do you feel? Pure tragedy? This was your plan. You just wiped out a million innocent people. Don't pretend to stand on some imaginary moral high ground."

He continued, voice rising. "At least what I did in Prague took out people who needed a lesson—the power elite, the smug aristocracy. Those who think they're better than everyone else. That was justice."

He turned and glared at the man seated beside Uriah, whose face was still hidden in shadow.

The man spoke calmly, his tone low and deliberate.

"Pavel, my dear misguided young sycophant… don't you realize? Our war is not against individual lives. It's against soulless governments—systems that grind people down. If we kill, it is not for revenge or shock value. There is a higher purpose—a plateau you clearly don't comprehend. Your obsession with pain and spectacle cheapens the cause."

He leaned forward slightly. "So either get a grip on your glee, or consider yourself no longer part of what comes next."

There was a long silence.

Then the man turned back to the computer screen. "Now, if you don't mind, it's time to send out the press release."

He hit Send.

The communique went live—broadcasting across global networks.

The modern world was now officially on alert.

And it had just been introduced to the Omega Collective Group.

52

The massive wall of floodwaters racing down the Yangtze River from the collapsed dam carved a half-mile-wide path of destruction, erasing everything in its wake—offices, houses, factories, neighborhoods, and entire villages. Its force was indescribable. As it tore through the valley, it surged toward the city of Yichang, sixty kilometers downstream, home to over 1.6 million people—all directly in the water's path. It swept away crop fields, fishing docks, roadside food stalls, and marketplaces, destroying critical pieces of what was once the world's third-largest economy. When the flood hit Yichang, it flattened everything, swallowing the city and most of its citizens.

As the torrent cascaded violently down the river valley, leaving devastation in its wake, a different kind of disaster unfolded—total darkness. The power once generated by the world's largest hydroelectric facility vanished. With the power grid crippled, even the simplest devices were useless. In an instant, 126 million Chinese men, women, and children were left without electricity. Roughly ten percent of the country's entire power grid went offline.

Most people didn't even know it yet. It was late at night, and many were asleep as outages rolled through community after community, city after city.

By dawn, it became obvious that a major power failure had occurred, but no one knew how vast it was. Communications were down too—cell towers, transmission sites, even emergency systems had gone silent. A mere trickle of information filtered out to the general population. Cities like Wuhan, Nanjing, Shanghai, and even Beijing heard vague reports of a seismic event and some sort of destruction, but no one understood its true scope. Emergency crews, including military units, were dispatched to assess the damage and the death toll.

Meanwhile, an emergency beacon flashed from a tower upstream of the dam, powered by its own backup supply. The signal was transmitted to a special uplink station equipped with solar-charged battery backups. This system was tied to seismic sensors that automatically alerted global geological agencies whenever a tremor above 5.5 on the Richter scale occurred.

The initial tremor at the dam, just before the collapse, registered 6.2 and triggered the beacon. Satellites began monitoring the area automatically. No one paid much attention—until the second wave of seismic activity began. A series of jolts pushed readings up to 8.2, stopping and starting in a pattern that drew the attention of a team of geologists and a volcanologist in Hawaii. They switched to infrared views of the area and watched in horror as the dam collapsed and a monstrous wave surged downriver.

The team leader immediately contacted the U.S. Geological Survey to report what they had witnessed. Within ten minutes, every major government and media outlet in the world was alerted to the catastrophe unfolding in China.

By morning, international agencies were in contact with Chinese officials, offering help in any form—search and rescue, emergency medical support, food and water, shelters, and evacuation assistance.

And then came a message from a group no one had heard of before.

The Omega Collective Group.

To: The People's Republic of China Government

Attn: The State Council and Disaster Response Agencies

Subject: Offer of Immediate Disaster Relief Assistance Following Earthquake at the Three Gorges Dam

Esteemed Members of the Government of the People's Republic of China,

We, the Omega Collective Group, a high-tech and philanthropic organization dedicated to the advancement of human well-being, extend our deepest condolences for the devastating earthquake that has struck the Three Gorges Dam region. In these extraordinarily difficult times, we stand in solidarity with the Chinese people and express our unwavering commitment to assist in every possible way.

Our organization possesses unparalleled resources, cutting-edge technology, and a global network of experts in disaster response, infrastructure rehabilitation, medical care, humanitarian aid, and financial mobilization. We are fully prepared to support efforts to mitigate this catastrophe and assist in long-term recovery.

Our proposed assistance includes, but is not limited to:

1. Advanced Search and Rescue Operations

2. Medical and Emergency Relief

3. Reconstruction and Infrastructure Solutions

4. Logistical Support and Resource Distribution

5. Psychological Support and Long-Term Recovery

We are deeply respectful of the sovereignty and cultural values that guide disaster management in the People's Republic of China. As such, we offer our aid in the spirit of cooperation and mutual respect. We are honored to coordinate with the appropriate government and humanitarian organizations to ensure our assistance is timely, respectful, and effective.

Please contact us via the channels listed below to initiate deployment. We are prepared to mobilize personnel, equipment, and resources immediately upon receiving your guidance and approval.

Together, we can work toward a swift, comprehensive recovery—rebuilding not only infrastructure, but also hope.

With deepest respect and solidarity,

Omega Collective Group

Global Headquarters

Phone: +1 (555) 283-6719

Email: mailto:disasterresponse@omega.collective.group.org

Website: http://www.omega.collective.group.org

Chinese officials immediately responded, accepting the aid and inviting this mysterious new player to coordinate relief efforts however they saw fit.

Back at the castle in Mallorca, Uriah Grovzny hung up the receiver at the conference table, turned toward the shadowed man beside him, and smiled.

"Well," he said, "that wasn't really so bad, was it?"

53

Sloane and the NATO commandos slowly made their way down what seemed like a labyrinth of hallways and corridors inside the castle, as did the other two teams that had breached the massive outer doors. They stopped frequently, listening for anything that sounded remotely like resistance from the internal security forces. So far, no such resistance had emerged for any of the three teams. Each pair took a different section of the castle: one NATO team moved through the northern wing, R.H. and his partner advanced through the southern wing, and Sloane and her teammate proceeded up the center of the castle.

All three teams remained in radio contact but switched to a keyed code protocol to eliminate verbal chatter, wary that even whispered communication might echo through the eerily quiet manse. Every step—despite soft-soled boots—made just enough noise to be noticeable if anyone were listening closely. For nearly a hundred more feet, they encountered only silence.

And then, the proverbial shit hit the fan.

All three teams came under fire simultaneously—from both single-shot and automatic weapons. Most of it came from defenders firing low from behind massive stone columns, darting out from either side to lay down suppressing fire, then retreating back behind their ancient cover. These towering obelisks, carved from local quarry stone, had stood since the castle's original construction—and now served as makeshift bunkers in a deadly exchange.

Fortunately for Sloane, R.H., and the rest of the commandos, they too had access to nearby cover. Fire was returned in calculated bursts from behind their own columns.

In each corridor, the defenders had a two-to-one or three-to-one advantage in numbers—but that didn't seem to faze the assault teams. They pressed forward using leapfrog tactics, covering one another while moving from column to column, trying to close the distance and deploy flashbang grenades to level the playing field.

In the northern wing, one commando crouched, readying to toss a flashbang. But as he leaned out, a hail of bullets shredded the column next to him, disorienting him. He dropped the grenade—it went off next to him with a deafening blast. Staggering to his feet, he was struck almost immediately—twelve rounds tore through him, killing him before he hit the floor.

His partner, now alone and pinned down, broke radio silence. The element of surprise was already gone. "I'm pinned!" he barked into the comms, reporting his status to both Sloane and R.H.

In the south wing, R.H. had better luck. He managed to roll a flashbang into position between a column and the wall. The result was devastating—two defenders stumbled into view, disoriented by the blast. Through the drifting smoke, R.H. and his teammate dropped all three with well-placed bursts. Seizing the moment, they dashed along the wall to the next set of columns. Three more defenders popped out to return fire, unaware of the advance. Four sharp bursts from R.H. and the NATO soldier dropped them instantly.

With the corridor clear, R.H. radioed to Sloane and the remaining teams and began looking for a route toward the northern wing to assist the pinned-down commando.

Meanwhile, in the castle's central corridor, Sloane and her teammate had taken out two defenders and wounded a third. Her sharpshooting and his steady cover fire kept the remaining attackers at bay, reducing them to wild, erratic bursts that only peppered the walls. It was clear to Sloane they had gained an edge, and she seized it—hurling a flashbang between the last set of columns before initiating her next move.

The grenade landed perfectly.

But just before it detonated, her partner dashed forward—and was struck down. A stray bullet from one of the defenders pierced the gap beneath his full-face helmet and tore through his carotid artery. He bled out in seconds.

Sloane didn't hesitate.

The flashbang's effect still rippling through the corridor, she stormed forward and dropped the remaining three defenders with surgical precision. With her path now clear, she pressed deeper into the castle, determined to reach the heart of it all—and, most of all, to find Pavel Grovzny.

Passing through the opulent great hall that overlooked the seaside cliffs, Sloane came upon a narrow stairwell descending into a plainer, more utilitarian section of the structure. The lavish trim and grandeur vanished as the space tightened into a featureless corridor. Only one door stood at the far end—long, dim, and lit by a single bulb overhead. The air was dry, still. Not a sound.

Sloane removed her helmet and listened. Nothing. She checked her weapons: her MK-18 was out of ammo. She placed it quietly against the wall and drew her Sig Sauer 9mm and her Gerber survival knife. One flashbang remained on her vest, but she kept both hands on the pistol—ready for anything. If needed, she could toss the grenade after breaching the room, but she had no idea what lay beyond the door.

That was the worst part: not knowing. In her experience, the unknown was always the biggest threat. Her heart thumped harder as she crept toward the door, each step deliberate, each breath measured. Just as she reached for the doorknob, she heard voices.

Raised voices—agitated. Three distinct tones: one deep and deliberate, one soft-spoken, and the third younger and sharper, growing louder.

Pavel.

That bastard.

Her pulse quickened again as she leaned closer, trying to discern the words. Most of it was muffled—except for one phrase that cut through clearly: "Price to pay."

Followed by Pavel's sarcastic laugh.

He was nearing the door.

This was it.

Sloane tightened her grip on the pistol, turned the knob slowly, and prepared to make her final move—on Pavel, and on whoever else waited in the room beyond.

Even if it was the last move she would ever make.

54

With the Sig in her right hand at the ready, Sloane thrust open the door and took a shooter's stance, sweeping the room back and forth as she entered. She spotted Uriah and the man in shadow, both turning to see who had just burst into their chamber. Neither man uttered a word as Sloane, not seeing who she had expected, demanded firmly, “Where is he? Where is Pavel?”

Suddenly, a voice came from behind the now-closing door.

“I’m right behind you, Harper, and if you move, I’ll put you down just like the stupid bitch you’ve turned out to be.”

Sloane froze at the sound. She slowly turned to face the man she now hated more than anyone in her life and replied sarcastically,

"Well, Pavel, looks like you're involved in something a little more than just Prague. And these two?" she gestured at the other men.

Pavel stared at her with pure hatred and growled, "They are of no concern to you. I'm the only one you need to worry about—but that worry will be over in short order when I finally take care of you. Now drop your gun."

Sloane paused, considering a move. But Pavel suddenly fired, nicking her in the right arm just outside her shoulder. She winced but maintained her grip on the Sig.

"Drop the gun," Pavel said coldly. "Or the next one goes in the middle of your forehead."

Breathing slowly, eyes steely, Sloane stayed calm, refusing to give him the satisfaction of a reaction—something that slightly unnerved him. She lowered the nine-millimeter to her side, and crouching as if to drop it, suddenly flung it upward—hard—toward Pavel's face. At the same time, she rushed him low like an NFL linebacker, crashing into his midsection with her left shoulder as he fired off an errant shot.

Caught completely off guard, Pavel had the wind partially knocked out of him. Sloane stepped back and lashed out with a front kick to his abdomen, doubling him over and causing him to lose his grip on his gun.

She pivoted into a sidekick aimed at his head, but Pavel managed to block it. Grabbing her ankle, he twisted it and shoved with all his strength, sending Sloane crashing to the ground in front of him.

He lunged. Sloane rolled, but not before catching a fist to the side of her head. The blow stunned her, and Pavel was on her in a flash, locking her in a chokehold. Gasping, Sloane bit his arm hard—savagely—and he loosened his grip with a howl. She slammed her head backward into his face, hearing the crack of cartilage as she broke his nose.

Screaming in pain, Pavel brought both hands to his face. Temporarily blinded, he gave Sloane the chance to roll free and stagger away, gasping for air.

She spotted the Sig on the floor and dove for it just as Pavel started rising. But as she aimed, a sharp click echoed through the chamber—a gun cocking.

"Enough!" Uriah's booming voice rang out.

Sloane froze, turning to face him. The elder Grovzny stood, a classic German Luger pistol pointed directly at her. Knowing she had no option, Sloane dropped the Sig and stood with a look of resigned defiance.

"Now, young lady," Uriah said, "if you'll please kick that gun toward my son and step over to the wall."

The word "son" hit her like a bolt. For a moment, Sloane's face showed clear shock. Uriah and Pavel—father and son. She felt a wave of astonishment and dismay, wondering if the father might be even more of a psychopath than the son. But it no longer mattered.

She complied, nudging the Sig across the room and moving to the wall beside the door.

Pavel retrieved the weapon as Uriah rose and addressed him. "Well, Pavel, do you think maybe—just maybe—you can do this without screwing it up? Or would you rather I take care of what you were supposed to do in Prague?"

The man in shadow rapped his knuckles lightly on the massive conference table and spoke calmly. "That's enough, Uriah. Pavel knows what must be done—and he'll do it. Maybe not exactly the way we'd planned, but it will suffice. Now, if you please—you've a plane to Rio to catch. The calls in response to our press release will be coming in soon, and you'll need to take the lead as discussed. The Collective is counting on you."

Uriah gave a mocking half-smile, his tone sarcastic. "Of course, Mr. Chairman. As you wish."

He turned and walked across the room as the elevator doors slid open. Without another glance, he stepped inside. The doors closed.

Pavel now walked with deliberate steps toward Sloane, gun raised.

"Turn around," he said. "Kneel. Face the wall."

Sloane slowly did as instructed. But as she knelt, Pavel rushed her and began pistol-whipping her—again and again—his rage boiling over. "This ignorant, cretinous ne'er-do-well has been the bane of my existence," he shouted. "She came this close to ruining everything in Prague!" He held up his thumb and forefinger.

The man at the table raised his voice sharply. "That's enough."

But Pavel didn't stop.

"I said, stop!" the man repeated, this time with cold authority. "She didn't succeed, did she? And the only reason she got close was because of your self-importance and overblown ego. You were sloppy—at every turn. That's why we never truly trusted you to be part of Omega in the first place. Now stop the histrionics and do what you're told. Finish it."

Pavel turned away from Sloane, pointed the gun at the man in shadow, and sneered, "You old has-been, failure of a spy. Between you and my father, you've both held me back from everything I planned to further this organization's goals. You always thought you were superior to me, but you've always been kidding yourself. You will never succeed without my actions. If it weren't for what I did in Prague, you wouldn't have had any cover for the cowardly acts you instituted. Without me, the Omega Collective Group would be powerless. I'm the reason you can make your future plans a reality, and you should never forget that you owe me a debt of gratitude. You all owe me, instead of barking orders at me like I'm some lackey or lapdog."

Calmly, the other man scoffed and replied, "But you are a lackey, Pavel. Don't you realize you were always just another puppet on our strings? Even your own father recognized that. In fact, he's the one who made it all happen by putting you in charge of Prague. We all knew we needed a scapegoat—and you were the natural choice, because of your reputation as a sociopathic mercenary. An easy-to-blame asset that could be pointed to for all the destruction and death that's befallen so many—starting with the Grand Prix. We even planted just enough incriminating evidence to aim the world's finger directly at you. Now, every law enforcement agency and government will be hunting you like the rabid dog you are."

Pavel's face turned red with rage. He pointed the gun at the man and screamed, "You're all nothing without me! Do you hear me? Nothing!" He raised the gun to shoot—but then expelled a sharp breath and froze, his expression shifting to shock and disbelief as blood welled at the corner of his mouth.

Behind him, Sloane had plunged her Gerber survival knife through the back of his neck and given it a twist. She shrieked at him as she pulled the blade free and plunged it into his back again—and again—then reached around and slashed his throat from ear to ear, still screaming. Even after he collapsed, Sloane pounced on him and stabbed him over and over in the torso until the man at the table shouted, "Dove, that's enough! Dove! He's gone and will never harm you again."

Sloane stopped and stared as the man emerged into the light—revealing a face she hadn't seen in years.

"Daddy? Daddy, it can't be. How can it be you? You were killed by the KGB."

Frank Harper stepped forward. "No, Dove. They never killed me. They just turned me—after our own government turned their backs on me. And then, just like our own, they betrayed me and my dear friend Uriah. Cast us out, discarded us like trash. We had to go into hiding for years, until we formed our own plans for revenge against all governments that treat their assets like garbage—thrown away when no longer useful."

He raised a gun and pointed it at Sloane.

"And now," he said, "I'm afraid you are just another piece of the puzzle. Another part of the problem."

Sloane's eyes welled with tears. "But I'm your daughter."

Frank Harper smiled faintly. "I lost my daughter years ago when the U.S. government betrayed me. I lost everything. You, your mother, our lives, and all that I believed in. And now it must come to an end."

He raised the gun and took aim.

As he slowly squeezed the trigger, Sloane saw his hand tremble. In that split second, she dove to the floor and grabbed the Sig from beside Pavel's body. Frank fired, but missed. Sloane came up firing and put a round straight through his heart.

Frank Harper's eyes widened. His mouth opened as if to speak, but no words came. He toppled to the ground—dead.

Tears streamed down Sloane's face as she let out a wail of anguish—a raw, uncontainable cry like a mother losing her child in wartime. She knelt beside her father's body, staring into the face she had once known in happier times, and bowed her head, sobbing.

Suddenly, she heard footsteps running down the hallway toward the chamber. She turned, preparing to confront whatever came next, no longer caring whether she lived or died.

Then she heard a voice—familiar, reassuring—speaking to others.

It was R.H.

She let out a breath, a heavy sigh of exhausted relief, as R.H. and two of the NATO commandos entered the chamber and found her kneeling beside the body of her now-dead father.

55

R.H. leaned down and gently touched Sloane on her injured shoulder. He gave her a questioning look, as if to ask if she was okay. She nodded silently and glanced toward the bloodied, lifeless body of Pavel Grovzny. R.H. walked over to the corpse and turned it over with the toe of his boot. His eyes widened slightly at the extent of the damage Sloane had inflicted in her rage. He shook his head and looked back at her—she appeared to be in a bit of shock.

Motioning to the two commandos, he instructed, "Check the entire room for any intel that might be here." Then he returned to Sloane and helped her to her feet.

"So… who is he?" he asked.

Sloane, finally regaining some composure, replied in a flat, debriefing-like tone, "His name is Frank Harper, and he used to be a CIA operative many years ago." She looked down at the body and paused. "He was also my father."

R.H. said nothing for a few seconds. Then he asked, "Is this how you found him?"

Sloane gave a quick, small shake of her head but said nothing.

R.H. glanced down and saw the gun still in Frank Harper's hand. Looking back at the shaken Sloane, he decided he'd asked enough questions for now.

"Come on, Sloane. There's nothing left for you here."

He nodded toward the commandos, who were now holding a laptop they'd recovered from the conference table. R.H. touched

Sloane's injured arm and, motioning toward the door, added, "Let's get out of here and get some first aid for that scratch."

Sloane forced something halfway between a grimace and a smile and nodded in agreement. As she, R.H., and the two commandos made their way to the door, she paused. Pulling out a miniature HD pocket cam, she quickly captured still images and video clips to ID both Pavel and Frank Harper, then followed the others down the hallway toward the waiting chopper for exfiltration to a NATO station at the "Jaime I" Army Base in Valencia, Spain.

Finding no resistance on their way out, Sloane, R.H., and the commandos rendezvoused with three other members of the Spanish special forces and were soon aboard the helicopter, flying away from the castle and the Mallorca coastline.

Once they were airborne, a call was patched through to Sloane from Eddie Stafford. She informed him that she had completed her mission and taken down Pavel. She also recounted the shocking revelations about her father Frank—and Uriah, who had turned out to be Pavel's father. Eddie listened carefully, clearly astonished by the news about Frank Harper.

He spoke in a consoling tone, admitting that Frank and Uriah had worked together years ago—and that Uriah had been the double agent who turned Frank for the Soviets.

Sloane told him she overheard something about "the Collective" and a mention of Rio before Uriah disappeared. She also let him know they had found a laptop and that it would be sent via military transport to Andrews Air Force Base and on to Langley for forensic analysis.

Eddie thanked her and said, "Get some rest, Sloane. I'll be in touch. Oh—and Collingswood will meet you in Valencia for an official debrief."

He ended the call, and Sloane exhaled, closed her eyes, and managed to doze off.

The next morning, every major newswire and media outlet released a story based on a press release from the Omega Collective Group regarding a global cyber threat:

FOR IMMEDIATE RELEASE

The Omega Collective Group Uncovers Global Cyber Threat Targeting Power Grids, Teams Up with Governments to Neutralize Threat

Present Day – Global

The Omega Collective Group, a leading high-tech cybersecurity organization, has uncovered a covert and sophisticated viral bug embedded in critical power systems around the world. This unprecedented cyberattack, designed to disrupt and destabilize the power grids of major nations, was discovered and neutralized by The Omega Collective Group's cybersecurity experts in a groundbreaking operation.

The malware—highly advanced and nearly undetectable—had the potential to cause widespread blackouts, disrupt essential services, and damage power-generation systems. However, thanks to The Omega Collective's cutting-edge tools and swift response, the threat was eliminated before it could be unleashed.

> “This was a global crisis in the making,” said Dr. Elara Thorne, CEO of The Omega Collective Group. “Our team worked tirelessly to detect, understand, and eliminate this threat. We recognized its catastrophic potential and are proud to have stopped it in its tracks. However, our work is far from over.”

Given the magnitude of the threat, the organization is now collaborating with governments around the world to fortify infrastructure and implement robust countermeasures. In the coming days, they will help roll out defensive protocols, monitoring systems, and new cybersecurity strategies to ensure long-term resilience.

The group’s actions have earned praise from cybersecurity leaders and global officials alike.

> “Cybersecurity is a critical pillar of national security,” said Max Greenfield, Director of Cybersecurity Affairs for the U.S. Department of Homeland Security. “The Omega Collective’s proactive engagement has been invaluable in preventing disaster.”

Ongoing efforts to remove residual malware are underway, with The Omega Collective Group providing round-the-clock support. Their experts are also assisting international partners in applying the lessons from this near-crisis to future defense models.

> “The partnership between Omega and global governments shows what’s possible when public and private sectors unite,” Dr. Thorne continued. “We remain committed to safeguarding civilization from increasingly sophisticated threats.”

For media inquiries, please contact:

Sarah Haines

Public Relations Director

The Omega Collective Group

Email: pr@omegacollectivegroup.com

Phone: +1 (555) 455-0001

Three weeks later, after some physical and emotional healing, Sloane stood once more in front of a full-length mirror inside the Prada Design Lab in Milan. Final adjustments were being made to the stunning new designer gown she would model for an exclusive show. Under a cover story about an automobile accident that had kept her from attending the Vogue shoot in Bali, the prestigious Italian fashion house had welcomed her back with open arms. They were thrilled she would be joining them for Fashion Week in New York in just two weeks.

As electronic dance music began booming across the venue, Sloane gently touched the healing scar from her gunshot wound, took her place at the front of the line, and—with a nod from the stage manager—stepped onto the runway to a sea of camera flashes and applause.

Later, backstage, seated before her makeup mirror and changing out of the designer gown, she stared at the seemingly expressionless face in the glass. Then her phone rang—its distinctive ringtone cutting through the backstage hum.

It was Eddie Stafford.

Prologue

"Uriah's Heap"

Approximately one kilometer south of Praia da Joatinga on the coast of Brazil lies the deserted island of Ilha Alfavaca. Beneath a thick canopy of trees, hidden from casual discovery, is a concealed entrance to an underground bunker carved into the bedrock during the early days of colonial Brazil, when the Portuguese were first establishing the territory as a center of trade. Originally, the island had served as an outpost, complete with a watchtower used to monitor approaching vessels—both friend and foe. It had long since been abandoned, left to the elements and forgotten by time, until two years ago, when a Spanish shell corporation called *Terminus Inc.*—operating on behalf of the Omega Collective Group—purchased it outright. They transformed the site into a semi-private underground fortress, perfectly suited for conducting operations away from detection or interference from local authorities.

Attached to the bunker, extending from beneath the surface, was a camouflaged access ramp leading to a discreet cove and small beach. Here, Uriah Grovzny now sat comfortably with a drink in one hand and a satellite phone resting beside him on an antique table fashioned from conch shells. As he sipped leisurely in the warm tropical breeze drifting in from the mid-South Atlantic, he contemplated the next strategic move for the Collective. Though their operations had been temporarily disrupted, the mechanisms they had set into motion were already reshaping the geopolitical landscape—each event part of their broader quest for global influence and control.

Still, Uriah remained puzzled by the silence. He hadn't heard from either Frank Harper or his son Pavel—surely, by now, they had neutralized the CIA operative who had infiltrated their chamber in the Mallorca castle.

What Uriah didn't know was that both Frank and Pavel were dead. Nor did he realize that the CIA threat wasn't just any agent, but Frank's daughter—Sloane—the very one he remembered hearing about so often in years past, before everything had unraveled for him and Frank.

And now, without knowing it, Uriah sat at the threshold of a new and unforeseen chapter—one that had begun with a shared vision, and was now cracking open the long-sealed doors of global change.

www.ingramcontent.com/pod-product-compliance
Lightning Source LLC
LaVergne TN
LVHW092000180526
839097LV00006B/5
9798897959198